BRIDE
OF THE
WINTER
KING

HOLLY ROSE

RED
SPARK
PRESS

BRIDE
OF THE
WINTER
KING

HOLLY ROSE

ALSO BY HOLLY ROSE

Legends of Imyria
Ashes of Aether
Storm of Shadows
Tears of Twilight *(Summer 2023)*

Winterspell
Bride of the Winter King
Heart of the Summer Queen *(Spring 2023)*

Learn more at:
www.hollyrosebooks.com

To my sister.
I would kill a king for you.

Chapter 1

Icy spires pierce the sky as the Crystal Palace beckons us. I grip the carriage window's ledge until my knuckles burn and fix my gaze on the frozen fortress, wishing all the hatred in my heart would melt this monstrosity to the ground.

Three years ago, I lost my sister to this icy hell. Now I return for one reason alone.

Vengeance.

Father shuffles beside me, his portly weight disturbing the plush emerald cushion beneath us. He too notices the Crystal Palace in the distance, crowning the mountain our carriage is ascending. Unlike me, he flinches, though the Winter King has called him here for meetings countless times over the last three years. I wonder whether he flinches every time he sees these icy spires.

"Adara," he whispers, his voice barely audible over the sound of our horses' clattering hooves and our carriage's rolling wheels. "We don't have to do this."

"We do." My words come out as cold and hard as the landscape around us.

Father shakes his head. The frost has branded his cheeks bright red. "We could run."

"To where?"

He frowns. Apparently his escape plan isn't well thought out. "To . . . Kadon. Or Hesta. I have contacts in both. People who owe me favors." Father pauses as he thinks, rubbing his chin. "We would be safe there. He wouldn't be able to take you, too."

"And if we were caught trying to escape, we'd be imprisoned for the rest of our lives. It isn't worth the risk, Father."

He sucks in a sharp breath. "What if he chooses you?"

"He won't," I say, doing my best to keep my voice steady. "Hundreds of other girls will be there tonight."

Father lowers his head and stares at his hands. I could offer him more reassurances, but what would be the point? All I have are false promises.

"He chose Dalia," Father finally murmurs.

"Dalia was beautiful and gentle," I say, each syllable clipped. "I am neither. I'll be lucky if the Winter King permits me inside his hall tonight."

"You are beautiful too," Father whispers.

I exhale deeply. "Not as beautiful as Dalia."

He can't argue with that. Dalia inherited Mother's appearance: lavish dark hair, thick fluttery lashes, and delicate cheekbones. I, however, received all of Father's charms: a freckled nose, flaming red hair, and ears which stick out too much. At least I have enough hair to hide them, unlike Father.

Father presses his lips into a thin line. "You must do every-thing you can to avoid drawing his attention tonight."

"I'll do what I can." The lie tastes like acid on my tongue.

Father holds my gaze. He looks unconvinced, and he's right to be.

I turn back to the carriage's window and peer into the distance at the Crystal Palace's formidable form. Dying sunlight gleams off its icy edges, making the turrets even deadlier. No matter how razor sharp they may look, they will not intimidate me.

Father knows not of the fire burning in my heart. Only once have I mentioned my plans to him: three years ago, shortly after the Winter King chose my sister as his Summer Bride. Father was sitting in the garden, staring at Dalia's favorite white roses through teary eyes. I took his hands in mine and squeezed them tight and told him I would make the Winter King pay for what he has done to us. Father just nodded in response. I don't know whether he heard me, since he was gazing at a spot somewhere far beyond, or if he did hear then perhaps he didn't believe that an eighteen-year-old girl would be capable of opposing an invincible, immortal king and decided to say nothing of it. Even if it sounded ridiculous, I meant every word I said to him that day.

The Winter King will die by my hand.

Many times I've considered telling Father my intentions. Ever since Dalia was taken, he's dreaded the day I would enter my twenty-first year and be forced to dance at the Winter King's Midsummer Ball, like all other twenty-one-year-old girls in the Kingdom of Avella. I worry that by telling Father, he won't look distraught enough when I am chosen. It's best he stays ignorant of the truth, even if it hurts him more now.

I must do this alone. For Dalia, and for every other girl the Winter King has stolen.

I grit my teeth and focus on the steel dagger pressed against my thigh. The weight of the vial strung around my neck. All my preparation won't be for nothing.

Whatever it takes, the Winter King will choose me as his Summer Queen.

And then I'll end his frozen reign.

Chapter 2

Deep within the Crystal Palace's walls, our carriage comes to a halt. The chill here is more vicious than when traveling up the mountain, and it bites through my layers of thick furs. I pull them tighter around me, but they do little to ward off the cold. My nose wrinkles.

I hate winter.

With a trembling hand, Father opens the carriage's door and helps me down. The two of us step out into the courtyard.

An enormous staircase towers before us, consisting of hundreds of steps. Each is carved from ice, like everything else inside the palace. Even the trees and hedges and grass are frozen solid and tinged with blue from the braziers strewn around the courtyard. No fire burns within them, only twinkling orbs.

When I first arrived at the Crystal Palace three years ago with my sister, I was so enthralled by the icy architecture that Father had to drag me away. Now I'm far from mesmerized. After scanning across the courtyard and the dozens of carriages arriving, my gaze settles on the door atop the staircase. I can almost see the Winter King from here, sprawled across his throne. My fists clench, and then I'm marching forward while Father is busy talking to our carriage driver. Snow dusts my curls, but I barely notice as I continue forth, all but pushing through the crowd to make my way to the stairs.

"Adara!" Father shouts, but his voice sounds hollow, as if it's coming from underwater.

He catches up with me a few paces later, panting as he recovers his breath.

"Adara," he says again, this time quieter. He shakes my arm, but I don't look at him as I ascend the stairs to the Winter King's hall. "Are you all right?"

"I'm fine."

His voice lowers a little more. "It's not too late to turn back."

"There is no turning back." My choice was made three years ago.

The dagger strapped to my thigh is heavier than it was in the carriage. And with every step I climb toward the Winter King, its weight grows.

I march faster. Father struggles to keep up and doesn't say another word until we reach the top of the staircase.

The doors open to a wide room. A queue of guests snakes around it, leading to the hall. Many lining up are girls my age, having received their invitation to the Midsummer Ball, and are accompanied by their families. As instructed by the Winter King, they all wear white cotton dresses like me. The reason we wear plain clothing to such an important Ball is so we all have an equal chance of being chosen as the Summer Queen, regardless of how rich our families are. We're also forbidden from wearing jewelry, and when I came here three years ago, I watched the steward remove a pair of exceptionally large diamond earrings from the girl in front of us. I don't know why anyone would want to draw attention and risk the Winter King choosing them, since each bride disappears before being crowned as the Summer Queen. No one knows what the Winter King does with his discarded brides. Some say he tires of them and orders their execution within the week, while others say he drinks their blood to preserve his immortality. Dozens of other theories rage throughout the kingdom, each ghastlier than the last. I don't know which version I hope is true, for Dalia's sake and for all the girls before her.

The chill becomes more relentless as we edge farther into the palace. The poorer girls have come without furs and shiver as they wait, but their faces aren't as bitter as those with furs. This Ball could change their lives. If they're unfortunate enough to be chosen, the Winter King will pay a handsome dowry to their families. Though their fate is unknown, their loved ones will live comfortably. And if they're lucky enough to avoid the Winter King's attention, they have the chance to win the heart of a rich noble and live happily ever after. For rich girls like me, the Midsummer Ball possesses no reward. Only risk.

Halfway through the queue, Father shoots me a pleading look. He says nothing, but I hear his unspoken words.

"Don't," I warn, my voice but a breath. It isn't just because I'm tired of listening to his pleas. There are other lords around us, all waiting for the chance to govern over our town of Brindale instead of Father. If they catch wind of his treacherous intentions, they will report him to the Winter King.

Father's eyes are heavy with solemness, but he's wise enough to keep his mouth shut.

Finally, we reach the front of the line and hand our invitations to the steward.

"It's good to see you, Lord Darrell," the steward says as he glances over Father's invitation. "It's been long since you attended the Midsummer Ball."

"Indeed." Father pockets the invitation back into his jacket, and when he looks up, he doesn't meet the steward's eyes. "It has."

Once, Father would attend the Midsummer Ball every year and leave me and Dalia at home. But since the Winter King stole my sister, neither of us has attended.

The steward doesn't seem to notice Father's grim expression and instead chuckles to himself. "Well, I can't say you've missed the weather," he says far too merrily and then glances down at my invitation. He frowns as he reads over it. Mine is different to Father's, marking me as a potential Summer Bride. Then the steward gestures to my furs. "If you will please remove your coat, Lady Adara. I must check your attire is suitable for the Midsummer Ball."

"Of course."

I shrug off my fur coat and hold it aside so the steward can see beneath. He scans over the white cotton dress, checking for any frills too fanciful for peasant girls, and my mouth dries. What if the thin cord holding the vial of Nightshade is peeking from beneath my dress's neckline? What if my skirts look too lumpy where my dagger is strapped to my thigh?

No. I checked my appearance carefully this morning before we left for the Crystal Palace. With every angle I turned, my dress concealed every trace of my weapons. If they're invisible while dancing, they'll be invisible to the steward's inspection—

no matter how sharp his eyes are tonight. I can't let my face betray my nervousness, or else he'll become suspicious. I must stay calm.

The steward's examination ends in the next breath, and he points to the hall beyond us. Steps lead down into a pit, and a balcony stretches all around it. The Winter King's Hall is more an arena than a ballroom.

I start down the steps, and Father hurries after me. Below, the enormous hall is already flooded with guests.

"Lord Darrell Lansford, Duke of Brindale," the steward calls out, his voice ricocheting off the high domed ceiling. "And his daughter, Lady Adara Lansford!"

Father is important enough that everyone ceases their conversations and watches us as we descend the stairs. Father's gaze roams across the dukes and barons and other lords gathered below, but I have no interest in any of them.

I lift my chin and turn my attention upward. On the third and highest tier, a frozen throne looms over the ballroom. This monstrosity is embedded into a cluster of razor-sharp icicles, each of which is thrice my height. Despite how formidable the throne looks, it's eclipsed by the figure sitting upon it.

With eyes such a vivid blue they glow in the faint light and skin so pale and flawless he seems to be carved from alabaster, there's no denying that our king is something *other*.

Winter born into physical form.

It is also undeniable that the Winter King is strikingly beautiful, but this only serves to make his appearance deadlier. Like a predator wearing a devastating guise to lure in unsuspecting prey.

The Winter King's bright eyes flicker across the ballroom and find me staring at him. It's bold and reckless to stare at him so directly, to face him head on, and yet I find it impossible to look anywhere else other than him. My feet are frozen in place, unwilling to descend another step. As if they have fallen victim to a strange bewitchment.

This is the first time I've seen the Winter King since he stole my sister.

Fire courses through my veins. The fury in my heart burns too ferociously to be quenched.

All I want is to wrap my hands around his neck and squeeze until his icy skin shatters and the eerie glow of his eyes extinguishes.

The Winter King leans forth, a brow raising with intrigue, and he rests his elbow on the arm of his throne. Wavy silver hair cascades over his broad shoulders with the motion, and the icy crown atop his brow gleams from the light of the braziers on either side of his throne. His strange eyes rake over me, and I fear that piece by piece he will undress the dark truth which rages through my heart.

I barely feel Father's hand as he grabs my wrist and pulls me down the rest of the stairs and into the ballroom.

"Adara," he hisses to me, his shoulders tauter than a violin's strings, "what are you doing?"

I jolt, his question shattering my trance.

I blink at Father, words impossible to form on my tongue. My gaze slips from him and back to the Winter King high above.

I can't tell what emotion lies on the immortal's face. His angular jaw is set tight. Is it with deliberation, or with irritation?

My breath shudders through my lips. What if, after my first few steps into the Crystal Palace, I've already ruined my plans? What if I've repulsed the Winter King?

I swallow. Regardless of which it might be, I must continue to enact my plan and pray I've captured his curiosity and not his wrath.

Wordlessly, I slip my hand from Father's.

It's time to make my next move.

For three years, I've investigated how the Winter King chooses his Summer Brides. I plowed through libraries and questioned those who've lived many more years than me. They say some girls are fair-haired, others have dark locks. Some are skinnier than brooms, others have lavish curves. There's no rhyme nor reason to whom the Winter King selects, and for a long time the randomness of his choices frustrated me. But then I met an old spinster with glazed eyes, and she told me of how her younger sister was chosen over sixty years ago. While it was clear she dearly missed her sister, the old lady bore no hatred. Not like me. For her, the Winter King choosing her sister meant her family no longer starved. She told me her sister was bright and beautiful and loved by all, and that was why the Winter King chose her. The description of her sister reminded me of Dalia, and then it became apparent every Summer Bride shines as brightly as the sun.

I must shine even brighter. Tonight, no one will shadow my light.

I march past Father and continue to the center of the ballroom. All the guests are gathered around the walls, leaving the middle empty. My heels click across the icy floor, echoing loudly enough to reach the Winter King. Only then does Father notice my absence from his side, and he beckons frantically for me to return. But he doesn't dare shout my name. Not here in the Winter King's lair.

Heads turn as I venture beyond the crowd's safety and into the center of the ballroom. I place my furs on the frozen floor and take a step back. Every eye is on me. Including the Winter King's.

No one moves. All wait with bated breath.

Dalia was talented at a great many things, and her deft fingers could play half a dozen instruments. I lack such dexterity. The only gift I possess is my voice, and it's far from an exceptional gift. Yet I've worked hard to hone what natural talent I have and sharpen it into the best blade as I can.

The song I choose is *The Stable Hand and the Rose* because it was Dalia's favorite and she sung it to me thousands of times. Verse after verse I sing, my sister's voice echoing in my ears, and my words bring to life this tale of star-crossed lovers. The girl in this song is to wed an old lord, and the stable hand can offer not a single coin for her dowry.

"Oh Father," she then pleas,
"Do let him marry me.
"Stable boy he may be,
"No lord is brave as he."

The young lovers escape to wed in secret but are caught by the girl's father. The stable hand disappears, and the ancient lord she is to marry dies of sudden illness. In the end, the stable hand slays a ferocious dragon and becomes a respected knight. Then he claims the girl as his bride and offers a mountain of gold for her dowry.

The Stable Hand and the Rose is well known throughout the Kingdom of Avella, and my audience knows the words by heart. Yet no one joins in, nor does anyone interrupt my singing. They listen to me line after line, my voice ringing out through the hall.

The Winter King watches me with his glowing eyes, and my stare doesn't falter as I sing with all my love for Dalia.

I reach the end of my song and fall quiet. The crowd remains silent. I don't know whether they are in awe of my song or fear what the Winter King will do. This isn't how the Midsummer Ball is supposed to go, and I've stopped the steward from announcing the guests. The Winter King could be maddened with rage from my interruption, but that's a risk I'm willing to take. Tonight is my only chance to become his Summer Bride, and if I'm not selected, I'll never avenge my sister. Our immortal king is never seen beyond these icy walls, and being chosen as his bride is the only way I can infiltrate the Crystal Palace. I must hope my bold entrance will engrave me deeply into his mind.

I offer the Winter King my finest curtsey, swallow down the bile rising in my throat, and retrieve my discarded furs from the floor. As I slip back into the crowd, no one offers me applause. But that doesn't matter. So long as I've shined brighter than the sun.

No one seems to know what to do next. The Winter King gives no indication of his current temper and stays so still it's as if he's become one with his frozen throne.

Eventually, the steward shatters the silence.

"Lord Holt Calverley of Fostan," he calls out. His voice is shaky and unsure, but when he announces the next name, the hall returns to normal.

Though I'm no longer standing alone in the center, I stick out among the surrounding masses. Eyes follow me wherever I go.

Father catches my shoulder and pulls me to the safety of the far wall. He'll want to lecture me for what I've done, but I don't writhe in his grasp. Too many are watching us, and I can't afford to make a scene. Not when my intended regicide hinges on my being chosen.

He brings us to a stop directly beneath the throne. From this angle, the Winter King shouldn't be able to see us.

"We must leave," he says, his words colder than the Winter King's frost. "Now."

He tries to pull me further along, to the doors on our right leading to the palace's gardens. I dig my heels into the floor, refusing to move even an inch. "No."

His face contorts with pain, as if the word has struck him through the chest. "What?"

I shake my shoulder free and fold my arms. "I'm staying here."

"Why, Adara?" Betrayal brands his round cheeks crimson.

"This is my choice." I don't wait to see Father's reaction before turning away. It'll hurt more than I can bear. Seeing the pain across his face will draw a confession from my lips.

He doesn't follow me as I start over to a group of finely dressed young men and infiltrate their ranks with fluttery lashes and shy smiles.

To ensnare the Winter King's attention tonight, I need a long line of dance partners.

Chapter 3

The steward announces the last guest, and the Midsummer Ball begins. The musicians on the balcony play their instruments, and the sweet song of strings fills the hall. Couples flock to the center and sway to the steady lull of the music. My first dance partner of the night—Tomald, Lord Edmond's son—takes my hand in his and leads me to where everyone else is dancing. Tomald was eager to offer to dance with me, but that isn't surprising since his father is keen for him to wed me. Though their initial preference was Dalia, given her grace and beauty.

My attention drifts up to the frozen throne high above, and I meet the Winter King's stare. I hold his gaze for a fleeting moment before turning back to Tomald as he twirls me around. Those bright eyes follow me across the ballroom floor, no matter how deep we delve into the crowd.

I don't look back up at the Winter King. After my grand entrance, displaying more boldness may risk him believing me to be a threat. The best way to maintain his intrigue is to blend with the rest of the ballroom. The stark contrast in my behavior should incite his curiosity.

Many steps later, when this dance ends, Tomald offers me a bow and a broad smile. "It's an honor to dance with you, Lady Adara."

"The honor is all mine," I say, returning his smile.

Tomald scans over my face, and then his smile falters, his expression becoming suddenly serious. He takes both my hands in his, clasps them tightly, and draws me closer to him. "Does the fact you accepted my dance offer tonight mean you've reconsidered the marriage proposal?" he whispers, his breath brushing across my cheek.

I jerk back. If the Winter King thinks me too familiar with another man, it may affect my chances of being chosen as his Summer Bride.

Then again, our king has little regard for how his taking of brides affects others.

"Lord Tomald!" I exclaim, though I keep my voice hushed. "Tonight is not the time to discuss such things."

Tomald's brow furrows. He's far from an unattractive man with his deep brown eyes and golden curls, and I know many daughters of Father's friends who have their sights set on him. If I wasn't determined to marry the Winter King and avenge my sister, perhaps I too would want Tomald as my husband.

It's hard to stop myself from imagining what a life like that would look like—whether with Tomald or with another rich lord's son. I would be well cared for and want for nothing, and might be fortunate enough to win my husband's affections, just as Father was enamored with my mother. But choosing such a life of luxury means choosing to turn my back on Dalia and forgetting the pain which the Winter King caused her.

I will do no such thing.

Maybe it's the intensity in my gaze that causes Tomald to take a step back. "You won't be chosen," he says, swallowing.

"Why not?" I demand. "Am I not beautiful enough?"

"Look at how many the king has to choose from," he says, gesturing to all the white gowned girls around us. "He took your sister only a few years ago. He can't possibly take you, too. Your father won't have an heiress."

Tomald's words voice my greatest fear. The Winter King saw me enter with Father, and there was no way I could avoid being announced with Father without raising his suspicion. All I'm counting on is that the Winter King is cold enough not to care if he takes two daughters from Father.

And if I'm wrong and the Winter King doesn't choose me, my plans will be over before they can truly begin.

I keep my face as steady as I can, preventing any trace of fear from leaking out. "I'm sure you're right."

Tomald nods, satisfied with my answer. "Would you care to grace me with another dance?"

I wriggle my hands from his grasp. "Maybe later. I already promised Ronan a dance." And Lyon and Danvil and three other lords, but I don't tell Tomald that. Depending on how terrible my other partners prove to be, I may need Tomald again later, so it's best to keep him sweet.

"Very well," Tomald says and releases me without another word. But I feel his eyes on me as I turn away to find Ronan. And his eyes aren't the only ones which follow me. From high above, the Winter King's bright eyes burn into me.

Ronan soon finds me, and we dance to the next song together. He isn't half as good as Tomald, but he turns out to be much better than Lyon, who I dance with next. The evening becomes a blur of dancing with a dozen partners, and I don't stop even once. My feet ache from my heels, and my throat grows parched from the exertion. Servants carry wine in icy goblets, and the deep ruby hue contrasts everything else in this frozen hall. I remember how sweet the wine tasted during Dalia's ball, though I could barely drink any under Father's careful watch. Tonight I dance without a single drop of wine on my tongue. Every second counts. I must shine brighter than every other girl inside the Winter King's Hall.

Tomald is the only partner I dance with more than once. I know dancing so much with him will cause him to think I'm interested in his marriage proposal, but it won't matter in the morning.

The Winter King will choose me.

Many dances later, the Ball reaches its conclusion. At the steward's command, the center of the hall clears. Only the potential summer brides remain, and those wearing furs now shed them. Hundreds of girls in white cotton dresses stand there, and all the other guests gather around the edges of the hall. I leave my furs with Tomald, who seems more than happy to bear the responsibility, and then fight my way to the middle of the hall. Some girls push me out of the way, trying to sabotage my chances. They're as desperate to be chosen as me. I give them the fiercest glare I can muster, and they soon find another girl to bother.

When we're all in position, the Winter King raises his hand, and the last dance begins.

Every year, the musicians close the Midsummer Ball with the same musical score. It's said the Winter King ordered this song to be written hundreds of years ago, and he entitled it Winterspell. Only once have I heard this music, but my ears have never forgotten a single note. It was the last time I watched Dalia dance, and to this day, the melody haunts my dreams. Throughout the dance, her eyes were fixed on me, and I remember wishing her to stop dancing so gracefully. I prayed to Mother that she would go unnoticed by the Winter King, but my prayers went unanswered. The Winter King called her name, his hollow voice ringing through the hall. My knees hit the icy floor, and I felt no pain, despite my skin bruising violently the next day. Dalia stared up at the Winter King in a daze, and then she turned back to me, her eyes flooded with tears. Not one escaped. Her lips pulled upward into a smile, and her eyes willed me to be as strong as her. That though the Winter King was separating us, she would be with me.

Always.

Now, as I dance for the Winter King, I imagine I'm dancing with Dalia and let her strength burn through me. My gaze remains on the throne, and my sister's spirit guides my every movement. She leads my arm out, reaching toward the Winter King, and then spins me around, granting me her grace.

I will be chosen.

A girl to my right dances almost as well as me. It's clear she also longs to be chosen. She might be more beautiful, but she is not me. She doesn't desire this with all the fury in her heart. She possesses grace, but not my burning passion.

Everyone will be eclipsed by my radiance.

The music ends, and the final note of a violin echoes through the icy walls. All girls drop to a curtsey, and I make mine the most elegant of all.

Silence seizes the hall.

The Winter King descends his throne and strides toward the balcony. His movements are slow and purposeful, carrying the weight of winter. His hands curl around the balcony, knuckles adorned with thick silver rings, and his grip is intense enough to shatter the ice. He leans forward and scans over all of us below.

One hand leaves the balcony. His finger extends toward me.

"Lady Adara Lansford." The Winter King's voice lacks any warmth or melody, cutting through the hall like a blade.

Me.

The Winter King has chosen me.

My heart soars while my stomach plummets into an impossible pit. Relief and fear wage war upon each other through my veins.

I've achieved what I've longed for so many years. A way to enter the Crystal Palace and face this villain head on. Yet the thought of becoming his bride chills me to the bone.

I swallow down all the bitterness and excitement swelling in my throat.

I will become the Summer Queen.

I will avenge my sister.

Father's anguished shout pierces through the stillness. The other girls disperse as he races to me. I always knew this is how he'd react, but it hurts so much more than I imagined.

He falls to his knees beside me and lowers his head to the icy floor in the deepest, most reverent bow he can. "Please, my king," he begs. Despite his pain, his voice is stronger than I expect. "Don't take Adara. You took my other daughter three years ago, and fate took my wife when both my girls were small. Adara is all I have left."

Guilt claws at me, constricting my chest. With a trembling hand, I reach out and squeeze Father's shoulder. "Father," is all I can manage, both syllables breaking in my throat.

I've brought him this pain. Even the truth won't mend it. It would only deepen the wound. He would tell me that slaying the Winter King isn't worth my life, that it won't bring back Dalia. And he wouldn't be wrong, but I refuse to do nothing. My sister's murderer must be brought to justice.

The Winter King is silent as he stares down at Father with his cold, hard eyes.

"Please," Father continues. "Take anything else I have. My manor, my wealth, my status. Take me. But please spare Adara."

What if the Winter King listens to Father's pleas? What if he decides to grant Father mercy?

This is too important to leave to chance.

I also drop to my knees and press my brow to the floor. The coldness sinks through my skin.

I lift my head and meet the Winter King's gaze. "Please forgive my father. It's my honor to be chosen as your Summer Queen."

Father clutches my arm, his fingers digging in deeply. Desperately. "Adara!"

I shake him off and return to my feet. "All I ask is that you spare my father for his words. He speaks only out of love and does not mean to speak against you, Your Majesty."

The Winter King's attention flickers between us both. I hold my breath, praying that he's as callous and cruel as I've always believed him to be. That he won't care for the pain he'll cause Father.

And my prayers are answered when the Winter King finally says in that frigid voice of his, "My choice has been made. Adara Lansford will be my Summer Queen."

Chapter 4

Maids lead me into the heart of the Crystal Palace. I expect the palace to be well-guarded, but we don't pass any servants. Nor do I spot a single item which isn't forged from ice. The frozen walls tower over us, each of our footsteps echoing through the high vaulted ceiling.

This deep inside the Winter King's domain, the chill emanates from everywhere. At least I have my furs back from Tomald. He was one of the last to leave the hall, along with Father, and the guards had to drag them both out of the palace. Tomald just stared at me dumbfounded, as if he couldn't believe I was chosen as the Summer Queen. Until tonight, I hadn't realized he was so infatuated with me. Being so focused on my plot to kill the Winter King seems to have blinded me to other things. As for Father, he begged me to reconsider, saying he'd plead with the Winter King on my behalf. Each time I refused, breaking him a little more. Now he'll be riding back in our carriage alone. Tears prick my eyes at the thought.

I wipe my eyes with the back of my hand. Luckily, both maids are walking ahead of me and don't notice my tears. Even if they did, plenty of Summer Brides will have wept over being torn from their families, never to see them again. I too cannot be certain I'll ever see Father again. Though I'm entering the Crystal Palace equipped with poison and blade, I don't know whether my plot will be successful.

Whether it will cost me my life.

It does me no good to dwell on my doom, so I shed those thoughts and shield my heart with icy walls thicker than the Crystal Palace's.

I haven't seen the Winter King since the Ball. He left as the first guests did. I wasn't surprised he left so readily without making a spectacle of my being chosen as the Summer Queen, since he didn't either with Dalia three years ago. Both Father and I clung to my sister until the steward ordered guards to drag us away. I wonder where the Winter King's chambers are and whether he's retired to them. Maybe he's already plotting my murder.

My hand brushes over the hilt of my dagger beneath my skirts, reassuring myself it's still there.

Whatever the Winter King intends, I won't go down without a fight.

The maids stop before an enormous set of double doors and usher me toward it. They haven't said a single word aside from introducing themselves in the Winter King's Hall. Considering I'm more a prisoner than a guest, I didn't expect a tour of the palace—even a brief one—but it would have been useful.

Maybe the maids suspect I won't be here long before I mysteriously disappear and know not to get attached. I've no idea how long they've worked inside the Crystal Palace, but they look old enough to have worked here for a few years. The shorter, plumper maid looks middle-aged, while the taller, willowy-limbed maid looks around five years older than me. How many Summer Brides have they escorted after the Midsummer Ball? Did they serve Dalia during her short time here in the Crystal Palace?

The question lies on the tip of my tongue, but I dare not ask it. Curious though I am, asking about such matters would raise suspicion and I can't afford such a risk.

The tall maid opens the doors and gestures inside.

"Your chambers, my lady," the other says. Elona, she said she was called when we were inside the hall.

I thank her and head into my room. Both maids follow me.

My chambers are grand, more than fitting for a queen. Or at least they would be, if not from the fact they're carved from frost and are as cold as the rest of the Crystal Palace. Both the vanity table and the armoire are made from solid ice rather than oak. Even the curtains are frozen sheets, thin enough to pass for gossamer.

The most pointless item is the large rectangular rug. It's made from ice like the floor and provides no protection from the cold. All four posts of the bed are forged from frost. What's most surprising is that I have real blankets and pillows, rather than blocks of ice.

Both maids stare at me, as if awaiting my reaction.

"It's . . . lovely." I worry my voice betrays my sarcasm, but neither maid comments on it.

They turn to leave.

"Wait!" I call after them, mostly from the shock that they'd leave me in this strange, frozen room with barely three words spoken.

The maids halt. "Yes?" says Kassia, the tall one.

"Um," I begin, scanning across the room. I had nothing specific in mind to ask. Only whether they really expect me to sleep in a room built from ice. "What about a change of clothes?" I ask, saying the first thing that comes to mind. "Do you have a nightdress for me to sleep in?"

I regret my words as soon as I say them. If the maids ask to help me change, I'll have to think of an excuse to stop them so they don't find the dagger and poison hidden beneath my dress. Though with how helpful they've been so far, it's unlikely they'll offer.

The maids exchange glances.

"Perhaps I might find a nightdress in the armoire?" I venture.

They hesitate.

"Sleep well, my lady," Elona finally replies.

Again, they try to leave.

"What of my belongings?" I demand as Kassia reaches for the door. "Can you have them sent here?" I'm not sure how long I'll stay at the Crystal Palace before I either assassinate the Winter King or die trying, but requesting my belongings won't be unusual for a newly chosen Summer Bride. Not asking would be more suspicious.

"You won't need them," Kassia says.

Elona shoots her a warning glare.

"Why not?" I dare to ask.

Elona quickly smooths her horror into a smile. "What Kassia means is you'll want for nothing inside the Crystal Palace. The Winter King has all you could ever need."

It's hard not to snort at that. All the Winter King has to offer is ice.

"But I understand you may desire certain home comforts," Elona continues. "In the morning, I'll send someone to collect your belongings."

Though I don't at all believe her words, I have no choice but to say, "Thank you."

This time, when the maids turn to leave, I don't stop them.

Chapter 5

When my maids are gone, I turn to the rest of my room and shiver, but not from the cold. The way the maids behaved unsettles me, though I prepared myself for the worst the Crystal Palace has to offer. How little concern they have for me suggests they don't expect me to make it to the morning. Otherwise, what sort of maids don't bring their future Queen a nightdress to sleep in?

I pace to the door and give it a firm shove shut. Then I draw my dagger from beneath my skirts, and steel whispers as I unsheathe the blade. Its metallic edges glint.

With how eager the maids were to leave, I fear that something may lurk inside my chambers and that I am to be sacrificed. Perhaps to the Winter King, or to another abomination altogether.

I grip the hilt of my dagger and scout my room. The first place I inspect is the armoire.

I tear open the doors and leap back, dagger at the ready. But nothing jumps out at me. When I open the other door, I find myself staring at empty shelves.

Both doors creak as I close them. The next place I check is my bed. I crouch, my dagger poised to strike, until my cheek is pressed to the floor. The gap beneath my bed seems to be large enough for me to fit through, but I don't dare try. Not until I'm certain there's nothing waiting amid the shadows.

I squint but with it being so dark inside my room, it's a struggle to see anything under the bed. Several beats pass, and everything remains still aside from my racing heart.

Though beneath my bed seems to be safe, I haven't checked inside it. Keeping my dagger close, I tear back the embroidered blankets and then the sheet beneath as well. The bedsheet peels off to reveal a slab of ice. There's no mattress in sight.

I press my palm to the surface, and as I fear, it's as cold as the Crystal Palace's walls. And as solid.

I groan inwardly. This will be worse than sleeping on a bed of stone—at least then I wouldn't freeze to death overnight. Even if I survive this first night, how will I defeat the Winter King while deprived of sleep?

A wry laugh bubbles in my throat. The Winter King has found yet another way to astound me with his hospitality. Is this how he murders all of his Summer Brides, by forcing them to sleep on ice? Are the blankets and pillows there for show since he plans to kill me before dawn?

I check the vanity and the curtains and every inch of my chambers, but I find nothing unusual. Only one thing is left to investigate, and that's the door next to the armoire on the far side of the room. I stride to it and push down on the handle, but it doesn't budge. It only numbs my fingers. I sheathe my dagger beneath my skirts, grip the handle with both hands, and try again. It's still no use. No matter how much strength

I apply—and my arm muscles are well-accustomed to the weight of a blade from three years' of training—I can't force down the handle. All I make is a slight crack, and then I let go of the handle, cursing under my breath. The edges dug deeply enough into my palm to bruise, and I squeeze my hands between my thighs to stop them from throbbing. I glare at the handle and the crack I've made in it. If I continue, I'll break the handle.

Or my hand.

When my fingers are once again warm and my palms have ceased throbbing, I opt for a different tactic. I trace the door frame and dig my fingers into the slight gap. Then I pull. But like with the handle, it's to no avail. All I come close to is freezing my fingers and breaking my nails.

I step away and fold my arms across my chest. The door stares back at me. I huff. It seems whatever I try, I won't succeed in opening it.

I glance over my shoulder at the door on the other side of the room: my only exit. What if I shut it too forcefully? What if, like this door, it will refuse to open?

I hurry to the other door and push down the handle. It resists. Panic jolts through me.

Am I locked inside these chambers?

Before fear can take root, the handle gives way, and I pull open the door. I open it just enough to know it isn't sealed shut, in case the maids are standing guard outside.

I close the door as silently as I can and turn back to the rest of my room, surveying my surroundings.

So far, it seems my fear is the most dangerous thing inside my chambers.

All that worries me is the far door. I don't know where it leads. Though it seems to be locked, that doesn't mean someone else won't be able to open it.

Someone else like the Winter King . . .

I run my hands through my red wavy locks. All the strands are knotted from dancing. Not that I care enough to find my maids and demand a hairbrush. Surviving my first night inside the Crystal Palace is my priority, and a hairbrush won't make for a suitable weapon.

In order to travel here for the Midsummer Ball, I woke well before dawn, and all the journeying and dancing has taken its toll on me. Staying upright is becoming increasingly difficult, and the chill isn't helping me to feel wakeful. Sleeping is a risk, but I also can't afford to grow weak with fatigue. I'll have to compromise by sleeping with one eye open. I've spent enough time training myself to become a light sleeper, since my previous habits of sleeping like the dead concerned me. Now even light rain pattering against my window panes is enough to wake me. The opening of a door should pull me from my slumber, but only if it makes a sound. I can't be certain these will make much noise.

My decision made, I return to the bed and remove my heels. My feet sigh with relief, and I stretch my toes, banishing the ache from dancing. I don't remove my furs as I slip under the embroidered blankets. The bedsheet beneath is thicker than I first thought, and my furs help to make the chill a little more bearable.

I unsheathe my dagger and clutch it to my chest. For a while, I lie there like that, staring up at the ceiling, until I realize that even if I wake to the sound of the maids opening the door in the morning, I won't hide the dagger in time. And then there's the matter of the vial of poison around my neck.

I have no desire to sleep unguarded in my enemy's lair, but I must plan for all possibilities.

The poison won't provide me with any defense against an ambush, since Nightshade takes several hours to kill. By then, I'd be long dead. That means my vial can be safely hidden away. As for my dagger, I must think of how to conceal it while keeping it within my reach. And come to think of it, the leather holster around my thigh will need removing before the morning.

I throw back the blankets and roll out of bed. My bare feet meet the floor, and the sensation is so unbearable it burns. If only I'd thought to demand a pair of slippers from the maids.

When I hid my dagger and vial on myself, I planned to hide them somewhere inside my chambers after successfully infiltrating the palace. In my room, there are plenty of nooks and crannies to hide such items. What I didn't account for is the lack of floorboards inside the Crystal Palace.

I browse the armoire and the vanity for hiding places the maids won't find, but it doesn't help that all the furniture is partially translucent. The only place which offers some shelter from the naked eye is my bed, thanks to the blankets. But there's a risk that the maids will want to change the sheets. That leaves under the bed as my sole hiding place.

I get onto my hands and knees and wriggle under my bed. It's a tight squeeze, and my furs add a few extra inches, so I have to shed them. The ice creeps through my thin muslin dress, but I grit my teeth and force myself onward until I'm completely under the bed. Using my elbows, I push myself forth and trace my fingers across the floor, praying I'll find a crack. It's only when I reach the wall at the head of my bed that I do.

The crack is wide enough for me to fit my fingers through and runs an inch deep. I press my dagger to the gap and dig. Tiny shards spray out as I claw my blade into the floor. After a while, I remove the dagger and feel the crack to check my progress.

I've not even made a dent.

At this rate, I'll be here all night.

I grimace and double my efforts. If I can't wrench open the floor, I'll have nowhere to hide my weapons and my intentions will quickly be discovered.

What will the Winter King do to me when he realizes I'm here to kill him? How will he choose to execute me? By frost or blade?

Those thoughts of my demise are enough to grant renewed strength to my weary limbs, and then I'm all but screaming as I carve into the floor. My efforts are so frenzied that once or twice, my blade slips across the floor, and I almost end up spear-ing my fingers with the tip. Other times, I apply so much pressure to my dagger I swear the blade bends. But that must be my imagination. I must be hallucinating out of desperation and exhaustion. Surely ice can't be stronger than steel?

I should be freezing, but my heart is pounding so furiously I'm burning up. Fire fuels my arms. My plans won't be ruined this easily. Not by the lack of a hiding place.

I will avenge my sister.

I will slay the Winter King.

A chunk gives way. Then another. Now the hole is large enough to fit both my vial and dagger inside.

Though I can't see what the hole looks like, I'm sure it's a mess. Even if I slot the chunks of ice back into it, the floor will be far from seamless. I'm counting on the fact my maids won't decide to clean under my bed during my stay here in the Crystal Palace.

I lower my blade and wipe away the bead of sweat gathering on my brow. Imagine that, sweating in a palace of ice.

My fingers are swollen as I reach for the cord around my neck and pull it over my head. It's too dark for me to fully see the glass vial, but enough moonlight filters under the bed that the indigo liquid glitters. I press the wooden stopper to my lips and whisper a silent prayer, begging Mother to bless this vial of poison.

I slip the Nightshade into the hole. My dagger should join it, but I must survive my first night here in the palace. Though I don't know what awaits me, it would be unwise to sleep without a blade to hand.

If the maids leave me alone long enough in the morning, I'll return my dagger to this hole. But I'll cross that bridge when I come to it. Right now, I need to focus on making it through the night.

I sweep the shards back into place and push them all down to compress them, applying gentle pressure in case the force shatters the glass vial.

Once done, I crawl from under my bed, wrap my furs around me, and slip back beneath the embroidered sheets. My best bet is to hide my blade under my pillow tonight and remove it in the morning. With my curtains wide open, the first light of dawn should wake me. I'll hide the dagger beneath my bed long before the maids enter my room.

I lie my head on my pillow and cling to my dagger. Its hard edges bring me comfort, and I drift to sleep sooner than I expect.

My dreams are haunted by Dalia—her singing and dancing. I dream she is here with me, in this strange bedroom. Over and over, I promise I'll bring her murderer to justice, but she only laughs and then we're both transported to our gardens. I watch as she picks a white rose and tucks it into her dark hair.

A creak rings out, and Dalia and her roses vanish.

Then I'm back inside my chambers.

Footsteps approach.

I'm not sure how long I slept, but it's still dark inside my room. Across from me, the moon shines brilliantly through the window. Dawn is nowhere in sight.

One pair of footsteps echoes through the room. That means it likely isn't my maids. Besides, they sound heavier, as if they belong to boots. And most importantly, they're approaching from the same side of the room as the sealed door.

By now, the footsteps are halfway toward me. I only turn my eyes, hoping the intruder will think me asleep.

The figure is tall and broad. The moonlight silvers their shoulder-length hair, and the frozen crown upon their head.

The Winter King.

Talons of dread rake through me. This is precisely what I feared most of all: the Winter King striking on my first night here in the palace.

I reach under my pillow. My fingers close around the hilt just as the Winter King reaches the bed.

I stop breathing.

His glacial blue eyes meet mine, and he then realizes I'm awake. His face betrays no surprise or hesitation. He reaches out and grabs my chin. His slender fingers are colder than anything else inside the Crystal Palace, and his touch embodies all the bitterness of Winter, sapping away my strength. I struggle in his grasp and try to pull away, but it's no use. His grip is stronger than steel.

I've never seen the king this close up, and he's more terrifying than from a distance. Stubble dusts his strong jawline like the powdering of first snow. His eyes glow so bright that his pupils are faint, and his skin takes on a glassy appearance, making it seem like he's made from ice rather than blood and bone. No one knows how the Winter King came to be. Maybe he was born from frost, rather than a mortal mother.

Has he come so late at night to kill me or to claim me as his wife? His expression is too stoic for me to tell which.

I squeeze the dagger. This wasn't what I had in mind when I vowed to slay the Winter King. In every version I dreamed, I was the one doing the ambushing. Not him. If I use the blade now at such an inopportune moment, I risk losing everything. But if he kills me now, I will lose everything either way.

The Winter King leans down, and the coldness builds to a crescendo. His lips brush mine, smoother and less chapped than I expect—though his stubble grazes my cheek. His kiss is so cold it burns.

Ice consumes my veins, devouring my blood. The last spark of warmth drains from me as he breathes Winter into me.

There is nothing passionate about his kiss.

This is a kiss of death.

As the Winter King lingers over me, I long to draw my blade from beneath my pillow and thrust it up into his icy heart. I will my fingers forth, but they ignore my command. They are frozen in place. Even my legs fail me, though I long to launch my foot into the king's side and shove him away.

Realization slams into me like a howling gale.

Whatever the Winter King has done to me, it's already too late to reverse it. To strike him back.

I have failed. My quest over before it truly begun.

The Winter King watches the struggle in my eyes. I wonder if he can see within them my burning hatred. I want to snarl at him and curse him in a thousand ways, but my lips won't move. His kiss has frozen them solid.

He tilts his head as he examines me, and disappointment flickers across his face. Perhaps he hoped I would offer him a fight instead of yielding so easily to his frost. But the emotion fades sooner than I can blink, and he turns away.

His cloak whispers across the floor as he strides toward the sealed door. He raises his hand and the cracking of ice echoes through my room.

The Winter King doesn't look back as he steps into the darkness and seals the door shut behind him.

Chapter 6

I don't know how long I lie there, my body but a foreign thing which refuses to obey my command. All I can do is blink and breathe, and even those become increasingly harder. My heart-beat wanes. Soon it will stop entirely.

Then I will die.

The worst part of this curse is I can still feel the dagger's hilt between my fingers. If only I didn't hesitate. If only I struck the Winter King when I had the opportunity. I might have failed, but it would have been worth trying. Now I lie on death's door. Never again will I have the chance to kill my sister's murderer.

My murderer.

Darkness washes over me. My eyes cease blinking. My dagger and the hard bed beneath me both disappear. All that remains is coldness. My breaths become hoarse rasps. No matter how I gasp, only a sliver of air finds its way into my lungs. Even that dwindles.

I stop breathing.

My heart stops beating.

In those final moments, between the edge of life and death, my sister's face flashes through my mind.

I scream her name into the all-consuming darkness.

I will not fail her.

The Winter King will pay for what he has done to me, my sister, and so many other girls. I will not let him take me this way. A mere kiss will not end me.

I refuse it with all the fire in my heart.

Then I'm burning. I am nothing but hatred and fury. A raging inferno. That will incinerate all in my path. I will melt this palace to the ground, and the Winter King with it.

The icy shackles binding my blood and bone thaw, unable to withstand the furnace roaring inside me. Air enters my lungs. My chest shudders with the shock of breath. I gobble up all the air I can in several greedy breaths.

I am not dead.

The Winter King did not kill me. Whatever spell he cast, I defeated it and freed myself from his frost.

With a shaky hand, I draw the dagger from beneath my pillow. My fingers are stiff and ache with how tightly I'd gripped the hilt, but I manage to free them from the steel. I stretch them out and marvel at the fact they now move, when minutes ago they were frozen solid. A fresh sheen coats my skin. I hold the back of my hand to my nose and sniff. I don't think it's sweat. Licking my skin confirms it's not. There's not even a trace of salt in the liquid. It tastes like pure water.

Which means the Winter King really did try to turn me into a statue of ice. And nearly succeeded.

I shudder and huddle into my furs. Tonight, I survived through sheer willpower. I don't know if I'll be so lucky next time.

If the Winter King ever again dares to ambush me in my bed, I won't hesitate to use my dagger. I'll plunge it straight through his chest.

I owe my thanks to my sister's spirit for surviving his spell. If she hadn't appeared to me when I was on the brink of death, I wouldn't have been determined enough to defeat it.

I slip the dagger beneath my pillow and don't release my hold on it even as I dream.

I awake to a door opening. This time it doesn't sound like the cracking of ice, and the footsteps aren't as heavy.

My eyes flutter open. Dawn pours in through the window with all its brilliance.

I didn't wake at first light as I wanted. The Winter King's spell must have left me weakened and exhausted. My dagger remains beneath my pillow. Both maids are approaching. I shut my eyes before they can see I'm awake.

The maids continue toward my bed, their shadows looming over me. Fine hairs prick across my skin as their stares burn into me.

"Is she . . . ?" Kassia begins.

Light fingers brush across my brow. Elona's, since she gasps and pulls away. "She's warm," she says. "So warm she's burning up."

There's a long pause. I imagine the maids are exchanging glances with each other, having a silent conversation.

Did they expect to come here and find me frozen? That would explain their complete disregard for me last night.

BRIDE OF THE WINTER KING

"We must tell His Majesty," Kassia says. "He needs to know about this."

"She'll also need a change of clothes," Elona adds. "I'll do that while you inform the king."

"All right," Kassia says. "I'll find him at once."

Light pours over me as their shadows turn away. Both their footsteps fade, and the door shuts behind them.

My eyes snap open. I must conceal this dagger. I should have a few minutes before they return.

Pulse quickening, I spring out of bed, and my bare feet meet the icy floor. I brace myself for the impact with the unbearable chill, but there is none. It's like an ordinary stone floor beneath my feet. Not cold at all.

With a frown, I crouch and place my palm to the ice. Not only are my feet immune to the ice but also my hands. I scratch the glossy surface, and a few shards of ice collect under my nails. I blow them away. The floor is definitely still frozen. What has changed is my ability to feel the cold. Is it because I overcame the Winter King's spell last night? Am I alone in this ability, or are my maids also immune to the cold?

I don't have time to contemplate these matters. I must hide my dagger while I have the chance.

I pull my blade from beneath the pillow and push myself under the bed. Without the ice creeping through my muslin dress, crawling across the floor toward the hole is much easier. Sparse light filters under the bed, illuminating my path enough to guide my way.

The crack I made last night glitters in the faint morning rays, and I can see the poison vial buried beneath thick layers of ice. I unsheathe my dagger and start digging, freeing the chunks. They soon come loose, and I bury my dagger and its scabbard and leather holster. I use the holster to pad the poison's glass and then sweep the ice back in place and press it all down.

I scramble from under my bed and dive back beneath my blankets. I resume my previous position, so the maids won't know I've moved.

I wrap my furs around me and wait. After a while, I become too hot and push my furs aside. Now that I can no longer feel the icy mattress, even my thin dress makes me too warm.

I draw in a deep breath and stare up at the ceiling and the floral pattern carved into its surface.

Last night was a close call. When Kassia informs the Winter King of the fact I still draw breath, how will he react? Will he storm in here with his sword at the ready and finish what he started?

I chew on my lip. The maids didn't seem horrified that I survived, but maybe they're sick of disposing of frozen bodies every Summer. Since the Winter King tried to kill me once, it makes sense for him to try again. Will he try to kill me in broad daylight? Or will he wait for the cover of darkness? If he strikes again tonight, I'll be ready with my dagger in hand.

And next time, I won't hesitate.

The icy doors swing open, and Elona strides through them with a yellow dress bundled in her arms. Though the design is simple, the color is beautiful and reminds me of buttercups and sunshine. Perfect for a Summer Queen.

With my dagger safely stowed away, I don't bother pretending to be asleep. Her brows raise as she draws near.

"You're awake, my lady?" she says, coming to a stop beside my bed. Her voice is much warmer this morning, and a faint smile plays on her lips. She looks happy to see me, though last night she couldn't wait to be rid of me.

I just nod, so surprised by her change in behavior that I'm momentarily lost for words.

"We have no dresses in the palace, so I sent someone down into the village to fetch one for you."

Since this mountain is plagued by eternal winter, the nearest settlement is the village halfway down the mountain. Those who live there are mostly servants, but a few smaller merchants have seized the opportunity to sell their wares there. Including a dressmaker's, apparently.

"It isn't the grandest dress," Elona continues, "but it should suffice for now. I've asked someone to send for Madame Bellmont from Netham. With some luck, she'll arrive at the palace tomorrow morning and can begin sewing more suitable gowns for you."

I peer at her eyes, which are a pale hazel, surrounded by faint creases. Though I search thoroughly, I find no malicious intent in them.

To have Madame Bellmont requested for me is an honor, and the most famous dressmaker in our kingdom wouldn't visit the Crystal Palace without the Winter King's blessing. Which means both he and my maids are deciding to treat me like a queen, rather than the prisoner I was last night. But why?

For now, I set aside my suspicion and offer her a smile. "The dress is more than lovely. But I thought the Winter King preferred his brides in plain muslin?"

Elona shakes her head. "His Majesty only demands such simplicity when choosing his Summer Queen, so that each girl shines from her own light and not from her dress's. Now you've been chosen, you must be presented like the queen you are."

"I'm not the queen yet," I say, though it's perhaps too bold. "I haven't married the king."

Elona doesn't flinch at my words. "Of course, but you will soon."

As far as I'm aware, no Summer Bride has ever married the Winter King and been crowned as the Queen of Avella. What Elona says is ridiculous. I might have survived last night, but there's no way the Winter King will let me live long enough to marry him.

I don't voice my lingering concerns and do my best to shed any doubt as Elona helps me out of bed. As soon as my bare feet touch the icy floor, she fusses over me and leaves to find slippers. I can't feel the cold, but I don't tell her that. All I know is that this mysterious change happened after overcoming the Winter King's kiss. Until I understand why, it's best to keep it to myself.

Elona returns a while later, apologizing profusely for the delay. With how long she's been gone, I was wondering whether she retrieved the slippers from below the mountain like the dress. These slippers are far from elaborate and look more like what a servant would wear. How peculiar it is that there are no clothes in the Crystal Palace from the previous Summer Brides. Maybe none made it through the first night. That would certainly explain my maids' surprise.

"Kassia is arranging for someone to collect your things from home," Elona explains as she helps me out of my muslin dress and into the bright yellow gown. "In the meantime, I'm to take you to the Winter King."

"The Winter King wishes to see me?" I blurt. I was under no illusion that I'd need to face this villain again, but I didn't expect I'd have to see him so soon.

"He's requested your presence this morning," she explains, tying the ribbons at the back of my corset's bodice. "You are to dine with him in his wing of the palace."

My blood runs cold. The man who tried to murder me last night wants to share breakfast with me. What is his scheme? Will he poison me and rid himself of me that way?

No. Poison will grant him no satisfaction. The Winter King is wicked enough to want to kill me with his own hands—or lips, as was the case last night. If he attempts to kill me this morning, it will be through his ice. Either an icy blade, or an icy kiss.

I shake away my fear. Even if he is more ancient and powerful than I ever imagined, I can't be afraid of him. I will hold my head high. Last night I overcame his spell, and I will do it again. In this game, I will be his equal opponent. Dining with him will allow me to better discern the monster behind the frozen throne. I will discover all his weaknesses.

And then I will exploit them.

Elona finishes dressing me and leads me to the vanity, where she brushes my hair. This hairbrush seems normal and isn't at all touched by frost. Its bristles appear to be horsehair and its handle oak. But a comb which is carved from ice catches my eye. It sits on the surface of the vanity and gleams in the morning sun.

I pick it out and offer it to Elona. "Would a comb not be best? The teeth look wide enough for my curls. I find a comb more easily tames them than a brush."

"I could try, my lady," Elona says, lowering her brush and eyeing the comb warily, "but I'm not sure it would be much use."

"The comb looks sturdy enough."

She shakes her head. "I'm sure it is, but that isn't what I meant. I wouldn't be able to hold the comb long enough to untangle your hair. Working in the Crystal Palace for so long has made the cold more bearable, but I am still only mortal."

"I see . . ." I put the comb down, it having already served its use. My maids aren't immune to the frost like I am. Did any other Summer Brides develop this immunity?

"I can find another comb," Elona continues, pulling me from my thoughts. "One which isn't made from ice."

Though I have little interest in a comb, refusing now may raise suspicion. "That would be perfect, thank you."

In the vanity's mirror, I watch Elona nod as she continues brushing my hair. "I'll send one of the other maids to look for one while you're dining with the Winter King."

Chapter 7

We arrive at the Winter King's wing sooner than I expect. His chambers aren't far from my own, and that explains how he easily entered my room last night. The door beside my armoire is likely a passageway leading to his chambers. If only I could slip through it and ambush him in his sleep.

If he sleeps.

No guards stand sentry outside of the Winter King's chambers. Father employed far more guards in our manor. This is only more evidence of the king's arrogance. And his incomprehensible power.

Elona comes to a stop beside the double doors and raps on them.

"Come in," the Winter King's voice rumbles from the other side. A chill washes over my skin at the sound.

Elona pushes down on the icy handles and holds the doors wide open for me as I stride through.

The Winter King sits at the end of a rectangular table, which is carved from ice like everything else. A chandelier hangs at the center of the room, and icicles plunge upward from each of the sprawling arms. Tiny blue orbs dance around the frosty candles, illuminating the room with their cool light.

Behind the Winter King is a wide window with frosted glass and the same gossamer-like curtains as the ones in my chambers. Beyond, the gardens stretch out and snow blankets every inch of grass. Not a spot of color is left, and the trees and bushes are all barren of leaves. Wherever the Winter King goes, death follows him.

"Your Majesty," Elona says, dropping to a curtsey. "I have brought your Summer Queen, as requested."

The Winter King points to the chair at the opposite end of the table, and Elona pulls out the chair and ushers me to sit.

Except I don't move.

Like last night, my limbs fail to obey. Except this isn't the result of any spell. Only my burning hatred.

The Winter King's bright eyes meet mine.

My hands clench behind my back, wringing together as they imagine squeezing his neck. I fight with my lips to stop them from curling up into a snarl.

All I can feel is the echo of his lips on mine, stubble grazing my skin as he breathed his frost into me. My face burns at the memory. With shame and rage and humiliation.

When my legs finally thaw, I have to drag my feet. All I can imagine is leaping forth, grabbing the frozen knife beside my plate, and hurling it into the Winter King's chest. I don't resist out of mercy, though. Attempting assassination with the element he presides over would be a foolish endeavor. Plus, it's broad daylight and my maid is here as a witness.

No. I must temper my wrath into a fearsome blade and bide my time. Then I will strike.

The Winter King watches me with cool indifference as I stalk toward my chair and sit. When I'm seated, I realize that I neither curtsied nor greeted him and that I've revealed how little regard I have for him. But surely that won't surprise him? He tried to kill me last night. Even if I weren't here to assassinate him, even if he hadn't stolen my sister from me, I would still despise him.

Elona glances between us, shuffling where she stands. The tension between the king and me grows until it suffocates the room. Swallowing thickly, she says, "I'll tell the kitchen servants you're ready for food to be brought up."

The Winter King inclines his head, and Elona hurries out of the dining room, the doors shuddering in her haste.

Then it's just the two of us. The Winter King and me.

There are no witnesses here now. I could murder him and flee. Perhaps his thoughts are mirroring mine. Perhaps he'll seize the opportunity to finish what he began last night.

My fingers inch toward my knife. I will them to still. A knife of ice won't have the same effect on the Winter King as a knife of steel.

The blue light from the chandelier pulses. I can't tell whether it's thrumming with the king's wrath, or whether my wrath is distorting my vision.

Calm. I must remain calm.

The doors swing open, and I jump so hard my head almost collides with the chandelier. Servants swarm in with wine. Surprisingly, the bottles are made of glass rather than ice. The liquid inside also isn't frozen. I've spent one night inside this icy palace, and it's already distorting my sense of normality.

At least the fact that the wine isn't frozen means I probably won't be expected to gnaw on an icy chunk of bread.

The servants fill both our crystalline goblets with wine, and the Winter King offers no words of thanks. He doesn't so much as look at them. His attention stays on me. Normally at home, I would thank my servants for even such a minor task, but I stay silent. Showing gratitude would be akin to showing weakness. I must show the Winter King I am as awful as him.

When the servants leave and we are once more alone, he reaches for his goblet and lifts it to his lips. Even while drinking, he doesn't break our stare. Ice claws down my arms, raising every hair. Luckily, my bright yellow sleeves are long enough to hide my discomfort. Who would imagine that drinking wine could be an act of intimidation? But I don't back down. I too raise my glass and drink, never once looking away from his glowing eyes.

The Winter King sets his glass back on the table. So do I.

Finally, he speaks.

"How do you find my palace?" Every syllable is laced with power, slow and heavy. Time bends for him. He has no reason to rush. Not when he has already lived so many generations.

I pause, considering his words. The question sounds polite, like one who is hosting a guest is expected to ask, but there must be a veiled knife behind his words.

I could tell the king exactly what I think of him and his palace: that he is a merciless tyrant living in a frozen monstrosity. But that won't edge me any closer to my goal. The Winter King must drop his guard before I reveal my claws.

"The Crystal Palace is striking, Your Majesty." I hope those words are neutral enough. Besides, I didn't lie. I didn't specify whether his palace was a striking eyesore or a striking beauty.

"Striking," the Winter King echoes, mulling over the word. "How so?"

"I've never seen a building carved from ice."

"And is that to your liking?"

It's hard not to glower. He really isn't letting this drop. Is he determined to draw pretty words from my tongue? Perhaps the immortal king possesses magic beyond the ability to manipulate ice and can sense the truth in my heart?

Either way, I will not crack. My mask will hold.

"I'm afraid I can't comment on it yet," I reply, my fingers playing on the icy stem of my goblet, "as I have so far seen only a fraction of your palace."

The Winter King frowns at me. I can see him trying to read my expression and what emotion lies behind it, but I give nothing away.

"I have meetings this afternoon," he says, "so I'll be unable to accompany you. I shall ask your maids to give you a tour of the Crystal Palace."

Perfect. An opportunity to scout the Winter King's lair and search for any advantage I can seize. Maybe I'll also be able to lure a few secrets from my unsuspecting maids.

"Thank you," I reply, forcing a small smile. My lips resist, and smiling for the Winter King is like thrusting a dagger into my chest over and over. "I would very much appreciate that."

"What of your chambers?" the king continues. "Are they to your liking?"

It seems he's tiptoeing around the incident of last night. Apparently he's too much of a coward to admit to his crime.

"My chambers are quite comfortable, thank you." I almost tell him I slept exceedingly well last night, but before the words can escape my tongue, I decide they'd prove too much of an obvious blade. Only a subtle knife will work on this ancient and powerful king.

But what I do say is enough to perplex the Winter King. A fog of confusion descends upon his bright eyes. "Do you not mind the cold, Lady Adara?"

"The cold has never bothered me, Your Majesty." I reply without hesitation, and I meet his stare straight on. My words are a challenge. A promise. No matter what forces of Winter he throws at me, I will overcome them all.

The Winter King reaches for his wine and drinks it, filling that brief silence. Then he settles back in his seat, his hands resting upon his lap. "Many believe they can brave a blizzard, but all succumb to it in the end."

I hear the threat laced in his words. Though I might have survived his frost last night, I won't be able to resist forever. But he's wrong. So very wrong. The fire and hatred in my heart won't be defeated.

I don't flinch and instead turn the focus back to him. "Even you, Your Majesty?"

The Winter King's expression darkens. Is he annoyed by the implied weakness, or is it something more?

Before I could prod him any further, the doors open and servants enter with embossed silver plates laden with warm food. Steam swirls up into the frosty air, and my mouth waters from the smell of salted ham and creamy butter. I can't remember the last time I ate. It might have been yesterday morning, before we left for the Crystal Palace before dawn. My stomach grumbles in protest at having to wait for the servants to finish setting the dishes down on the table. At least the clanging of silver plates is loud enough to disguise my mortal weakness.

The servants retreat, bowing as they leave the room. The Winter King points at the food set before us. There is a variety of fruit and cheese and meat. "Eat," he says, the word more the demand of a tyrant than the invitation of a hospitable guest. And yet, with how famished I am, my treacherous stomach obeys without question. I pile my plate up higher than is polite with all the scrambled egg, ham and sausage I can fit on it. The Winter King puts substantially less food on his plate and eats it slowly. I'm surprised he even eats, since he's made of ice. Maybe he's like us mortals in some ways. I dearly hope this extends to sleep.

"Why *The Stable Hand and the Rose*?" the Winter King asks after a few bites.

I begrudgingly look up from my food and blink at him.

"At the Midsummer Ball, you sang *The Stable Hand and the Rose*," he continues. "I was wondering why."

Does he think me daft enough to not remember which song I sang last night? But if he thinks me stupid, he won't expect my capacity for cunning.

"It was my sister's favorite song," I say after swallowing a mouthful of food.

"Your sister," he says, cutting into a chunk of ham. "Her name was Dalia, was it not?"

Breath shudders through my lips. How dare he mention my sister when he is the one who murdered her?

I clench the icy handle of my knife. "Yes, Your Majesty."

The Winter King looks down at his plate once more and continues eating. Despite how famished I am, I've already lost my appetite. My eyes burn into his. I wish my hatred would be enough to melt him.

"It's unconventional to sing at the Midsummer Ball," he says, his attention still on his food.

"I pride myself on unconventionality," I reply, my words clipped. I know I must conceal my wrath, but he is making it increasingly difficult. Did he bring my sister up on purpose? Was it an attempt to force me to reveal my traitorous heart? I must better manage my temper, or I'll play straight into his hand. If only it wasn't so hard.

The Winter King's eyes twinkle. Or do they pulse? I can't tell whether he's amused or annoyed. "The Midsummer Ball is the most important celebration of the year and has certain regulations which must be maintained."

"Are you scolding me, Your Majesty?" If my singing at the ball displeased him, then why pick me as his Summer Queen? Unless he chose me as a punishment. That would make sense, except my research showed all Summer Brides are chosen for their virtuous qualities.

"No," the Winter King replies. "I am merely curious why you sang."

"I desired to sing, so I sang." I can think of no better response. And I certainly can't tell him the truth. That I sang because I wanted to be chosen. No noble lady would ever want to be chosen, and even he must know that.

"Were you not at all afraid of any repercussions?"

"Being punished does not scare me," I say, lifting my chin. "I sang from my heart, for my sister."

"To remember her?" the Winter King asks, tilting his head as he regards me.

I swallow down my hatred. It scalds my throat. "Yes."

The Winter King turns back to his plate and picks at his food as if it's beneath him.

My stomach is far from full, but I set my knife and fork on my plate and push them all away. I won't manage a morsel more when all I can imagine is murdering him in so many ways.

"Did you wish to be chosen, Adara?" The Winter King's words are quiet. He looks up at me and meets my eyes. "Did you wish to become my Summer Queen?"

What does he have to gain by asking such a question? Does he derive pleasure from my torment? If only he knew why I wanted to be chosen.

"Of course, Your Majesty," I reply sweetly. "It's my honor to be chosen."

And it will truly be my greatest honor when I drive my dagger through his heart.

Chapter 8

After breakfast, my maids show me around the palace. They first take me to the banquet hall, which is an extended version of the Winter King's dining room, and then we spend the next half hour touring a row of bedrooms. All are small and nowhere near as impressive as my suite, so I suspect they are servants' quarters. None seem to be occupied, and when we reach the end, I turn to my maids and ask, "Where do the servants sleep? In another part of the palace?"

Elona shakes her head. "No servants sleep in the Crystal Palace, my lady."

"Not even yourselves?"

"We can't," Kassia replies.

"Why can't you?" I ask. It doesn't surprise me that servants don't sleep in the palace. After all the conditions are dire and no one would wish to be subjected to them. But *can't* is an interesting choice of words. I'm supposed to be their queen and yet even I am expected to sleep on a bed of ice. Why would the

Winter King decree for his queen to sleep here, but not his servants?

Elona presses her lips together. My question must broach a topic they aren't to discuss with me. The Winter King must have given them a list of what I'm allowed to know and what I'm forbidden to know. Regardless, I will know them all.

"All these rooms are unsuitable," Elona quickly says. "We can't sleep in them because they're frozen and inhabitable."

I offer her a slight nod and don't point out that my own chambers are just as frozen, if not more so. I could prod her for more information, but I won't squeeze anything else out of her. Elona's guard is up, and only cunning questions will work. Kassia seems to be the easier target. If I find myself alone with her, I'll see if I can get her to slip up.

My maids lead me up several spiraling staircases, and I try to form a mental map of the Crystal Palace. The image I have of it is hazy, but if I can stroll through the palace again tomorrow, then it will all become more solid.

They show me grander bedrooms than the ones before, and I suspect these are designed for guests, though none would find these rooms hospitable. Then they take me downstairs to the armory, which features dozens of swords and axes and bows, all carved from ice. I doubt anyone but the Winter King uses these now, and he probably could fashion himself a weapon out of ice whenever he likes. With how everything is arranged, I'm suspecting that once, centuries ago, the Crystal Palace wasn't made of ice. Why did the Winter King freeze it all? Maybe he likes it this way and being surrounded by ice makes him more powerful, but surely a palace of ice is inconvenient? All these frozen, useless rooms seem such a waste.

At the end of the corridor, we come to a large bathing room. The bath is surrounded by pillars with three small steps leading to it. The sides are all engraved with ornate detail, and the pillars feature the same decorative touch. My maids say nothing as I climb the few steps and peer at the water. As expected, it's completely frozen.

I lean over and press my palm to the ice. Even when I apply some pressure, it doesn't crack. The frosty bath seems as solid as the palace's walls, and I even see some petals suspended in the still water.

"What a lovely bathroom," I remark, descending the steps and returning to my maids. "It's a shame they're all frozen. Can His Majesty not let them thaw, even for a day? I would much like to bathe here."

"Even if we could melt the water," Kassia replies, "and fill the bath with boiling water from the kitchens, it would quickly lose heat. You would freeze in there, my lady."

I glance back at the frozen bath. As with everywhere else inside the Crystal Palace, I couldn't feel the ice's chill when I pressed my hand to it.

"But of course we can arrange for you to bathe," Elona says, ushering me out of the bathroom. "Madame Bellmont should be here tomorrow morning, so I'll send for a bathtub to be brought to your room before your fitting."

I thank her as we step out of the room, and the maids close the doors behind me.

We browse through a few more rooms, and then start back toward the Winter King's chambers. My maids don't show me around any of his rooms, and I know better than to ask. On our way back down from his wing of the palace, we pass a flight of spiraling stairs, which I'm certain we haven't ventured up. I pause, gazing to where the steps lead. My maids take a few paces to realize that I've stopped.

"What's up there?" I ask.

"Nothing," Elona replies too quickly.

My brows raise. If Elona doesn't want me to see this part of the palace, then it must be something the Winter King is hiding. What dark secrets could he possibly be concealing up here?

"I suppose there's no harm in looking if there's nothing up here," I say and then ascend the stairs. Out of the corner of my eye, I catch the maids exchanging glances, but they don't try to stop me and just hurry after me, fearing what I might find.

The stairs open to a chamber. On either side, stairs lead to the palace's uppermost floor. But it's the double doors opposite which intrigue me the most. Given the frosted swirls laced across them, the room inside must be grand.

"My lady!" Elona calls as she reaches the top of the stairs. I pretend not to hear her and dive straight for the double doors.

My shoulder collides with solid ice. I stagger back, dazed, and clasp my throbbing shoulder. My maids continue toward me. Before they can reach me and drag me away, I give the doors a shove with all my might.

They don't budge. Just like the door beside my armoire, these are sealed with ice. And my guess is that the Winter King alone can open it.

Whatever ugly truth he's trying to hide, I will uncover it.

I whirl around to my maids. "Can we go inside?" I ask, struggling to hide my impatience.

"It's locked," Kassia says. "Only the Winter King can open them."

"Come on, my lady," Elona pleads. "There's nothing interesting to see here."

With how desperate my maids are to leave, it's clear they know the truth behind this door. But it's unlikely they'll shed any light on this mystery. I could stay and keep trying to open the door, but if it's sealed with the Winter King's frost, then brute force won't work.

An idea sparks in my mind.

Last night, my burning hatred for the Winter King was what enabled me to overcome his spell. What if flames will work on these doors?

All I need is flint or matches. So far, I've found neither in this icy palace, but hopefully there will be some inside the kitchens.

I press my palm to the doors once more and silently vow I'll pry them open tonight. Then I pull myself away and follow my maids back down the spiraling staircase.

Soon after, we finish our tour of the Crystal Palace, and though I'm sure we've scouted every corridor and room on every floor, we don't come across the kitchens. Unless I can find the required tools to start a fire, I won't be able to attempt my task of melting down those doors tonight. My maids lead me back to my chambers, and I stop them before they can open the doors.

"We haven't seen the kitchens yet," I say.

"They're outside the palace," Kassia replies.

Outside? What an odd location. Though with what they said about warm water quickly losing heat, it must be impossible to cook inside the Crystal Palace.

"You should wrap up before we head out," Elona says. "The gardens are covered in snow, and you'll freeze to death if you go out in only a dress."

With my newfound immunity to the frost, a bit of snow won't bother me. But I remain silent as my maids lead me to my chambers.

They bundle me up in my furs and find me a servant's boots, which offer more warmth than my slippers. With all my layers, the heat is sweltering, and I want nothing more than to strip down to my yellow dress.

They lead me down several flights of stairs and out into the gardens. An icy path runs through the center and is lined by hedges on either side, their naked branches like a nest of spindles. A few benches are dotted here and there, and farther in, I find a fountain. Three doves perch on a pillar, spouting ice from their beaks. I lean over the side of the fountain and brush my fingers across the frosty droplets. How long has the water been frozen? Why won't the Winter King allow even a fountain to flow or flowers to grow? Such a place is so lacking in life.

I leave the fountain, and we continue through the gardens. Eventually, we reach an icy wall which marks the Crystal Palace's perimeter. Beyond that, a lush forest of pines crawls down the mountain. The wall isn't too high, and a few branches hang over it.

With how low the wall is, I should be able to scramble over the wall and make it into the forest beyond. Firewood will allow me to make an even bigger fire than with matches alone. Hopefully, one large enough to melt down the sealed doors.

I bite back the satisfied grin threatening to curl onto my lips and turn back to my maids. "We've still yet to see the kitchens."

"We'll take you there now, my lady," Elona says, beckoning me forth. We head back through the gardens and follow a narrow path around to the left of the palace.

Large square buildings emerge from the heavy blanket of snow. Unlike the rest of the Crystal Palace, these are made from stone and are glazed with ice, making them glitter in the noon sun. Snow dusts the tops.

My maids lead me to the largest building, which sits between the other two.

"Is this where the kitchens are?" I ask, pointing at the building ahead of us.

"It is," Kassia replies.

"What about the rest?" I gesture to the other buildings around us. "Are all these kitchens as well?"

"That one is a library," Elona says, pointing to the building on our right. "And the rest are storehouses."

I understand how the palace's conditions might affect food, but I'm surprised the Winter King houses his library inside an external building.

"Have these buildings always been here?" I ask.

"They've been here since I started working in the Crystal Palace," Kassia replies, and then looks to Elona.

"As with me," Elona says. "From what I've heard over the years, it seems His Majesty ordered these buildings to be constructed at the beginning of his reign."

"Which was when?" Though I've consulted many books, I've never been able to find an accurate date of when the Winter King assumed his throne. Our history books don't remember a time before the Winter King, no matter how crumbly a book I find.

"I believe it was over three centuries ago that the Winter King took his throne," Elona replies.

"Do you know where he came from before that?"

"Not even the oldest of servants know His Majesty's origins, and his past isn't something we gossip about."

I suppose that's my hint to stop asking such questions. I just nod and cease my prodding. We continue toward the largest stone building, and when we reach it, my maids hold the doors open for me.

We enter the kitchens, where servants are busy chopping vegetables or tending to stoves. Though I've been in the Crystal Palace for less than one day, all this warmth radiating out is unfamiliar. Steam escapes through the open windows, a stark contrast to the frosty air beyond.

Kassia and Elona don't edge farther into the kitchens, so I make a show of being interested in what the servants are doing while searching for matches. I scan the shelves and counters between greeting the servants who notice me and stop their work to bow their heads.

Finally, in the far corner of the kitchens, I find a pack of matches sitting on a shelf so high I missed it at first glance. When I pause and lean on my tiptoes, I glimpse the shadows of several more packs behind it. Perfect. There are enough on the shelf that no one will realize if I take one.

Tonight, I will strike. Whatever secrets the Winter King is hiding behind those frozen doors will be mine.

Chapter 9

The Winter King's meetings continue until late so I'm not granted the invitation to dine with him this evening. I eat my dinner in my chambers, with Kassia and Elona fussing over me. It's a wonder to think that only last night they looked at me as though I were mud sullying a new pair of shiny boots. Now they're both like doting mothers.

I spend the rest of the evening reading in the frozen armchair beside my fireplace. As the sun sinks into the horizon and darkness emerges, the flickering blue light illuminates my pages. Unfortunately, this book and the stack Kassia and Elona helped me retrieve from the library are mostly fiction. I wanted to search for more interesting works which may shed light on the Winter King, but I couldn't risk that with my maids looking over my shoulder. The only ones I smuggled up here are a few about the history of our kingdom. I doubt they'll reveal any new information, but there's more of a chance of that with them than the other books in the pile.

So that my maids don't suspect my reading habits are for anything more than pleasure, I select the most innocent book in the pile—a fictional romance—and make a show of being engrossed in reading it. Before long, they should associate me with being an avid reader and won't bat an eyelid as the weeks go on and I progress to more unusual reading material.

And in all honesty, reading is an activity I value. It was only through smuggling books out of Father's library that I could discover poisons like Nightshade and learn to distill the herb myself into a potent liquid form. It was also the main way in which I learned about all the Summer Brides which have come before me. As well as the academic value of reading, it also offers me a much-needed respite from my scheming. An escape from the reality where I've bound myself to my sister's murderer to avenge her death.

Soon it's time to retire to my chambers, and tonight my maids offer me a nightgown to change into. I wait for a long while after they leave, staring into the moonlight as it pours through the thin curtains. When I'm sure they won't return, I slip from my blankets and crawl under my bed to retrieve the dagger I buried. Since I don't have my blade to hack at the crack, I have to use my fingers to peel back the ice. It takes longer, but the chunks soon come loose.

I reach into the hole and retrieve my dagger and poison, holding them both to the faint moonlight filtering under my bed. Whorls of frost decorate the glass vial, and when I give it a shake, the poison doesn't swirl around. Only when I tip the vial upside down does the liquid trickle to the wooden stopper, though the motion is painstakingly slow. The poison isn't entirely frozen, but it won't be long before it is. I shouldn't be surprised. It's more than clear by now that the Crystal Palace slowly freezes everything in its walls.

I draw my lips into a thin line. How will I pour my Nightshade into the Winter King's wine if it's frozen solid? I could try to thaw it, but then I'd risk ruining the poison and losing its potency, rendering it useless.

Having no alternative, I pull the cord over my head and tuck the vial beneath my dress, hoping that my body heat will melt the poison slowly. My dagger also hasn't escaped the frost, though it isn't as icy as the small glass vial. A fresh sheen coats the hilt, soon turning to water in my palms. I draw the blade from its sheathe, and the steel glints, sharp as ever.

I shove it back into its scabbard and secure it around my thigh with the leather holster. Then I scramble from under my bed and nestle back into my mound of thick blankets.

I fold my arms over my chest and wait even longer still. I don't know whether the Winter King will appear in my chambers again tonight, but if he does, it'll be late. And that's the time I intend to slip from my chambers unnoticed.

Those hours seem to drag on for a lifetime, and my thoughts turn to Dalia. Glimpsing her face always fuels the fire in my heart. It reminds me of my cause. To see the Winter King dead at my hands.

When the moon reaches its zenith, and I roll out of bed. I don't reach for the boots my maids gave me earlier tonight and continue barefoot across my icy floor. Both my options of footwear, boots or heels, will slow my strides and add weight to my footsteps. Neither of which I can afford. I also go without my furs. No chill seeps through my skin, and the layers would diminish my stealth.

I pause as I reach the other side of the room and glance back at the sealed door beside the armoire. What if the Winter King comes tonight when I'm stalking through his palace? Since he made no remark about last night's murder attempt at breakfast this morning, I doubt he'll say anything if he finds me missing from my bed. Then he'll regard me with suspicion, while I'll be none the wiser.

I need a way of knowing whether the Winter King arrives in my absence.

My gaze sweeps around the room.

If I take those icy chunks from beneath my bed and distribute them across the entrance to the sealed door, I'll be able to check them later to know if the Winter King entered my chambers. Assuming he arrives like he did last night.

My mind made up, I return to my bed and slide under it, retrieving several chunks of ice. I spread them out before the sealed door and take a few steps back to survey my work. The chunks are small enough that the Winter King won't see them before stepping on them. And it won't raise too much suspicion. A few shards of ice won't look out of place here.

Content with my strategy, I stride across my room toward the exit and pause before opening the door. I gently push down the handle, and it gives way beneath my hand. I pull the door open slightly, and then peer beyond into the slither of darkness. The corridor is empty.

I slip into the shadows and close the door behind me, making sure the ice doesn't so much as whisper as I pull it shut. Then I hurry down the corridor, moonlight filtering through the few small windows. I keep to the walls as much as I can and hope the shadows will offer me some coverage, despite my stark white nightgown. Though my other dress, the bright yellow one, wouldn't offer more subtlety.

Before turning each corner, I slow my pace to a halt and peer beyond, checking for any approaching guards. When I hear no footsteps, I continue through the palace, my pace hastening.

I don't pass any servants before I break out of the palace and into the night. Overhead, a few guards patrol the wall, looking out over the palace's gardens. I hug the walls, and as soon as they turn away, I sprint toward the long shadows cast by the frozen bushes and crouch behind them.

Since the ground is covered with snow, my white night gown offers me camouflage and should render me nearly invisible in the shadows, especially from high above.

On my hands and knees I shuffle through the snow, following the bushes which weave through the gardens. As I draw farther from the palace and the guards above, I quicken my pace until I reach the kitchens' stone building.

No amber light radiates from the windows. That should mean no servants are inside. If I do run into anyone, I'll just have to say I woke up hungry and came in search of food.

The bushes stop a few yards short of the kitchens, so I have no cover to make it all the way. When I'm sure no guards are looking, I bolt across to the kitchens and slip through the doors. They barely make a sound as I close them behind me.

My eyes struggle to adjust to the lack of light. I linger by the door, listening carefully. The kitchens are still and silent. All I can hear is the wind brushing against the walls and the hooting of owls in the forest beyond.

Certain I'm alone, I stalk through the kitchens until I find the shelf I spied the matches sitting on and swipe one from the back.

I adjust the buckle on my holster and tuck the pack of matches between the leather band. The matches are bulkier than my dagger, and when I smooth the skirts of my nightgown, there's a slight bump where the pack sits. But it's dark, and I don't intend to run into anyone tonight, since the mere fact I'm out of bed is enough cause for suspicion.

I leave the kitchens and open the steel doors to a slight crack. One guard on the palace's walls turns in my direction, and it takes some time before he looks away. When he does, I seize the opportunity and slip out of the kitchens. Blood roars in my ears as I dart for the bushes. I'm just in position, swathed in shadows, when he turns back. Fearing he may notice movement, I hold as still as I can until he looks away again. Then I follow the bushes through the gardens, crawling through the snow. It's fortunate I no longer feel the cold, or else this would be much more challenging.

I reach the wall on the far side of the gardens without alerting any of the guards. This far away from the palace, I'm certain they won't be able to see me amid the shadows.

When I was younger, I used to climb the trees in our gardens and took pleasure in frightening Dalia. Her face would turn bone white at the sight of me reaching the highest branches of a great oak, and she'd rush into our manor, screaming as loudly as her lungs would allow. Then she would return with an army of servants, all yelling at me to come down, and sometimes the boldest of them would try to climb up. They could never reach me, and it would take Father standing at the bottom and giving me one of his sharpest glares for me to finally come down. By then, it was usually dusk.

It's been years since I climbed a tree, and I'm sure scaling a wall has a few of its own nuances, but I'm optimistic I'll figure it out. With my matches alone, I will only have a small flame, and that won't be enough to melt open the doors. Collecting a few fallen branches from the other side of the wall will enable me to make a far greater fire.

I search the wall for grip and begin to climb. The wall looks to have once been made from stone, and each is now a block of ice. Some jut out and a few are cracked or hollowed out, so I use them to hold my footing.

When I'm halfway up the wall, the nearest icy slab to grab is too far away, and I have to stretch above to reach it. My fingers claw at the ice as I try to secure my grasp, and I nearly succeed, but my right foot slips from the crack I've shoved my toes into. I tumble from the wall.

My shoulder hits the ground at an awkward angle, but the blanket of snow beneath pads my landing. I stare at the guards patrolling the palace's wall in case the thud was loud enough for them to hear, but none turn my way. My shoulder aches, but it isn't enough to deter me.

I will scale this wall. I will find firewood. And then I will melt down the Winter King's doors and unleash all his dark secrets.

I haul myself up from the snow and attack the wall with renewed effort. This time, I dig my toes even deeper into the cracks as I stretch for the next icy stones to grip. Again, I almost fall, but my toes cling with all my strength and I manage to steady myself.

I reach the top of the wall and scramble onto the nearest branch.

Scaling this pine is much easier than scaling the icy wall. I descend the tree slowly, lowering myself from branch to branch.

Despite my care, as I climb down the last few branches, I catch the ends of my skirts on a sharp twig. The thin fabric tears, but the damage is slight, and I hope my maids won't notice it.

I leap from the last branch and race into the forest, searching for fallen branches. There are several, but most are too large for me to hoist up the tree. After many more paces, I find a few smaller ones and hack them apart with my dagger.

With firewood bundled in my arms, I follow my footprints through the crisp snow until I arrive back at the tree I climbed down. Then I ascend it, resting the wood on the branch above before hoisting myself up.

Near the top, two pieces of wood lose their balance and tumble. The first falls all the way down and lands in the snow. I react quickly enough to catch the other, but splinters dig into my palm. I grimace and carefully return the piece of firewood to the branch above and haul myself up.

I reach the top without losing any other pieces. I perch on the wall and gaze at the gardens beneath. There's no way I'll make it down with my firewood. It was hard enough on the way up without having to carry anything. I can try but from this height, I risk hurting myself. My shoulder aches from the impact before and will undoubtedly leave a bruise. I can't afford another injury. This alone will raise enough suspicion.

My only solution is to toss both pieces over and hope the snow softens the fall enough that they don't make a sound.

I lean forth and release the first piece of wood. I watch with bated breath as it plunges to the ground. The resulting thud is louder than I like, but is disguised by the wind rustling through the trees. I watch the guards for several moments. None whirl around.

I release the next pieces, angling them away from each other so they don't collide. Thanks to the wind, they blow closer to each other than I want, but none land too noisily.

Now it's my turn.

I slide down the wall, my toes searching for cracks. When I find some, I grip them and begin lowering myself down the wall.

I make it two-thirds of the way down before leaping off the wall. I swipe the firewood into my arms and then, dropping to a crouch, hurry to the cover of bushes and shuffle through the gardens, slowing my pace as I draw near the palace.

The door is still open from before. When the guards aren't looking, I dart from the safety of the bushes, trying not to drop my firewood in my haste.

Chapter 10

Once inside the Crystal Palace, I gently close the door and hurry through the corridors and up the spiraling staircases. Like before, I keep to the shadows and pause behind each corner but I pass not a single servant. My maids were truthful about no servants staying in the palace at night. I assumed they only meant sleeping here, but it seems that extends to them working over-night. Except for the guards.

The Winter King is far from merciful, so it's strange he would treat his servants so leniently. Maybe it's because he doesn't want any to bear witness to his wicked secrets.

Like attempting to murder me.

Knowing he could be in my chambers by now, I pick up my pace and bolt through the palace at double speed.

Soon I arrive at the sealed doors I spied earlier today. The torches pinned to the nearby walls highlight the ornate pattern carved into the ice with their twinkling blue light. The doors look undisturbed from earlier today, though with the Winter

King's magic, I doubt they'd look any different even if he'd slipped inside after his meeting. The sealed door beside my armoire certainly looked no different after he opened it.

Fearing he might come marching up the stairs, I dash to the door and deposit my firewood before it. I reach beneath the skirts of my nightgown and swipe the matches from my holster.

I pluck one from the box and run it across the side, but nothing happens. No spark crackles. I try again and again until the match snaps, and I curse under my breath as the sharp point pierces my finger. I cast the broken matchstick to the heap of firewood and lift my finger to my mouth, nursing the wound. The warm, metallic tang of blood washes over my tongue.

When my finger has mostly slowed its bleeding, I pick the next match from the box and run it across the edge. It sparks, a small flame blooming. I lower it to my firewood but, as soon as I do, the flame extinguishes.

Frowning, I inspect the match.

Did I move too quickly, causing the air to extinguish it? Or didn't I light it properly?

I toss the match into the heap and select my third. This one takes two attempts to light it, and I take care to lower it slowly to the firewood, but the flames refuse to spread. Even by the time the match runs out down to my fingers and scalds my thumb, the firewood doesn't ignite.

My eyes narrow at the sealed doors. Could it be that the Winter King has placed an enchantment on these doors which prevents any fire from being lit? If his spell engulfs the entire palace, that would explain why all braziers and torches and fireplaces are filled with his strange blue orbs rather than flames, as well as why the kitchens are in an external building.

Clenching my jaw, I grip the box of matches.

Even if the Winter King has cast such a spell, it won't stop me. One way or another, these icy doors will be wreathed in flames.

I withdraw yet another matchstick and set to work lighting it. Over and over I fail, and before long, I whittle the pack down to the last two sticks. I hold both matches, pinching them between my fingers.

Two chances remain. If both attempts fail, I can't return to the kitchens. I'll be lucky if these missing matches go unnoticed by the kitchen staff, and if I steal yet another box, then I'm sure that luck will soon run out.

These matches must succeed. Failure isn't an option.

With steeled resolve, I take both matches and swipe them simultaneously across the box's edge in a single sharp movement. Both spark into small flames. I lower them and press them firmly against the firewood.

I hold my breath. The flames dance back and forth, brushing across the wood. I plead for them to take fire. The flames flicker agonizingly slowly, as if to taunt me.

Then the wood catches fire. Both matches spread far and wide. Soon my two pieces of wood are engulfed in flames.

I grab the edges and bolt upright. I lift the flaming pieces of woods as if they are swords and scan the doors from top to bottom for any weakness, such as where the ice may be thinner and easiest to thaw through. But as far as I can tell, the doors are uniform thickness all the way down. The only place at all that the ice thins is in the very center, where the two doors meet. It isn't much of a weakness, but it's the best chance I've got.

I lunge forth and drive the flaming wood into the gap between the doors. I shove the pieces as far as they'll go, my heels rooted into the floor.

My flames diminish. They are no match for these doors.

I urge my flames on, begging them to gnaw through the ice.

A small drop of water trickles down the doors. Despite its size, its meaning is significant. This drop proves that my fire is affecting the doors, if only slightly. As long as my flames don't extinguish, I can stay here all night, melting open these doors one drop at a time.

I remove my pieces of wood so they can recover from the ice and fan them with my hands until they're reinvigorated. When the flames are restored, I wield them against the doors once more. A second drop rolls down. Then another.

Soon the doors are weeping. A satisfied grin curls itself onto my lips. I'm sure if my maids saw me now, wielding fire and grinning maniacally, then they would both shriek and flee down the stairs.

After longer still, I remove the flames and notice that a small dent has been made. The gap stretches wider between the doors, and I bend to press my eye to the hole. I can't see anything beyond. Just darkness.

What if there isn't anything in that room? What if I've struggled and risked being caught for nothing?

No. With how the maids acted, the Winter King's secrets must lurk behind these doors.

I straighten and hold the fire once more to the doors. They continue weeping, their tears falling faster.

Footsteps sound behind me. They echo through the chamber, ringing all around me in a macabre rhythm.

Plumes of smoke billow through the air. If I flee with my flames, the trail of smoke will allow my pursuer to follow me. I have no choice but to leave the evidence here.

I drop the flames, and they hiss as they meet the icy floor. A pool of water forms. If the floor is melting this fast, it proves the Winter King has spelled these doors shut. But I don't have time to consider this matter. The footsteps are already upon me. Like last night, they're slow and purposeful. Mighty as a glacier.

I glance down the corridors on either side of me. I can't remember where they both lead. But it doesn't matter which path I take. As long as I escape.

I lunge right, diving into the mass of shadows. But my shoulder slams into something solid.

In my haste, I'm thrown off balance and hit the ground. I scramble up, the ice offering my hands little grip, and struggle to my feet.

I find myself face to face with a solid wall. The frozen mass is translucent enough for me to see the shadowy corridor beyond. The ice distorts my view, and the shadows writhe around, tormenting me.

I press my palm to the wall and push, but it doesn't yield. It's several inches thick, and I don't have the time or strength to force my way through.

I glance back. My other exit is also sealed. I whirl around, facing the staircase behind me.

The Winter King stands there, his hand raised and his face contorted with glacial fury.

Last night, when he tried to kill me, he bore no anger. Fear lances through my stomach. What will he do now I've antagonized him?

Instinctively, I shrink back into the icy barrier, though it makes no sense to cower before a wall he can manipulate at his will. The more rational part of me reaches for the dagger beneath my skirts. The press of metallic edges against my fingers tempers my fear.

I refuse to be a cornered deer. Whatever the Winter King tries, this time I'm not going down without a fight.

He takes one step toward me, his hand lowering, and then he takes another.

I fight the urge to draw my blade. I must wait for him to strike first. Or else I risk unnecessarily exposing myself.

The Winter King comes to a halt halfway through the chamber. I suck in a sharp breath. His bright eyes sweep across the floor and settle on the discarded firewood before the door. They've formed an impressive puddle, but the ice has caused their intensity to wane. An unnatural draft blows through the chamber. There are no windows, and the room is sealed aside from the stairs behind the Winter King. His magic must be responsible for extinguishing my fire.

When the flames are dead, his glowing eyes find me. I grit my teeth and meet his stare, daring him to come closer. He doesn't.

"Why are you here?" he demands.

"I . . ." I swallow, my mind racing too quickly to produce a reasonable excuse. With the blood pounding in my ears, it's impossible to concentrate. All I can feel is the dagger at my thigh. My fingers itch to draw it and drive it into his chest. "I couldn't sleep."

It's a pitiful explanation, but what else can I say? The Winter King has caught me quite literally red-handed, trying to melt open his enchanted doors.

His forehead creases. "And so you came up here to start a fire?"

There's nothing I can say to that which won't incriminate me any further. My lips stay sealed.

His attention sweeps to the doors and then back to me. "Did your maids not tell you that this room is strictly off-limits?"

I consider my response carefully, even as the Winter King's eyes narrow with impatience. It would be best to play ignorant, but that wouldn't explain why I came here in the dead of night to start a fire. And if I say my maids didn't tell me the room is forbidden, I'll only subject them to the Winter King's wrath. While I've known them for just one day, I wouldn't wish that upon anyone.

"They made a fuss about my coming up here," I say slowly, "so I was curious what the fuss was about."

The Winter King says nothing. I wait for him to take a step closer, my heart thundering. But he stays right there. I wait for his first move, certain it will come when I least expect it. He must be infuriated by what I've done. The punishment will be great, for he has no mercy.

I press my lips together. Even if he doesn't decide to kill me for what I've done tonight, I've delivered a fatal blow to my quest for vengeance. It will take months to regain his trust. If ever.

This was a terrible mistake.

He lifts his head. His angular jawline gleams like the edges of blades in the dim blue light. My nerves are so taut that the movement, though slight, almost causes me to unsheathe my dagger from my skirts. Luckily, I stop myself.

"You are not to come here again," he grinds out after a long silence. "Is that understood?"

Is he letting me go without a fight? Does he believe me but a curious, harmless fool? Or does he plan to deal his punishment when I least expect it? Like later tonight, when he believes me to be fast asleep.

I wonder what he will do if I come here again. Though I have my suspicions, I want to hear him admit what a monster he is. I have to bite my tongue to stop myself from asking the question. Now is not the time. Especially not when I've done enough damage.

I give a quick, shaky nod. His threats don't scare me, but the girl I'm pretending to be would be frightened.

Tension seeps from his broad shoulders. "Good," he says, satisfied by my answer. He believes he's terrified me into obedience and though his emotions are usually impossible to read, this time the relief in his expression is obvious. Whatever lurks behind those doors, he fears its discovery.

The Winter King raises his hand, and the walls sealing the corridors disintegrate. Specks of ice glitter into the darkness. "You should return to your chambers."

I hastily drop to a curtsey, hoping politeness will help to remedy some of this situation. "Yes, Your Majesty." I don't wait for him to tell me twice. Any hint of disobedience will only make matters worse. I start to the burned-out fire and bend to pick up the charred wood and snapped matches.

"Leave it."

I do as he commands, straightening at once, and hurry past him toward the stairs, though turning my back to my enemy makes my spine crawl. He could choose to freeze me now, and I wouldn't see the spell coming. I hope it requires skin contact like last night, but with how he conjured those frozen walls to block off my escape route, but I can't be certain his magic is limited in such a way.

My nerves are pulled so taut that when he speaks again, I nearly whirl around with my dagger at the ready.

"Lady Adara," he says. I turn to see him picking up the heap of firewood and matches. His bright eyes twinkle. "Do try to stay put in your chambers for the rest of the night."

I'm certain I see the ghost of a smile dancing on his lips, and the sight unnerves me. His smile reminds me of a cat toying with the mouse it caught, watching in fascination as it runs around between its claws.

Not knowing what to say, I scurry down the stairs and cling to the dagger through the fabric of my skirts all the way to my chambers. Only after I slam the doors shut behind me do I relax my grip.

I stay there with my back pressed to the doors, my breaths shuddering into the frosty air.

I lift my head and peer at the sealed doors beside my armoire on the other side of the room. The shards of ice I deposited there are intact, and when I move to crouch beside them, I see no evidence of the Winter King entering my chambers tonight. At least not through this door. I was suspecting he searched the palace for me after finding my bed empty, but now I'm not sure that's the case. Did the enchantment he cast over those sealed doors let him sense my efforts to thaw them open? Or did he simply want to visit his forbidden room? Either way, I can't risk trying to thaw this door open as well. Even if it leads to his chambers, like I think.

I throw aside the curtains so that dawn will wake me and then I crawl beneath my blankets, blood still pounding through my veins. I sleep with my blade and my poison vial both resting on my chest, and it takes a short eternity to fall asleep, since every gust of wind or hooting of an owl has me bolting upright and arcing my dagger in front of me.

But the Winter King does not come. Not tonight.

Chapter 11

I wake to shafts of dawn streaming through the window. By the time my maids arrive, I've long stowed away my dagger and poison and swept the translucent curtains back over my window. After having both on my person for an entire night, the effects of the frost have vanished. It seems my immunity has reversed the freezing and I hope that continues to be the case, even if I must sleep with my dagger and poison every night to prevent it from happening.

Though I'm grateful for it, I don't understand why the Winter King didn't come to my chambers last night to unleash his wrath upon me. He certainly seemed angry enough outside the sealed doors. I suppose striking last night would be much too obvious, and I already overcame his first attempt. Perhaps he's biding his time, waiting for the opportune moment. Like I am.

Servants swarm into my room with a copper bathtub and a folding screen. They set it all up in the far corner, and more servants scurry in with wooden buckets. Tendrils of steam swirl upward as they deposit the warm water into my bath. When the tub is filled, they bow themselves out of my chamber, leaving me with Elona and Kassia. My maids help me undress and lead me behind the screen. The bathtub's metallic sides are engraved with ornate detail, fine enough for a queen.

My maids hold my arms to steady me as I climb into the bath, and it's only when I'm sitting in it that I realize they're both staring at my shoulder. Elona's fingers brush over my skin as she inspects the blemish. Until now I forgot about the injury from falling off the wall last night. Though it doesn't hurt too much, it's a sickly yellow hue which is darkening to an indigo.

"What happened, my lady?" Kassia asks. "How did you get this bruise?"

All thoughts vacate my mind. I watch the steam dancing along the water's surface, desperately trying to conjure an excuse.

"The bed post," I say, the words tumbling from my mouth before I can fully consider them. "I woke up to use my chamber pot and bumped my shoulder on the way back to bed."

I'm not sure why I lie. After all, the Winter King will have informed the maids of what happened last night. I'm surprised he hasn't already scolded them for it.

"Be careful," Elona chastises. But neither maid prods the excuse.

They present me with an array of perfumes and soaps, lifting each bottle and jar to my nose and asking me to choose which herbs and flowers I prefer. I opt for rose and patchouli, and they deposit several large drops of each into my bath. Then they take to scrubbing at my arms, using a considerable amount of force, as if they're trying to scrub off my skin. Yet when it comes to my shoulder, they take more care and skirt around the swollen area, their tenderness surprising me.

Soon they move onto my hair, lathering soap into my nest of red curls. They pluck out more twigs and pines than I realized were there.

"My lady," Elona says, after finding what must be the twentieth pine, "what ever happened to your hair?"

This question is much harder to answer than the first. The only excuse which comes to mind is continuing the tale of my clumsy visit to my chamber pot and claiming that I fell out of the window, and that is too absurd.

I sink into the warm, soapy water and hope Elona will drop the question without me having to answer it.

Elona glances up at Kassia, but keeps quiet. Neither maid presses me for a response, and the sloshing of water instead fills my chamber.

"Your belongings came this morning," Kassia says. "I told the other servants to leave them in the storehouse, where they'll be safe."

"Can we go down to look at what has been sent from home?" I ask.

"I'm sure they'll be time later," Elona says. "You have a busy morning ahead of you. Madame Bellmont arrived a few hours ago, and she'll need to take your measurements before she can start making any dresses."

With all of last night's antics, I forgot about Madame Bellmont coming to make my dresses. Though Dalia and I begged Father to hire Madame Bellmont, he would always refuse, and no amount of persuasion could convince him otherwise. He claimed I was the reason he refused, since I'd ruin my gown anyway in a single afternoon with all my tree-climbing and rolling through meadows, and that he wouldn't let one of us have such an expensive dress and not the other.

Then the Winter King took Dalia, and I never asked Father again.

To have Madame Bellmont create my dresses is rather exciting, even though I'm only here to destroy my sister's killer. If everything goes to plan, I won't keep the dresses for long, but at least I can enjoy twirling around in them once or twice before then.

Elona adds, "And before you see Madame Bellmont, His Majesty has once again requested your presence at breakfast."

At the thought of facing him again, my stomach plunges. I grip the bathtub, my fingers digging into the metallic edges. I hope Elona doesn't notice my elevated pulse as she scrubs my wrists.

Has he requested my presence so that he can continue scolding me? Regardless of what reason he wishes to see me, I must compose myself. After last night, I need to mend the damage I've caused. That is, if he doesn't want to murder me, anyway.

My thoughts drift to what Kassia said about my belongings. "Why don't we ask for my things to be brought up here while I'm having breakfast with the king?"

"If there's something specific you want," Elona replies, scrubbing my nails clear of dirt, "then we can send for it."

My eyes narrow. "Why don't we just ask for everything?"

"We could," Kassia says, pouring water over my hair to rinse away the soap, "but then we'll have to send everything back to the storehouse."

"Why? Can't my things stay in here?"

"We wouldn't want the ice ruining your belongings, my lady," Elona says quickly. "It's safer for valuable items to stay in the storehouses."

"The palace," I say, thinking of the frost coating my poison vial last night. "It turns everything to ice, doesn't it?"

Both maids glance at each other, but say nothing. Elona hastily finishes and brings me a towel, ushering for me to climb out.

"Am I right?" I press as she wraps the towel around me.

"You should ask His Majesty these questions," Elona says, drying me. "We are but humble servants."

I scan her face, and Kassia's as well, but they reveal none of the Winter King's secrets.

When I'm dry, my maids help me into a dress. This one is an emerald hue, plain like the last, but I like the way it contrasts my hair. If only the sleeves weren't so long. I'll have to be careful not to get them covered in jam during breakfast.

Elona and Kassia comb through my damp hair and secure it in a neat bun with a matching green ribbon. Once I'm presentable, they whisk me off to the Winter King's chambers.

Like yesterday, the dining room is barren of color. My green dress is the only pop of color amid the ice. The Winter King wears a deep navy tunic which is heavily embroidered with a pattern reminding me of twirling snowflakes. His icy crown doesn't budge in the slightest as he lifts his head to look at me, perfectly crafted for him. I wonder if it's frozen solid to his head and that he even has to sleep with it on.

Though being in his presence still makes my blood boil, today I remember to curtsey before sliding into the chair Kassia holds out for me. Either I'm becoming accustomed to him, or to the sensation of fury burning through my veins.

"Good morning, Lady Adara," the Winter King says.

I return his greeting, and then Elona and Kassia leave to tell the other servants to bring us food and wine.

"Did you sleep well?" the Winter King asks. I can't tell whether it's the flickering blue fireplace or his bright eyes twinkling more than usual as he speaks.

"I did, thank you," I reply as casually as I can. But he mentions nothing more of my exploits last night, and just like that, the matter is brushed over. He makes polite conversation about my stay here in the Crystal Palace, and I hesitate before answering each question, taking great care in my response.

I want to demand to know the Crystal Palace's secret, for him to confess that it freezes everything within its walls and why. But I can't. Especially not after last night.

"Madame Bellmont arrived a few hours ago," he says as servants pour us wine.

I raise a brow, surprised that the immortal king would be interested in a dressmaker. "My maids mentioned it before."

"Have her make however many dresses you want. If you require twenty or fifty, then I shall spare no expense."

I force a smile. "Though I'm very much grateful for your kindness, I won't require many dresses. Kassia said my belongings from home arrived earlier, so I already have plenty of my own in the palace."

He frowns. "You are to be the Summer Queen, and you must be dressed appropriately."

"Do you fear my gowns won't be up to your standards?" I do my best to make my tone light and teasing, but it's hard with the bitter lump in my throat. In the gleaming edges of his crown, I glimpse Dalia's reflection.

"Of course not," he says quickly. "I'm sure they are more than lovely. But if you are to be presented as the queen, your gowns must demand respect. It is not a matter of vanity. Appearances can be powerful weapons."

I don't mention that none of his three hundred odd previous brides have ever been crowned as Queen, and that my lowly gowns from home will never have to fear being shown up by such a spectacle. "I see, Your Majesty."

"Elaric," he says.

I blink.

"You may call me by my birth name, rather than address me as Your Majesty. You are, after all, to be my wife."

I sit back in my chair and knit my hands together, regarding him carefully. Though I've seen the Winter King's name mentioned in passing in a few books, I almost forgot what it was. It seems absurd to give the embodiment of Winter a name. And his birth name, as he called it. Does this mean he wasn't born from a lump of snow and ice, but from a mortal mother?

The Winter King watches me, and his lips twitch as if he's in possession of some unseen joke.

I can't tell the reason for his humor. Is it because he knows I will not make it to our wedding? I am surprised that he's requested I call him by his name, rather than his title. All this familiarity must be to lure me off-guard. Maybe I'm his most challenging bride yet, and he's trying an alternative tactic on me to lure me to my doom.

"As you wish," I say, though I much prefer calling him the Winter King. Giving him a name like Elaric makes him seem human, which he is most definitely not.

Our conversation is interrupted by the servants as they bring us food, similar to what they brought yesterday. The Winter

King, or rather Elaric, stares at me from across the table. No matter what mouth-watering dishes they set before him, he doesn't look away from me even once. Heat crawls up my neck.

"Have you ever been to the capital, Lady Adara?" he asks, when the servants retreat.

"A few times." I pause, frowning. "Adara is fine. If I am to call you by your name rather than your title, then it seems you should not address me so formally either." Only by reciprocating such pleasantries will this faux relationship grow.

He smiles at that. "Of course, Adara." He reaches for his glass. "What did you think of Netham?"

I'm not sure what he expects to gain by asking me this, so I consider my response carefully before speaking. "Busy. There were many wonderful balls and operas and stalls, but I prefer the quieter streets of Brindale. And I certainly prefer the country-side."

"Then the seclusion of the Crystal Palace will not bother you." He leans back in his chair and glances over his shoulder, staring out wistfully at the barren landscape of his gardens. "Although I suppose you will still miss the countryside."

That's what he was wondering? I could tell him I don't miss home, but he won't believe it. Who wouldn't miss home when caged in this icy behemoth?

He turns back to me. "Do you like flowers, Adara?" He speaks my name slowly, as if savoring fine wine.

"Flowers?" I repeat, unable to hide the incredulous note in my voice.

"Roses, tulips—"

"I know what flowers are, Your Majesty—"

"Elaric."

"*Elaric*," I correct. "I was just surprised you'd ask me about flowers." It almost sounds like he's attempting to court me. Unless asking about flowers is merely passing conversation. If he intends to court me, it's only either for appearances' sake or to lure me off-guard.

"Why does it surprise you?"

"I didn't think you particularly liked flowers," I reply, "since there are none here."

The Winter King's eyes shadow at that, and he reaches for a platter of meat. I realize then that the food has been sitting before us for some time and neither of us has touched it, both too occupied with our conversation. But food doesn't interest me as much as the emotion flickering in the Winter King's glowing eyes.

"Do you wish there were flowers here in the Crystal Palace?" I dare to ask. I know it's a bold question, but it's phrased innocently enough. If he wishes there were flowers here, then it implies he has no control of the Crystal Palace's frost.

The Winter King takes an age to reply. When he finally answers, he says, "I'll ask the servants to bring you some flowers."

Chapter 12

When I return to my chambers, Madame Bellmont is already there, sitting in my armchair beside the flickering blue fireplace. Given her widespread fame, I expected someone as established as her to be a little older, around Elona's age. But she looks barely a decade older than me.

She's a tall, lithe woman with deep brown skin and high cheekbones. Her dark hair is braided into a voluminous bun with two shorter wavy pieces hanging down and framing her face. Her eyes narrow as I enter, as if she is taking my measurements with her gaze alone. Given her talent, I wouldn't be surprised if she actually could. Am I what she expected as a Summer Bride? Has she ever made gowns for any Summer Brides before me?

"Your Majesty," she says, rising from the armchair and curtseying before me. She wears a plainer dress than I expected, burgundy in color, and though the fabric is undecorated, it looks like high-quality cotton. "It's a pleasure to meet you."

"Thank you, Madame Bellmont," I reply, returning the gesture. "Likewise, I am honored to meet you, but you needn't address me as 'Your Majesty'. I'm not yet officially the queen."

"Of course," she says, her eyes sweeping over me. It's clear from her somber expression that she's recalling the fact no Summer Bride has ever been crowned as Queen.

Madame Bellmont is a woman of little words, and we exchange only a few more pleasantries before she whisks me behind the screen in the corner of my room and begins taking my measurements. I expected her two girls to take my measurements, but she insists on doing it herself. One girl holds the measuring tape in place, while the other furiously scribbles down all the numbers Madame Bellmont barks at her. To gain the most accurate measurements, she insists on taking them in my chemise.

"Are you sure that's necessary?" Elona asks, glancing over me. "Lady Adara must be freezing in her chemise."

"Unfortunately it is," Madame Bellmont says, not looking up from the measuring tape. "Careful measurements will ensure my dresses need little alteration."

Elona looks across to me, and I give her a nod to reassure her. It isn't as though standing here in my chemise inconveniences me, since I can't feel the cold, anyway. But to avoid drawing suspicion, I shiver once or twice.

Madame Bellmont takes my measurements thrice to get the most accurate numbers. By the time she finishes, my back aches from standing so rigidly. She orders her girls to bring over an enormous chest, and they open it on my table.

An assortment of fabrics fills the chest, each cut to a square piece that measures only half a foot on either side. She spreads the pieces across my table, forming a rainbow of velvet, satin and silk.

"I have full bolts for each sample," Madame Bellmont says, gesturing to all the fabric. "Were there any particular colors or finishes you had in mind?"

"I was thinking warm colors would be best." I pick up a square of golden brocade and rub it between my thumb and index finger, relishing the softness of the fabric. As expected, Madame Bellmont has only the highest quality of material. I spot a piece of crimson silk and hold it beside the golden brocade. "My dresses should resemble fire."

"Fire?" Madame Bellmont gestures for her assistant to come forth. "I have a few suggestions for such gowns." She takes the notebook from her assistant and begins sketching out the draft of a dress. The result is remarkable, with flouncy skirts and sleeves which remind me of dancing flames. She says the dress will be of golden brocade I selected, and that the hems and sleeves will be of the other fabric, giving them a crimson hue. The only change I suggest is a more daring neckline, which will capture the Winter King's attention. She implements my suggestions, redrafting the dress on the next page with the changes, and then we repeat the process for several more dresses—all of which embody Summer.

We design six dresses, and it takes us until late in the afternoon. By the time we finish, a servant arrives at my room with a bouquet. Tulips and pansies and roses are bunched together and secured by a ruby ribbon. The petals remind me of tiny blooming flames, arranged together to look as fiery as the midsummer sun.

"For Lady Adara," he says, handing the bouquet to Kassia, who answered the door. He bows himself without another word.

Kassia's brown eyes gleam as she crosses the room and hands them to me. "What a pretty bunch of flowers." In a hushed voice, she adds, "Does my lady have a secret admirer back at home?"

I turn the bouquet around, searching for any writing which would indicate who they're from. They couldn't be from Tomald, could they? I thought he'd have given up all hopes of marrying me when the Winter King chose me at the Midsummer Ball.

That's right. The Winter King. He mentioned flowers this morning, that he would send me some. At the time, I didn't believe he really would. The nearest town unaffected by the mountain's eternal winter is several hours away, so whoever he sent would have needed to ride there and back, just to buy a bunch of fresh flowers. Surely such a trivial task isn't worth that amount of effort?

Elona flocks toward us and peers at the vibrant flowers. "As exciting as an admirer might be, you should write home and tell them not to send you pretty gifts. You are to wed the Winter King, my lady."

"They are from the Winter King," I reply, holding up the flowers to the faint light streaming through the window. With the sun sinking into the horizon, the amber glow makes the bouquet look even more fiery.

My maids only glance at each other and look thoroughly unconvinced by my words. I would be too, if the Winter King hadn't mentioned it this morning. Even now, I'm sure the flowers will vanish in my fingers.

If my maids are shocked by the Winter King sending me flowers, then maybe this is the first time he's sent any to a Summer Bride.

Elona and Kassia must think I'm marveling at the pretty gift, but I'm instead marveling at what it represents. Despite trying to thaw my way into the Winter King's forbidden chamber, he's sent me flowers. Is this a clever ploy to lure me into a false sense of security, or is he not as infuriated by last night as I feared?

I send Kassia and Elona to find me a vase, and I specifically request one forged from ice. I arrange the flowers inside the vase and set it on the small table before my window, displaying it proudly like the spoils of war. The flaming petals above the solid ice depict the scene of what is to come: Summer vanquishing Winter.

When my maids escort me to the Winter King's chambers for dinner that evening, I can't help the bounce in my steps. I hope they think my enthusiasm is over receiving the Winter King's attention, and not relief over last night having less effect on my plans than I feared it would.

"Were the flowers to your liking?" the Winter King asks as soon as I'm sitting opposite him.

Without turning, I can feel my maids' surprise behind me. "I did," I say. "It's very kind of you to send me flowers, especially when you must have so many other matters demanding your attention."

My maids take a moment to snap out of their disbelief before leaving to call for other servants.

"If they please you," the Winter King says when they're gone, "I will have a bouquet sent to you every day."

I'm unable to stop my surprise from showing. I quickly smooth it into a smile and hope he will think it's pleasant surprise rather than suspicion. "Thank you, Elaric. I truly appreciate your kindness." I decide not to add the fact that having a servant ride to the nearest city and buy me flowers isn't the same as him doing it himself. I'd be surprised if he even saw the bouquet before the servant handed it to me.

A part of me doesn't believe he will follow through with his words. But he does. Every afternoon, a servant knocks on my door and presents me flowers from the Winter King. The flowers are different each time, and the petals of pansies, lilies, daisies and magnolias form a rainbow in my chamber. As much as I brushed it off when the Winter King first suggested it, I can't deny that it makes my icy room look much more hospitable. By the time Madame Bellmont returns a week later, I'm already running out of room to display all the flowers.

During these days, the Winter King doesn't creep into my room even once. I sleep with my dagger every night nonetheless, certain that each night will be the night when he sheds his mask and once again embraces the monster he is.

The gowns Madame Bellmont brings with her are so heavy that several servants have to carry them up to my room. They lay them all out across my bed and Madame Bellmont allows me a few minutes to admire her work.

Each gown is remarkable, and all of them are inspired by Summer. My favorite is the one we designed first, which looks even better than it did in Madame Bellmont's sketches. The golden dress is fitted to the knee, flaring out into crimson ruffles. The sleeves follow the same design as the skirts. My second favorite surprises me, since I thought little of it when Madame Bellmont drew it. The fabric is powder blue, like a clear summer sky, with tiny blossoms sewn onto it. The most daring feature is the backless bodice, which I don't remember from Madame Bellmont's sketch.

"I added that in last minute," she says as I examine it. "I hope you don't mind the alteration to our original design. I thought with the suggestions you made to the other dresses that a bolder style would be more to your liking."

"I don't mind at all," I reply, my fingers brushing over the finely embroidered petals. "It's stunning. As are the rest."

She offers me a broad smile. "I'm glad you're pleased with them, my lady. But come now. We must get them fitted. Despite my care with taking your measurements, it's possible some slight alterations will be required to ensure a perfect fit, depending on the cut and stretch of each gown."

Elona and Kassia help me change into the gowns, with Madame Bellmont's girls carrying them back and forth to my bed. Madame Bellmont examines every inch and somehow finds bunching fabric under my arms or around my waist, all of which escaped my notice since I was so enthralled by the dresses.

I want to twirl around in each and look at them in the mirrors, but Madame Bellmont is too focused on her fitting. As she tucks pins into the fabric, my heart aches with longing for my sister. I wish more than anything that Dalia was here and that she too could have extravagant dresses made for her by Madame Bellmont. I can only imagine how beautiful they would have looked on her.

When Madame Bellmont has examined me in each dress, she and her girls set to work with cutting and resewing the seams. Though the adjustments are slight, they still take several hours to implement, even with three pairs of hands. Elona and Kassia take me down to the library, and since we haven't visited since my tour of the palace last week, we return the books I finished and then take a stroll through the gardens.

On my way back to my chambers, we come across the first crowd I've seen in the palace since the Midsummer Ball. The Winter King must have held a meeting inside his audience hall, since all the lords and dukes are flocking out. They stop to look at me, brows raising in surprise. Have they never seen a Summer Bride in the Crystal Palace?

I pause as they pass, hoping to glean any useful information or gossip, but the lords stay remarkably silent upon sighting me. Then I spot a bald head and a flaming red beard.

Father.

He notices me at the same time that I notice him, and he turns against the tide of lords and hurries to me. I stand rigid, neither stepping away nor edging closer to him. My heart both dreads and cherishes seeing him again.

"Adara," he gasps as he reaches me, gripping my forearm. "You're here."

"Of course I'm here, Father," I say with a smile. "I'm to become the Summer Queen. Where else would I be staying but the Crystal Palace?"

He shakes his head in disbelief and cups my cheek. "You're not cold. Not at all. Your cheek is so warm, as if you've been basking in the sun."

"I must be getting used to the cold."

Father leans nearer and lowers his voice, though my maids are close enough to catch fragments. "Does he treat you well, the Winter King?"

The question catches me off-guard, and I'm too slow to stop hesitation from slipping through. I can't help but think of how the Winter King tried to freeze me on my first night here. It's enough for Father to see the truth. His face contorts with worry.

"He brings me flowers," I say quickly, conscious of my maids behind me. "Every day—"

"But—"

"And he's ordered Madame Bellmont to make me splendid gowns. Speaking of which, I must be keeping her waiting." I pry his fingers from around my arm and slip from his grasp. "You needn't worry about me, Father. The Winter King treats me well." I turn and leave before he can discern any more truth from my expression.

"Adara!"

I don't pause as he calls my name. I sprint all the way through the icy corridors to my chambers and only stop once I'm safely behind the doors.

Chapter 13

Back in my room, Madame Bellmont has already finished making the adjustments to my dresses. She wastes no time in having me try on all my gowns, and they fit perfectly. I keep the last dress on: the powder blue one with embroidered flowers scattered across the silk. After I thank Madame Bellmont for her work, Elona takes her to arrange payment. Kassia stays with me, and once I've finished twirling in front of all the mirrors inside my room, I ask her to tidy my hair and make it look as beautiful as my dress.

Kassia sits me down in front of my vanity and brushes my red curls into an updo, securing it with pins and ribbons. Elona returns shortly after we finish.

"You look lovely, my lady," she says with a smile.

I glance at the window. The sun has nearly sunk into the horizon and casts shadows across the snowy gardens. "Will the Winter King be free for dinner?"

Elona shakes her head. "He has an audience with the Duke of Walsworth until later this evening."

"How late?"

"I don't know, my lady. As late as the duke decides."

I turn back to my vanity's mirror and inspect my appearance. I certainly look more radiant than usual, and though I could ask Kassia to style my hair again, it seems a shame to waste her efforts.

"I'm sure the duke won't stay all night," Elona continues. "So His Majesty should be free at some point this evening. If you'd like to see him later, I can ask on your behalf?"

"Yes, please."

Without another word, she leaves in search of the Winter King. Though I don't yet know whether our meeting will be guaranteed, I ask Kassia to search my belongings from home for cosmetics. She brings back two tiny ornate tins and uses their contents to powder my nose and rouge my lips.

Elona soon returns with word from the Winter King. He doesn't know what time he'll be free, and whether another matter will unexpectedly arise, but he'll send for me as soon as he's finished.

I spend the afternoon reading, and it grows so late that I end up dining alone in my chambers. I do my best not to let my soup smear my makeup, but despite my efforts my maids will need to fix my rouge before I meet the Winter King.

The evening continues to drag on with no word from him. There's no clock inside my chambers, and even if there was, it would be a useless piece of ice, but I suspect it's well past nine o'clock. Beyond my window, the full moon shines at its peak, like a luminous pearl sewn into the dark canvas of night.

"It's late, my lady," Elona says after a while. The two of us sit beside the fire, me reading while she knits. Kassia left around half an hour ago, returning home for the night. Elona assured her that she would manage alone for the remainder of the evening. "We should get you changed into something more comfortable, ready for bed." By now, it must be ten o'clock. If not later.

"We'll wait a little while longer," I say.

Elona presses her lips together. "I'm sure you'll see His Majesty at breakfast tomorrow morning. You don't need to stay up so late to see him."

I suppose she's right. But I've already decided that tonight I will make progress with the Winter King. We've exchanged plenty of polite conversation, but in this week I've grown no closer to getting him to lower his guard. We only ever talk across a dinner table, and how will I ever assassinate him when I'm several arm's lengths away from him? Tonight I plan to suggest some other activities, where I will hopefully be able to poison or stab him sooner rather than later.

"If we hear nothing from the king within the hour," I say, "then I'll go to bed."

Pacified by my answer, Elona continues knitting, her needles clinking together. With the whisper of parchment as I turn the pages of my book, the two of us form a peculiar rhythm.

"What are you making?" I ask a few pages later, looking up from my book. I point at the ball of crimson wool in her lap.

She holds up the rectangle she's shaped her wool into, her needles plunged into it. "A scarf," she replies, "for my grand-daughter."

"You have a granddaughter?"

Her pale eyes twinkle. "Why? Don't I look old enough to be a grandmother?"

I laugh. "No, not really."

"I'll take that compliment, my lady," she says, lowering her wool and continuing her knitting. "My eldest daughter had her first child two years ago. It's my granddaughter's birthday in September, so I thought I'd start knitting her a scarf. She's only a small, delicate thing, and a scarf will keep her warm during the Winter months."

"Winter months? Isn't it always Winter here?"

"They no longer live with me beneath the mountain," Elona says. "My daughter grew up here, since I've worked for the Winter King before she was born. She married a blacksmith's apprentice, who has now become a master of his craft. His business was booming so much that they recently moved to Netham."

"It seems she chose him well, then."

Elona smiles. "He chose her. Every morning, he would leave a flower on our doorstep and my husband would chase him away. He persisted for so long that even Dorin softened to him." Her gaze trails across to the vibrant flowers sitting in the vase on the low table between us. "I suppose His Majesty is rather like my son-in-law."

Elona is wrong. A monster like the Winter King can't be compared to her sweet son-in-law.

"The gesture His Majesty makes every day is no mere matter," Elona continues, when I say nothing. "I have served in the Crystal Palace for the last two decades, and I have served over twenty Summer Brides during my time, but never once has the Winter King ordered any flowers to be sent."

My head snaps up. I let her words sink in slowly, savoring each nugget of information. I want to ask her how long each lasted, and whether any have survived a week like me. What does she know of my sister's fate? Does she know how the Winter King disposed of my sister's body after he murdered her? My fingers claw into the old leather cover of my book so deeply I'm sure my nails will leave crescent shaped marks. It's all I can do to stop the question from unraveling on my tongue.

Elona then seems to realize what she has revealed, and she quickly looks back down and resumes her knitting. The gentle clink of her needles is a stark contrast to the thunderous rhythm of my pulse.

Even Elona, who is tighter lipped than Kassia, is letting more and more information slip. And I've only been here for a week. In a month, how much more comfortable will she be with me? It's just a matter of time before she reveals critical information about the Winter King. Information which will be his undoing.

A few minutes later, when my pulse has finally settled to a normal rhythm, a knock sounds at my door. Elona puts aside her knitting and rises from the armchair. She opens them to a servant and exchanges a few words with him before returning to me.

With a smile, she extends her hand. "You were right to wait, my lady," she says as I put down my book. She helps me to my feet and brushes out the creases in my skirts. "The Duke has finally left, and His Majesty is ready to receive you."

Before we leave, I have her tidy the strands of hair which have loosened from my updo, and she also reapplies my rouge and powder. Then we're off, whisking down the icy corridors to the Winter King's wing of the palace.

Throughout the week I've been staying at the Crystal Palace, I've never ventured deeper into the Winter King's chambers than his dining room. I thought I might discover something more of him from the contents of his rooms—like his origins—but there is only ice to be found. Like my bed, his is entirely frozen. Except his is a third of the size and has no blankets of cotton or silk or fur. They're made from ice, just like the curtains. Those are pulled back, tucked behind once metallic holders, and the double doors, which have a dozen frosted windows carved into them, are spread wide open.

The Winter King stands out on the balcony, elbows resting on the icy balustrade, gazing at the gardens beneath. The ends of his wavy hair dance in the evening breeze, flowing like molten silver. So lost in thought, the Winter King doesn't stir until Elona steps out onto the balcony and says, "Your Majesty, your bride is here to see you."

Though I've not once forgotten what I am, what I have chosen, the reminder makes me swallow.

The Winter King turns, his eyes drifting across Elona before settling on me. His attention sweeps across my face, then down to the glimpse of cleavage offered by my gown before snapping back up to my eyes. He holds our stare briefly and then returns to the gardens behind him.

"Come," he says, gesturing beside him.

Elona retreats wordlessly as I start over to the Winter King. I stop around a yard away from him, close enough to be polite but not too close. Yet even at this distance, I'm swept up in the raw power emanating from every ounce of his being. His aura feels like wispy tendrils curling around me, trying to pull me in, pulsing at a steady rhythm.

I'm certain that if not for my newfound immunity to his frost, standing this close to him would freeze me immediately—no kiss required.

The Winter King is as silent and pensive as he was when I arrived. I follow his gaze down into the gardens, watching as snow whirs in the night wind. A few flakes brush my cheeks, but they're not at all cold.

"What are you pondering so deeply, Your Majesty?" I ask, when I can bear the silence no longer. The Winter King glances up at me, a brow rising, so I quickly correct myself with: "Elaric."

"The gardens," he replies, gesturing to them beneath us. The embroidered hem of his navy sleeve flicks out with the motion. "I was considering how you must find them."

"They're fine." I silently curse myself after speaking, since 'fine' is such a paltry word. "More than fine," I add hastily.

"Despite them lacking even a single drop of color?"

With the incredulous note to his voice, I decide it best not to lie on this occasion. I make a show of leaning on the balustrade and examining the gardens, giving myself a moment to think.

"I suppose they would benefit from a dash of color," I say carefully, unsure why he deems this a matter of importance. Maybe he's once again trying to lure out my true thoughts of his palace.

The Winter King nods. "They would, but nothing will grow in frozen earth, and any flowers planted would freeze within a day."

I stand straighter at his words. Here is yet more evidence that the palace's frost is an inconvenience to the Winter King, that he can't control its spread. "Have you tried?" I ask.

"Many times," he says. "But there is one idea I've yet to attempt."

"What idea?"

"To paint the frozen flowers. There is no rain here in the Crystal Palace, only snow. And that snow never melts. Any paint should last years."

"The Crystal Palace has been frozen for so long," I say. "Why bother now? It'll take the servants weeks, if not months, to paint every flower in the gardens."

"Elona tells me you enjoy strolling through them, barren though they are. This is your home now too, Adara, and I wish to make it as pleasant for you as I can."

"Didn't your other brides enjoy strolling through the gardens?" The words are out of my mouth before I can stop them. And I fail miserably at disguising the barb behind them.

The Winter King stops and stares at me. My breath catches in the back of my throat. He steps toward me. This is it. I've finally incited his wrath.

As he closes the distance between us, I have to grip the balustrade to stop myself from retreating.

The Winter King's bright eyes burn down into mine. He reaches for my cheek. I expect him to grab it like he grabbed my chin, right before he kissed me and breathed Winter into me but instead, his touch is soft as he brushes my skin. "You are not like any other bride," he whispers. Does he believe that the sharpness in my words was because I'm jealous of his past brides and not because my heart weeps endlessly for them? "You do not feel the cold."

It's then I realize I didn't flinch at the Winter King's touch. That first night, his fingers were ice, but now they burn across my skin.

"I—" I begin, but the Winter King tucks a loose strand of hair behind my ear and the gesture erases every thought. Even my hatred vanishes, leaving only the feeling of his fingers on my skin and the frantic beating of my heart.

"I noticed the other night, last week," the Winter King continues. "Though you were barefoot, the frost didn't seem to bother you while hurrying down the stairs."

I barely hear his words, my mind otherwise focused on his closeness. On the absence of my disgust. I should loathe this feeling, and yet, for some inexplicable reason, warmth rushes through my entire being. I find myself unable to look away, mesmerized by how his eyes shine as brightly as a morning sky, how the softness of his full lips offers a stark contrast to the unyielding angles of his cutting jawline.

It's as if I'm ensnared by a nightmarish bewitchment.

"And you succeeded in lighting a fire," the Winter King murmurs. "In all these centuries, not a soul has ignited so much as a spark."

"I don't understand," I say, because I don't understand any of this. What the Winter King is saying, why my body is burning with something other than hatred and fury. An emotion I don't dare to name in fear that doing so will grant it more power over me.

"You are my Summer Queen," he says, as if this explains everything.

"We're not married," I reply, keeping my voice as level as I can. "I'm not your queen yet."

His fingers slip from my cheek, and he instead takes my hand in his, squeezing gently. "I've been meaning to discuss this with you," he says. "The date of our wedding."

My stomach dips. "We have a date?"

The Winter King's grasp loosens around my hand, and he takes half a step back. My reaction has likely offended him, but I don't have the courage to grab his hand and pull him back close.

"No," he says quietly, "we have no date yet. I was wondering what your thoughts were, so that we could arrange one."

Even if the feeling of his hand in mine isn't as unpleasant as I imagined, I have no desire to marry an enemy I've hated for countless years. The thought of walking down the aisle to him sends bile rushing up. I swallow it down, though it scalds my throat.

I've always known this would be the price of vengeance, that I would have to marry this man, that I might even have to lie with him as his wife. I hoped that my chance to kill him would come before that, but during this past week, no such opportunity has arisen. How long can I delay our wedding without raising suspicion?

I've hesitated long enough. The fog of wariness is already creeping into his eyes. I need to mend the damage my reluctance is causing, but my mind is currently buzzing with hundreds of conflicting thoughts.

All I can think of to say is: "This kingdom has been without a queen for so long. We should not delay our wedding."

The Winter King frowns at this. Was my response not satisfactory?

To my relief, he closes the distance he created and his fingers tighten again around mine. "It does not matter what the kingdom wants. It matters what you want, Adara."

I chew on my lip. I could ask him to wait several months, during which I'd likely find a chance to assassinate him, but how will he react if I ask such a thing? Is it better to play along with this, to give my body and soul to him if I must, all in the name of vengeance?

Before I can reach a conclusion, the Winter King says, "Don't decide now. It's late. We'll discuss it more in the morning."

"I'll sleep on it," I say, my stomach churning.

The Winter King smiles and then, before I can step away, leans down and presses his lips to the top of my head. This kiss isn't cold like the first. Warmth seeps through my hair and into my skin, rushing down to my toes. It bothers me even more than the matter of our wedding.

Even after bidding him good night, I still feel the burning mark of his lips all the way back to my chambers.

Chapter 14

That night, sleep eludes me. All I can think about is the feel of the Winter King's lips. His fingers brushing across my cheeks. The warmth consuming me, even now.

I shouldn't feel like this. Not for the man who has taken so much from me, who has caused me so much pain that an entire lifetime wouldn't be enough to erase it.

I should hate him.

I *do* hate him.

I feel nothing for him but fury, and I'll remind myself of this over and over until anything *else* is obliterated. All I can pray is that it'll be enough.

Then there's the matter of our wedding. Of what will come after if I don't soon find the opportunity to kill him.

I clench the hilt of my dagger, its weight balancing on my chest. My other hand clutches the poison vial, relishing how the glass presses into my palm.

If he comes tonight, I will kill him. But over this past week, he hasn't once returned, and I'm not sure tonight will be any different. Why, I don't understand. Surely I infuriated him enough last week when I tried to melt down those doors? Yet so far, I've received no repercussions for my actions. Only flowers.

A shadow of doubt snakes through my heart. What if for all these years, I've been wrong about the Winter King? What if he isn't the villain I've always believed him to be? Could Dalia's disappearance be a misunderstanding? Could the Winter King be innocent?

No. He took Dalia. He came to my room on that first night and tried to freeze me. There can be no mistaking that. The Winter King is responsible for all of it.

I must rid myself of any doubt. It'll only hinder me.

Deep into the hours of night, I drift into a light sleep. Dalia dances in my dreams, as she always does, reminding me of my purpose and granting me the strength to tolerate the Winter King and his frost day after day.

The darkness shatters at the sound of a door opening. I bolt awake. My fingers instinctively unsheathe my blade, steel whispering through my room.

The Winter King?

I hold my breath and listen carefully to the footsteps. More than one pair approach. From their rhythm, I guess three. And they don't sound proud and steady like the Winter King's. Nor do they sound light like my maids'. These footsteps are foreign.

I dare to open an eye. The moon is but a thin crescent, only a slither of light penetrating my curtains. My eyes struggle to adjust to the darkness. When they do, I make out the forms of three men. I can't see their faces. Their hooded cloaks conceal their identities. Silver flashes beneath a cloak.

A sword.

Has the Winter King sent his men to execute me? Has he decided that since his ice won't work on me, he'll instead use steel?

The men stalk through the darkness, moving slowly and quietly.

I don't so much as twitch. I let them believe me to be asleep. Then I wait as they draw closer. Until they're looming over me.

One reaches down for me. In a flurry of steel, I throw aside my blankets and swipe out for him. My dagger connects with his shoulder. I feel my blade sinking into flesh, deep enough to draw blood.

The man lets out a sharp yelp and leaps backward. As do his comrades.

I seize the opportunity their surprise offers and spring to my feet. The silken skirts of my nightgown swirl around me with the motion. I grip my dagger.

At home, I spent nearly all my free time training with Father's guards. Though it's three against one, I've faced worse odds in duels. One may think the guards went easy on me, lest they injured me and faced Father's fury, but being beaten by a teenage girl on many occasions does wonders for inciting a man's temper. After countless humiliating defeats, it's safe to say all the guards came at me with their full strength.

But tonight, I wield only a dagger and not a sword. It reduces my reach substantially and means I'm going to have to get closer to them than I would like. At least my usual fighting style relies on speed and clever feints.

Surprisingly, my ambushers don't draw their swords. Even when I twirl my dagger, they don't rise to the challenge. I don't waste time contemplating my luck. I strike first.

As I lunge to my nearest enemy, he takes a step back and narrowly avoids my blade. I swivel and aim for his stomach. He raises his hands before I can. In surrender.

I stop and frown. I don't loosen my grip on my dagger, fearing this may be some sort of trick. But the other ambushers also raise their hands. None make any sudden movements.

"Lady Adara," says the one nearest me. His gravelly voice is familiar. "Only you would sleep with a dagger cradled to your chest."

"Orlan?" I ask.

He answers by lowering his hood and revealing his strawberry blond beard and shoulder length hair. I lower my dagger at the sight of Father's guard captain, the man who taught me everything I know about swordsmanship. The one guard I have never beaten.

A grin cracks across his face, creasing the weathered lines around his green eyes. "Took you long enough, my lady." He points to the other two men. "Fillon and Tierley."

Fillon and Tierley don't lower their hoods and both give me a nod. Now that Orlan has said it, I can recognize both of their statures. Tierley is taller and broader than Orlan, and he's the one I cut. The wound doesn't seem to be too deep, though. Fillon, the youngest guard in our household, is shorter and thinner than both Tierley and Orlan. He often offers to help our servants with unloading and carrying heavy crates. The other guards tease that he's so desperate to add some bulk to his shoulders.

"What are you doing here?" I demand, turning back to Orlan.

"Your father sent us to rescue you."

I hook the vial's chain around my index finger and dangle it. Like a pendulum, it swings back and forth. "Do I look like I need rescuing? Like I'm some sort of damsel in distress?"

His smile vanishes. "My lady, now's not the time for fooling around. We encountered a patrol on the way into the palace, and though we defeated them, it won't be long until the other guards realize they're missing. We must hurry."

I dig my bare heels into the icy floor. "I'm not going anywhere."

Orlan draws out a heavy sigh. "Adara," he warns, losing formality as we do in sparring. "Don't be foolish. There's no such thing as a Summer Queen. The Winter King may not have hurt you yet, but he will. The prospect of becoming Queen isn't worth death."

My grip tightens on my dagger. "You think I'd risk everything just to sit on a pretty throne? Considering you spent years chasing me through meadows and up trees, I thought you knew me better than that."

"Then why stay?"

"For Dalia."

Orlan's attention falls on the vial swinging in my hand. His eyes widen. It seems he only now realizes what lies within. "Madness!" he exclaims. "You can't possibly think you'll succeed in killing the Winter King?"

I tighten my hold on the vial's chain. It stops swinging.

"Dalia would never want you to throw away your own life like this!" he continues.

"Dalia isn't here," I grind out.

"We must get you out of here before the Winter King discovers what you're plotting."

I lift my chin. "You can return to my father and tell him I refuse to leave the Crystal Palace, no matter how many guards he sends to collect me."

"I'm not leaving here empty-handed."

"You don't have a choice."

Orlan's expression hardens. "Your father instructed us to retrieve you, even if you refused."

I pull the chain over my head and tuck the vial beneath my nightgown. "I suggest you leave before I call for the guards."

Orlan shakes his head in disbelief. "It doesn't need to be like this."

My hand tightens around my dagger. "It does."

I lunge for him as he unsheathes his sword. My blade arcs through the air. He steps out the way, and I narrowly miss him. With the longer reach of a sword, I'd have had him. My best chance of defeating the guards is to disarm one of them and steal his sword. Orlan isn't a suitable target. One to one, I've never beaten him. I'll have more chance at defeating Tierley or Fillon. Especially Fillon. Besides, Tierley's broadsword is too heavy for me to wield with case. Fillon's will be perfect.

Orlan sweeps his sword toward me in a single fluid movement. I duck. The blade sails overhead. Tierley and Fillon draw their weapons, and the three of them circle in on me.

Still low, I jab at Orlan's thigh. But he parries.

I swivel around and kick Fillon's knee. My foot connects with him, and he stumbles.

Tierley's broadsword descends on me. Air thunders as it crashes down.

I lunge to the side, and Tierley's sword plunges into the ice. It bites through several layers of frost, creating a gaping crack. Shards splinter off. Orlan pauses and narrows his eyes at Tierley. They're here to rescue me, not kill me. Though I suspect Tierley may actually want to. Most of our sparring matches end with him on his backside and me standing over him with my sword at his throat.

With Orlan hesitating and Tierley yanking his blade out of the ice, I turn to Fillon. And not a moment too soon.

Sword first, he charges at me. I lean back. His sword sweeps over my chest, slicing through the air.

I dig one heel into the floor to keep my balance and shove my other foot into his knee again. I must have struck him hard enough the first time, since this blow sends him toppling over. The blade slips from his grasp. I lunge for the sword before it hits the ground. My fingers scarcely find the hilt. I clench it.

Orlan's blade races toward me. I catch it between my sword and dagger. He withdraws. The shrill shriek of steel ricochets through the room. I release his blade. My weapons are in the wrong hands, my dagger in my dominant one rather than my sword. Offering resistance will cause me to lose my balance.

I leap away and use the distance gained to switch my hands. I've barely secured my weapons before Tierley swings again. This blow is less devastating than the last. Either it's because of Orlan's silent warning or because he's favoring speed over strength. But it'll still hurt if I get caught.

Luckily, Tierley's fastest strike is too slow for me. I step around him and shove the pommel of my dagger into his wounded shoulder. He howls with pain. With the window of opportunity, I could strike his exposed side. But I'm doing my best to avoid injuring them too severely, or else they'll struggle to escape the Crystal Palace. My aim is to wipe the floor with them and send them running back to Father with their tails between their legs.

If I can beat Orlan, that is.

I evade Orlan's next blow by stepping right and then sweep my sword toward his side. He sees the counter coming and parries. Before he's even blocked, I jab my left hand at his gut. Though I've been lenient with Fillon and Tierley and wouldn't dare deal them such a critical blow, I can't afford to show Orlan any mercy. If I attack him with anything but my full strength, I have no chance of beating him.

Orlan leans back. For a split second, I hold my breath as the blade lurches toward him. But it continues past, and I miss by a hair's breadth. I shouldn't be surprised the feint didn't work. Orlan is the one who taught me this move.

The tiniest breeze of relief washes over me. I crush it and focus on the present. No mercy. I won't let Orlan stand in my way and stop me from slaying the Winter King and avenging my sister.

Tierley is too busy nursing his wound to bother with us, and Fillon is still unarmed and looks scared to approach. Only my blades and Orlan's clash in the center of the room, teacher against student.

"Give it up, Adara," he urges. I hate that he doesn't sound the slightest bit out of breath. "If we leave it much longer, there'll be no chance to escape."

"No," I hiss.

His jaw clenches, and he attacks me with renewed strength. Before, we were evenly matched, but desperation fuels each of his blows. They come at me faster and faster, forming a volley of steel. I can barely keep up with him, and leaning on the defensive myself means I have no chance to retaliate. I can only keep focusing on each incoming blow, and they come so quickly and from every angle, it's as if he is wielding ten swords rather than one. Even with two blades, I stand no chance against him. Orlan is a master swordsman, and it's the reason I'm as good as I am.

Several strikes later, I find myself with my back to the wall. No, not a wall. A corner.

Between the storm of steel, I see Orlan's eyes glinting. I can hear his unspoken words, a lesson from long ago.

Never be so focused on your opponent that you lose sight of your surroundings.

I should have known better. Playing the offensive and forcing his opponent into a corner is Orlan's favorite strategy.

I must fight my way out of this.

I stop focusing on where the blades are coming from. Instead, I *feel* them. I attune myself to the rhythm Orlan is forming, the hum of battle guiding my hand. Then I'm fending off his blows from instinct alone, my moves quicker than before. It gives me enough time to think. To devise a strategy that will disrupt his rhythm and take him by surprise.

Finally, I find my opening. A chance to slip my dagger past his defense.

I parry with my sword and thrust my dagger into his side. He notices, but his blade is locked with mine. Horror bubbles in my throat. A scream that struggles for release. I've held back no blows with Orlan, and he wears only leather. My attack contains my full strength, and this wound will be fatal.

Despite the fact he's currently my enemy and is standing between me and vengeance, I do my best to slow the blow. To reduce the power. But my blade is singing through the air with far too much momentum for me to control.

Orlan's sword arcs down to my dagger, just as it collides with his side. Every part of me screams. Even to avenge my sister's death, it isn't worth murdering the man who spent thousands of hours training me to wield a blade. The man who raised me like a second father. And Dalia, too.

But the blow isn't as devastating as I feared. Between my attempt to weaken the blow and Orlan's sword absorbing some of the impact, the resulting injury is barely more than a scratch.

My hands tremble. The dagger slips from my fingers, and clatters onto the icy floor. The blade is red and sticky from Orlan's blood.

This isn't the first time I've wounded someone during sparring, but it's the first time I've struck with the intention to hurt. And it terrifies me. Yet another part of me whispers that if I cannot bear the sight of a scratch on Orlan's side, how will I possibly have the courage to strike the Winter King through the chest? I tell myself it's completely different: Orlan is like family, whereas the Winter King is a monster. But deep down, I fear I'm just a silly girl meddling with affairs far above her. I'm no assassin. How can I expect to slay our monarch?

When I look up, I expect Orlan to be glaring at me. But he isn't. Though I've hurt him, he isn't the slightest bit angry. Not even annoyed. He only looks at me with his brows drawn together and eyes heavy with pity.

It's then I realize his sword is at my neck. The flat edge of his blade rests against my chin.

Chapter 15

My entire body is numb as Orlan and the guards lead me through the Crystal Palace. Coldness washes my limbs in a way that I haven't felt this last week, not since overcoming the Winter King's spell. But I know the ice crawling across my legs has nothing to do with the frozen walls around me and everything to do with my current situation.

I could try to escape, but I can see no way out. They've bound my wrists with rope, and Orlan tied the knot as tightly as he could. I try to wriggle my wrists free but the fibers burn my skin. Since they need me to walk, they've left my legs unbound.

I could kick them and struggle like an unruly colt, but I doubt it would lead to my escape. They're armed and I'm not, and Orlan is more than my equal. All kicking will accomplish is causing a ruckus that might alert the Winter King and his guards. While that would guarantee the failure of this rescue mission, it would also mean condemning Orlan and his men.

And Father too, if the Winter King searches for accomplices and finds him lurking outside the palace's walls.

No matter how hard I try, I can't think of a solution. If I refuse to stop walking, Orlan will tell Tierley to chuck me over his shoulder, and then I'll have less chance of wriggling free. That's why I have no choice but to follow Orlan and the others and do as they say. All the while praying that an opportunity presents itself.

We reach a corner. Orlan raises his hand, signaling for us to halt.

Footsteps ring out down the corridor. We all press our backs to the wall, leaning into the shadows as best we can. We're just in position when guards race past, their armor gleaming in the blue light of the braziers lining the walls. I hear Fillon suck in a breath. He goes rigid beside me. The guards shout out to one another, their words so frenzied I can scarcely decipher them. The fragments I pick up involve 'infiltrators' and 'search the palace' and 'alert the king'. Fortunately, they're all so busy running to their stations and securing the palace that they don't glance down the dark corner we're huddled in.

When they're gone, Orlan's lips draw into a thin line. "We need to get moving before they block all the exits."

Without wasting another second, he slips around the corner and heads the opposite way to where the guards vanished. Tierley nudges me forward, and with him at my heels, his form towering over me, I have no choice but to dash after Orlan. Fillon takes the rear, constantly glancing over his shoulder to make sure no guards suddenly appear.

Orlan picks his way carefully through the palace, weaving in and out of the quietest corridors and pausing before making any more daring moves. Somehow, we make it outside without colliding with any guards. Fillon shuts the small servants' door behind us, and we stalk out into the gardens, using as much of the foliage to cover us as we can. Guards are patrolling the walls, far more than when I sneaked out of the palace last week, and all of them are alert.

We crouch behind the hedges, waiting for the guards to turn away before delving deeper into the gardens. Then we move as quickly as we can, until they turn back in our direction.

It feels like it takes all night to make it to the other side, though I reasonably know it can't be more than ten minutes.

Eventually, we arrive at a small door carved into the palace's outer walls, shrouded by a tangle of branches. It's so well hidden that I didn't spot it during my tour with Elona and Kassia on my first day here. If only I had. It would have saved me from having to scale up the wall and climb pine trees.

But given the lack of handles, it must be frozen shut.

My lips curl into a wry smile. "Good luck cracking that open."

My sarcasm doesn't dampen Orlan's spirit. Then I notice it's been left ajar.

Orlan's fingers find the edge, and he pulls the door toward us. "It was harder to open on the other side," he says, holding the door open for me. "But it wasn't anything Tierley couldn't force his way through."

I glance up at the brute with a frown. Surely the door hasn't been sealed with the Winter King's magic if Tierley has barged the door open? If it was, then it seems employing Tierley to work on the door to the Winter King's forbidden chamber would have been a superior tactic than attempting to thaw it open.

But Tierley offers no clues, and Orlan lets out a sharp hiss of breath, indicating another patrol is likely coming into view. When I glance back, I see my suspicions confirmed. I don't waste another second before lunging forth into the tangle of trees beyond, hoping Orlan and his men have enough time to make it through.

They do. But barely. Just as Tierley is pulling the door shut behind us, a guard shouts something. Then all their frantic footsteps rush toward us.

"This way," Orlan says, pointing to the left.

I race after him, stepping over hundreds of pines. They feel like a bed of needles underfoot.

"You know," I say between breaths when I've caught up with Orlan, "if you're worried about being captured, I could just hand myself over to the guards. That would give you all enough time to escape."

Orlan smirks. "Nice try, my lady. Tierley, make sure she doesn't get lost in the trees."

Tierley only grunts in response. I roll my shoulders in a shrug. It was worth a try.

All these pine trees look the same as the last, but Orlan guides our way. Shouts echo from behind us, muffled by the branches. It sounds like there are more guards than before. Maybe the entire palace is already pursuing us. Does the Winter King know what's happened yet? How will he react to my disappearance?

I stub my toe on a gnarled root and seethe in pain. Then I focus my thoughts on my surroundings instead of the Winter King. Running downhill makes it harder to control my footing, especially when countless roots and branches riddle my path.

We break into a clearing. Half a dozen men are waiting on horseback, joined by three horses with no riders. Like Orlan and his men, they all wear black leathers, and hooded cloaks obscure their faces. But I recognize the man in the middle from his silhouette alone. He's shorter and rounder than the rest, lacking the broadness of a warrior's shoulders.

"Father," I breathe. Though my words are quieter than the wind shaking the pines, he seems to hear me.

"Adara!" He pulls on his horse's reins and charges toward us. When he reaches us, he comes to a halt and gazes down at me, taking in my torn nightgown and the rope around my wrists. "Remove her restraints," he says to Orlan. "I won't have my daughter a prisoner."

Orlan hesitates. "With all due respect, my lord, Lady Adara was rather hard to persuade—"

A glare from Father silences him.

"As you wish." Orlan narrows his eyes at me as he cuts my ropes, pleading with me not to do anything stupid. But I won't. As much as I long to avenge Dalia, I won't do anything that will cause them to get caught.

"I won't run," I promise. And I mean it. My opportunity to run is long gone, and I can't bear to see any of them get hurt because of me.

Orlan gives a small nod and slices through the last of the rope's fibers. The remnants fall to the floor. He unclasps his cloak and drapes it around my shoulders. I go to protest and say I have no need of it, since I no longer feel the cold like him, but then I remember I'm in my nightgown. And surrounded by the company of nearly a dozen men. I accept the cloak with a

BRIDE OF THE WINTER KING

brief word of thanks, and then he helps me up onto Father's horse.

Shouts ring out through the trees. The guards aren't far away now. We've delayed long enough. If the guards are also mounted, I fear we won't outrun them.

Father kicks our horse's flanks, and then we're off, galloping through the sprawling mass of trees. Orlan takes the lead, navigating his horse through the maze of pines. We stomp over fallen trees and over a sliver of a stream, barely trickling. The clatter of hooves thunders through the forest. The shouts grow farther into the distance.

I gaze up at the canopy of pines, moonlight flashing through at various intervals, and cling to Father. My emotions are too tangled to unravel. Though I'm relieved we've all escaped unscathed, bitterness broils in my heart. I've failed Dalia. I've failed to avenge her murderer. And I hate most that I can breathe easier here with Father. As if a weight has lifted from my shoulders. For the past week, I've lived as though treading across a barely frozen lake, fearing one wrong move will plunge me into the icy depths. I squeeze my eyes shut and hug Father tighter, focusing on his warmth rather than the glass vial branding my skin.

"You shouldn't have saved me," I whisper.

"How could I leave you, Adara?" His voice sounds like fabric stretched too thin, barely holding onto the seams.

"You could have been caught," I say. "Then what would have happened?"

"I haven't slept a single night since he took you. All I could think about was him hurting you."

"You saw me today in the palace. Was that not enough to know I was well?"

He shakes his head. "Though you were well today, that didn't guarantee you'd be well tomorrow. Or the day after. I had to get you out of there while I could."

I don't reply. How can I when I myself couldn't guarantee my safety? I don't know when the Winter King would have next struck.

"Did you ever see Dalia?" I ask after a moment. "After he took her?"

"No. Not once."

It was so long ago that I can't remember how soon Father returned to the Crystal Palace after the Winter King took her. It might have been a week. Or a month. I don't know whether my sister survived her first night, or if she also gained this strange immunity to ice.

"Why did Orlan bind your wrists?" Father says. "Why did you refuse your rescue?"

My plan is already ruined. What difference will it make if he knows the truth? At the very least, it'll be better than him believing I forgave the Winter King for my sister's death just so I could be crowned Queen and wear pretty dresses and sit on a throne of ice.

"So I could kill him," I say. "The Winter King."

Even over the howling wind and thundering hooves, I hear Father's sharp intake of breath.

I continue before he can say anything. Even my name. For I fear that alone will be enough to break me.

"I wanted to be chosen so I could kill him. So I could make him feel our pain. But now my plan is ruined."

Father is silent for a while. "I'm glad I ruined it," is all he eventually says.

We say nothing more. Though he's ruined all my scheming, I cling to him. Because deep down I fear I'd have never pulled it off, anyway. How can a girl who can't stand the sight of blood kill a king?

A tear escapes. I don't bother lifting my arms from Father to wipe it away. I let it roll down my cheek, heavy with despair. Disappointment in myself. If only I'd acted sooner, instead of putting off killing the Winter King, waiting day after day for a better opportunity to land on my lap. Now any opportunity I had is gone, and I'm left with nothing. Nothing but a still bleeding heart, without vengeance to cauterize it.

I'm sorry, Dalia.

I whisper the words to the wind, hoping it will carry them high into the Heavens so she can hear them. I've failed her and I've failed myself and I've failed every other girl the Winter King has snatched away. All I can hope now is that she and every other Summer Bride will one day forgive me. That I can learn to forgive myself.

And that's when I hear it. The beating of wings. They're too strong to be a bird's, even a hulking eagle. I know in my heart who it is, long before I see him.

We burst from the trees, the midnight sky breaking free of the pines and brambles. I tilt back my head and gaze upward.

Gleaming among the stars are enormous wings sculpted from ice. And frosted hooves and a silken mane. The sight is as chilling as it is breath-taking. Like *him*.

But no matter how beautiful the winged horse might be, I feel only horror when it descends close enough for me to see its rider.

The Winter King. With a cloak of ice billowing behind him and his glacial eyes focused on me.

Chapter 16

Father pulls on our horse's reins, turning us back toward the trees. Though the cover of branches will shroud us from above, I doubt it'll make much difference in escaping the Winter King.

The world is a blur of pines around me. It's all I can do to hold on to Father and not slip off our horse. This fate is worse than failing my mission. If we are caught, I will lose Father. And it will all be my fault. If I hadn't drawn the Winter King's attention, he would have never chosen me.

Orlan and his men whirl around, urging their horses after us toward the trees. But it's too late. The ground trembles as the Winter King's fearsome mount lands. Even from atop the saddle, I feel the shockwave shuddering beneath.

I glance back. The Winter King's eyes lock with mine. He doesn't look away as he raises his hands. The pines before us turn to ice, their branches growing until they tangle too thickly for us to squeeze through.

Our escape is cut off.

Our horse rears, just before it collides with the branches. Father pulls on the reins again, and our horse settles down and veers right.

Orlan and his men don't follow now. They halt and turn back to the Winter King. All draw their swords.

"Go, my lord!" Orlan shouts, gripping the hilt. If he fears facing our immortal king, he's brave enough not to show it. "We'll cover your escape!"

Determination hardens his face. I squeeze my eyes shut and dig my nails into my palms, unable to look at him and hating the truth I see.

That he's willing to die for Father and me.

If I throw myself off this horse and race over to the Winter King and tell him that everything was just a misunderstanding, will he be content to let them all go and take me alone back to the Crystal Palace?

No. The Winter King isn't known for his mercy. Even if I beg him to spare Father and Orlan and their men, he will kill them. Then they'll die for nothing. If Father and I escape, Orlan's death won't be in vain.

Or if I were braver, stupider, I'd charge dagger-first at the Winter King.

Father must feel my fidgeting or know me well enough that he says, "Don't, Adara."

"But Orlan—"

"Is doing his duty."

His duty. Like my duty to my sister. Which I failed.

I force myself to look back. To remember his face. All their faces. They've surrounded the Winter King now, but their horses tremble. As if they can't bear to be so close to his terrible aura.

Father rides us around the frozen branches. Though the Winter King only gave the slight wave of his hand, he's turned many of the trees to ice. It takes several strides to reach some that are still green, and Father forces our horse through the narrow gap between the pines. Just as the branches grow dense enough to restrict my view, I catch a final glimpse of Orlan and his men facing the Winter King. The Winter King summons six wolves made from ice and unleashes them.

They're monstrous things, thrice the height of normal wolves, coming shoulder to shoulder with the horses. Their fangs are as long and wide as my forearm. My stomach turns to lead as I imagine those wolves ripping Orlan and his men apart.

"Father," I gasp, "we must go back. Please."

He says nothing. But I know he hears me from how his shoulders tense.

The clanging of metal echoes from beyond the trees.

"We can't let them die like this!" I exclaim.

"As our guards, it is their duty to keep us safe," Father says, his voice harder than I've ever heard it. "And as your father, it is my duty to keep you safe."

Those painful moments drag on. The sound of fighting grows distant.

Guards or not, duty or not, I can't do this. I can't abandon them.

Before Father can stop me, I yank his sword from its scabbard and throw myself off our horse, Orlan's cloak swishing behind me.

I cover my head with my left arm, bracing myself for landing. Father's sword slips from my grasp. I hit the ground at an awkward angle, lightning sparking up my side. Then I'm sent rolling downhill.

I stop rolling by digging my fingers into the frozen earth. One knee is badly grazed, while my skirts shielded the other. Both my palms are torn and bloodied.

"Adara!" Father shouts. Hooves drum toward me. He's only a few paces away.

I force myself up, no matter how much my body protests. I scan the area, searching for Father's sword. Silver flashes to my right, just as Father closes in.

His hand sweeps out, trying to grab me. I duck and fling myself under his horse, narrowly avoiding being trampled by hooves. I scramble toward the sword and grab the hilt just as Father spins his horse around and charges again. Then I run, my lungs burning. I throw myself through brambles and over giant roots. I stumble several times and surrender myself to the momentum, allowing it to propel me.

The path is narrow, and Father is forced to ride around it. I glance back to see how far he is, and misjudge my step. I tumble over a bank and slide straight down it. My skirts offer little padding from the stones and twigs, which jut into my legs and backside. Each painful bump after another blurs into one. Ahead, the pines lessen. I reach the end of the bank and am deposited a few paces away from the edge of the trees.

I shove myself back onto my feet and sprint, clasping Father's sword with all my might, refusing to drop it again.

I break from the trees, the torn and sullied skirts of my night gown fluttering around me. I pause, assessing the situation. The wolves are gone. Several icy statues are gathered around the Winter King.

One man of flesh and blood remains. Bowed over before the Winter King, entirely at his mercy.

"Orlan!" I shout, charging across the grass. Hooves pound behind me. Father calls my name. I don't look back.

I raise my sword, though I'm too far away. I won't stop the Winter King in time. I won't save Orlan.

Orlan doesn't look up at my shouts. But the Winter King does. He watches me as magic swirls in his hands, as it engulfs Orlan. No matter how much I shout, the Winter King doesn't stop his spell. Not until Orlan is rendered to ice.

I stagger. Hopelessness and grief drag me toward the ground.

The Winter King has stolen someone else from me.

All I can see is red. As if someone has smeared blood across my eyes. As if my bleeding heart has finally bled enough to blind me.

I will kill him.

Now.

This was never how I imagined I would face him. I always imagined that I would have the advantage. That I would get to savor the look of shock and despair on his face right before I plunged my dagger into his chest.

Now I'll be lucky if I even cut his arm.

I force myself onward. For Dalia. For Orlan. For every life the Winter King has seized.

He doesn't even twitch as I charge toward him. Father's shouts are muffled, more distant than I know him to be.

"Adara," the Winter King says as I reach him. I grip Father's sword with both hands, my breathing ragged with hate and rage and pain. "What is the meaning of all this? Have I treated you unfairly? Why do you wish to run?"

The metallic edges of the hilt dig into my palms. "Do I look like I'm running now?"

The Winter king pauses, taking in my heaving chest, my furious expression, my steel grip on the sword. "No," he says quietly. "No, I don't suppose you do."

"You killed them," I spit, no longer bothering to mask my hatred. My rage is too wild to restrain. "You killed them all."

"What else would you have me do? Roll over and allow them to plunge their swords through me?"

My nostrils flare. I hate how innocent he claims to be. That it's natural and fair for him to turn men into ice.

He is a monster.

A monster that must be slain.

The hooves of Father's horse pound toward us. Before he can reach us, the Winter King raises his hand and surrounds us in ice. The dome is as clear as glass. A window which enables me to see Father's horror-stricken face. His hands tremble around the reins. He shouts my name, but I can only see the syllables on his lips. The barrier is thick enough to silence all sounds. There's no way Father will bash through. And for that, I'm grateful. This fight is between the Winter King and me, one which is three years overdue. If Father has any sense, he'll turn and flee while he can. But I know he won't. He's as stubborn and reckless as me.

I twirl my sword and assume a fighting stance. I scan across the Winter King, searching for any weaknesses and grasping for a strategy to defeat him.

The Winter King extends his hand, drawing a sword from blue light.

Though he stands there with a blade in his grasp, he makes no move. He doesn't so much as assume a fighting stance. I wrinkle my nose. Arrogant. He sees me as so beneath him that he won't make the first move.

Father bangs on the icy dome. Though he puts all his strength into shoving the wall, it sounds like light rain pattering against a window. His horse has the sense to run. It's almost vanished into the trees.

Now Father has no escape. Unless I defeat the Winter King, he'll kill Father like he killed Orlan.

"Well?" The Winter King arches a silver brow. "Shall we dance with our blades, or shall we return to the palace? What will it be, my queen?"

My queen.

Those two words make every hair on my spine and neck shudder. Disgust propels me forward. Without thinking, without a proper strategy, I charge for him in a storm of blind rage.

I swing my sword at him with all my burning fury. The attack is wilder and clumsier than I know to be sensible, but at least it isn't lacking in strength.

The Winter King just stands there, watching my sword sail toward him. Only at the last second does he raise his icy blade and parry my attack. He stares down at me, his expression stoic. Yet his blue eyes glitter. As if daring me to strike again.

I withdraw my sword in a careful, controlled motion. My blade scratches over his. I pause and narrow my eyes, determined to make my next move less reckless than my first.

The Winter King doesn't move.

This time I try feinting right. My sword arcs toward his left, and he parries again with frightening precision. But that wasn't the move I was counting on. I hurl my left foot at his groin. I move as quickly as I can, hoping to catch him unaware. Yet he steps away. I try to redirect my kick, but he moves completely out of my range. Then I'm left stumbling forth. But the Winter

King doesn't take advantage of my brief loss of balance. He waits for me to correct my stance, and then I swing at him again. Once more, I don't come even close to striking him.

Over and over, I swing and jab and kick. No matter what I try, I can't break his defense. He moves too quickly and predicts my every feint. Never have I fought an opponent this skilled. His abilities are a world apart from Orlan's.

With a sinking heart, I realize he isn't fighting me properly. He stays on the defensive, not so much as countering my attacks. Nor is he using his magic on me. My stomach knots. If he fought me with his full strength, this fight would be over within minutes.

If he insists on underestimating me, I'll have to use it to my advantage and make him regret thinking so little of me.

I make the show he expects, letting my movements grow weaker, projecting fatigue onto my face. At first, I'm not sure it's working, but then the Winter King slows to match me. And when I appear to be seconds away from giving into my exhaustion and collapsing to the ground, I snap back to life. In a burst of speed, I slash at his arm. He tries to evade the attack but steps away a moment too late. My sword catches him.

At the sight of his silk tunic ripping, my heart skips. But it's such a small victory, the blow little more than a scratch. Nonetheless, I have wounded him. And that is a sight I've waited so long to see. Determination sends a fresh wave of strength rushing through my body.

I'm so focused on his injury that I'm late to notice his counter. I dodge and narrowly avoid the attack. His blade is sharp enough to sever a lock of my hair. The crimson strand falls to the icy ground.

I sweep my blade up, but the Winter King blocks the blow. When he breaks our parry, I realize just how much he's been holding back. He pushes my blade away, and though my muscles strain, I lack the strength to resist.

Then he releases my sword. I try to counter, but he's already taken advantage of the opening. The icy tip of his blade rests against my sternum. Half an inch lower, it would have grazed against my poison vial. I hope he doesn't see the slight bulge under my nightgown, that the silk is opaque enough to hide the incriminating hue of nightshade.

Shame brands my cheeks. I've failed my quest to slay the Winter King. I've failed to avenge both Dalia and Orlan. Now I'm forfeiting not just my own life, but Father's too.

"Kill me," I hiss.

The Winter King considers me. I begin to think he really will drive his icy blade through my heart. I wait and wait, but the end never comes. Instead, he lowers his blade and closes his eyes. He presses his lips together and regards me again. "You are my Summer Queen, Adara," he says, his words solemn and heavy, "and I have waited three hundred years for you. Even if you wanted to throw away your own life, I would not let you."

The most humiliating part of my defeat is this supposed mercy. He will not kill me because I belong to him. Because he needs me for whatever reason he needs a Summer Queen.

I say nothing. He lifts his hand and conjures shackles. They wrap around my torso and my legs, and force my arms to my sides. They bind my legs so tightly I'll be surprised if I can even walk. Though my arms are useless, I hold on to my sword with all my might. If we return to the palace and he doesn't find my poison vial, I may regain his trust and strike another day. The most logical next step would be reining in my hatred and donning the façade of an innocent flower and apologizing profusely for striking him, but I can't. I am surrounded by the icy statues of Orlan and his men, and besides, I've already shown him my thorns. Never again will I be able to resume my role of a shrinking violet.

The Winter King releases his sword, which disintegrates into thousands of tiny shards, and steps toward me. I don't flinch. My glare doesn't relent. He reaches for my hand and lifts my fingers from the hilt one by one. He does so lightly at first, until it becomes apparent that I'm clinging on with all my might.

"Adara," he whispers. "Release your sword, and let us return to the palace."

I refuse and grasp the hilt harder. But then reason pierces through the fog of fury, and sense crashes down on me like an avalanche.

I release the blade, and the Winter King catches the sword, and it turns to ice at once in his hands. He doesn't wield the sword against me, but instead snaps his fingers and the dome shatters.

Father is still trying to barge his way in and stumbles forth when the barrier gives way. I want to run to his side, but I can barely move with the shackles. I manage just half a step. The Winter King doesn't move as Father races toward us. I glance between Father and the sword in the Winter King's hand, and dread twists through my stomach.

"Don't," I gasp, the word shuddering through my lips before I can realize. I hastily add, "Please don't kill my father. Whatever you need from me, I will give it to you freely, so long as you spare him."

The Winter King's stony gaze trails across to me. He watches me for a second and says nothing before turning back to Father. A lump swells in my throat. These shackles render me useless. Whatever the Winter King chooses, I cannot stop him. How I wish Father would run.

He wields no weapon. I stole his sword and now the Winter King wields it, frozen in his hand. And all the blades of Orlan and his men remain in their grasp, one with them for eternity.

Father drops to his knees a few paces away, just where the ground stops being ice and starts being grass again. He presses his head to the ground. "Please, Your Majesty. I beg you to release my daughter."

The Winter King tilts his head as he examines Father. "You sent your men to break into my home and steal my bride, and now you demand I hand over that which I've searched for more than thrice your lifetime. Tell me, Lord Darrell, why I should not kill you where you stand."

An unintelligible sound escapes my throat. Something between a sob and a scream. I shake away my fear. It will not serve me here.

"If you kill my father," I blurt, "I will not give you what you seek."

I don't know what the Winter King wants from me. I don't know what bargain I'm striking. But it's all I can say to stop him from murdering Father as he murdered Dalia and Orlan.

The Winter King's attention flickers to me. "And you know what it is I need?"

I clamp my mouth shut. Whatever I say may make matters worse. The three of us stay silent, and my heart thumps so loudly I'm sure the Winter King will hear it and know my fear.

Then he raises his hand. Blue light sparks. Horror constricts my chest too tightly for me to breathe. My mouth opens, but no sound escapes. I can only watch as the magic washes over Father, as it turns him to ice.

Except it doesn't. By some miracle, I'm wrong. When the blue light fades, Father is left as flesh and blood. What the Winter King has done instead is to bind him with shackles, ones which are even tighter and thicker than mine.

"I will not kill you," the Winter King says, "but neither will I let you walk freely. Tonight you have paid me a grave insult, and not even the most merciful of kings would allow this to escape without retribution." With his free hand, he beckons to the icy chains, and they come rushing forth, pulling Father until he is beside me.

Father opens his mouth to say something, likely to continue pleading for my freedom. I silence him with a glare. If he isn't careful in what he says, the Winter King may change his mind about sparing his life. Besides, I need to stay in the Crystal Palace and continue playing my part as a Summer Bride for as long as I can. I'm prepared to wait however long it takes to regain the Winter King's trust.

Magic flashes in the Winter King's hands again, and he summons a pegasus carved from ice. This time it's accompanied by a sleigh, bound with frost. The Winter King says nothing as he gestures for us to step in. I don't wait for him to force me in with his magic because that would be even more humiliating than waddling over to the sleigh as best I can with my shackled legs. Father is more stubborn, and the Winter King narrows his eyes. Being pulled forth by his icy chains must have been uncomfortable enough, because Father then shuffles into the sleigh beside me.

Once we're inside, the Winter King raises his hands once more, and ice crawls up over the sleigh, forming the bars of a cell. At first, I think it's so we can't escape, though neither of us can go anywhere with these shackles. But then the pegasus beats its enormous wings and lifts us into the air, and with how the sleigh shudders, I realize the bars are there to stop us from falling out.

Father says nothing as we fly through the air in our icy sleigh. He just stares at me helplessly. I can't bear to look at him, and instead, I turn my gaze to stars twinkling high above, promising Dalia and Orlan and all Summer Brides before me that I will slay the Winter King and avenge their deaths.

Chapter 17

It takes us barely more than five minutes to fly back to the Crystal Palace. Though the Winter King has proven more powerful than I ever imagined and Father is now his prisoner, I momentarily shed my worries and instead let myself enjoy the view. The trees slope down the mountain in a lush sea of pine needles, their tips powdered with snow. The Crystal Palace looks like a toy sculpture from this height, its walls glittering in the moonlight.

When I was younger, I used to spend much time lying in the grass and staring up at the birds soaring high above, wondering how they perceived the world below. Even the tallest oak in our garden was only as high as our manor. Now I finally see that the world is smaller than I ever imagined, and that I am even smaller still.

It feels too soon that we descend. The Winter King directs his steed toward the Crystal Palace's central courtyard. The square is teeming with guards, and they all clear the center as we land in their midst. None look surprised by the Winter King's winged steed and must have seen such feats countless times before.

The Winter King dismounts and the icy steed vanishes into the night, along with the caged sleigh around Father and me, leaving us kneeling on the frosted cobblestones. Our shackles are intact, though.

"Take him to the dungeons," the Winter King says to his guards, gesturing to Father.

The guards march forth and drag Father to his feet, pulling him away.

"No." I bolt upright, though the shackles binding my arms to my torso make it a struggle. Pain burns through my left knee. I didn't realize I hurt it this badly when I threw myself from Father's horse. Until now, adrenaline must have been numbing the pain.

My single word commands more power than I expect, since the guards halt halfway across the courtyard. They look to the Winter King for guidance.

"Take him," is all he says.

My fists tense as I watch them continue leading Father away. I could argue with the Winter King and demand for him to release Father, but I can't risk angering him any more. Not when Father's life is in his hands.

I force my fists to relax, though they resist.

When Father and the guards are gone and it's just the two of us standing out here in the cold night, I dare to ask, "How long will you keep him as your prisoner?" I don't look at the Winter King as I speak.

"As long as I must."

Those icy words cause me to whirl around, barely contained fury blazing in my eyes. "And what of me?" I demand, my lip curling. "Will you also have me thrown into your dungeons?"

"No," the Winter King says quietly, his voice soft against the evening breeze. "You are my queen, not my prisoner. The dungeons are no place for you."

I can't help the bitter laugh which escapes me. "I'm not your prisoner?" I repeat, shrugging my shoulders in an attempt to move the shackles around my chest. They don't budge. "These would certainly suggest otherwise."

The Winter King stares at me, scanning across my face and the shackles binding me. Then he raises his hand, and the icy chains vanish. The sudden release causes me to stumble, weight bearing down on my bad knee, and I clench my jaw to stop myself from seething in pain. I straighten myself soon after, giving the Winter King no need to assist me.

"Shackles or no shackles," I continue, though I know I should stop, "it doesn't change the fact that I'm a prisoner in this icy cage, no matter how big it might be."

The Winter King doesn't reply. He just watches me, and the two of us stand there, snow dancing around us. The night wind tugs on the ends of Orlan's cloak, which is still wrapped around me.

Finally, he turns away. "Come," he says, starting toward the steps on the other side of the courtyard.

At first, I resist the command and watch him walk for several paces. Then I imagine him conjuring those icy chains once more and forcing me to follow, and I hurry after him. Every stride aggravates my knee, but I do my best to ignore it, refusing to reveal my weakness. Despite my efforts, the Winter King notices by the time we reach the stairs. He grasps my arm, preventing me from taking another step.

"You're injured," he says, peering at my left leg, though the wound is invisible beneath the layers of my nightgown's torn and dirtied skirts.

"I'm fine." I pull my arm away and start up the steps. I walk as normally as I can, but stairs are much harder to walk up than level ground.

For several steps, the Winter King doesn't move. I feel his eyes burning into my back.

Then I hear his footsteps as he catches me up, having had his fill of watching my misery for tonight.

In the next moment, the steps slip from my feet and I'm hoisted into the air and deposited across his broad shoulder.

"I will not have my queen limp to her chambers," the Winter King says.

I go rigid in his grasp, conscious of every place his arm is touching around my waist. Warmth seeps through the thin silk of my nightgown, reaching to my skin.

The Winter King steps forth, and I instinctively cling to him to keep my balance, able to feel the hard muscles of his back beneath his tunic. But I soon realize there's no need. The Winter King's arm is secure around me.

"You don't need to carry me," I say when we reach the top of the stairs. My face burns with a volatile mix of conflicting emotions, which I'm becoming far too familiar with.

"I do," the Winter King replies, stepping through into the palace. I don't dare to protest again, in fear of angering him any more than I have so far tonight.

The Winter King carries me to my chambers and raises his hand when we reach the doors of my room. They yield to his power at once, shuddering wide open, and he continues through into my chambers, where he sets me on my bed. I expect him to throw me onto it, but he lets me down with surprising gentleness.

He pauses beside my bed, his shoulders rigid. The last time he set foot in my room was my first night here. All I can think of is his lips on mine, his frost consuming me.

I swallow and avert my gaze, scanning across my room to distract me from my anger. My chambers are still in disarray from my skirmish with Orlan and his men. A crack runs through the icy floor, decorated by a splatter of blood.

My attention catches on the glint of metal in the far corner. My dagger, hidden amid the shadows.

The Winter King takes another step forward and drops to his knees before me. The sight causes a breath to hitch in the back of my throat. It's unfathomable to imagine the Winter King kneeling before someone else, and yet this is what he's doing right now.

"May I?" he asks, gesturing to my left leg.

Stunned, I find myself nodding before fully considering the implications of his question: his hands on my bare skin.

The Winter King hesitates, scanning over my face, as if I'll change my mind. Maybe I should. But after tonight, I can't afford to push him away. Even if he froze Orlan and took Father prisoner. Even if everything confuses me.

When I don't pull back, he tentatively pushes my skirts up to my knee, and the softness of the silk against my skin sends a chill rushing through me. I contain it as best I can, not letting myself so much as twitch.

My knee looks as awful as it feels. A streak of dried blood runs down my shin, and dirt surrounds the torn flesh. The Winter King examines the wound briefly before rising.

"Wait here," he says, starting to the door.

Silently, I watch him leave, and when he's gone, I bolt from my bed and over to where my dagger lies on the other side of the room. I grab it and whirl around, searching for a hiding place. I can't be sure how long I'll have before the Winter King returns, and I don't want him to come back and find me crawling under my bed, especially when my knee is as bad as it is. I could hide my dagger under my pillows or my blankets, but what if he decides to tuck me into bed and finds it hidden there? It's a ridiculous thought, and I doubt the Winter King would do such a thing, but I can't risk losing my sole weapon in the Crystal Palace.

The large painted vase sitting on my vanity catches my attention. It's filled with peonies and carnations, all petals powdered with frost, and I hurry to the vase and pull out every flower. The vase's neck is just large enough for my dagger to fit through. I sheathe the blade and lower it through hilt-first until it reaches the bottom. Then I return all the peonies and carnations to the vase and arrange them like they were before. Unfortunately, they don't look as good as how Kassia placed them. I've never been one for flower arrangements. I try shuffling a few of them around, but it doesn't do much to improve it. Hopefully, the Winter King won't notice a few flowers out of place.

I dart back to the bed and lift my skirts over my knee like before.

The Winter King returns a short while later, equipped with a bowl of water and a tin. He sets them down on the floor and kneels before me once more. He dips a cloth into the bowl, wrings out the excess water, and dabs it across my skin. Though I brace myself, it's impossible to keep from hissing in pain.

The Winter King pauses and glances up at me. "It needs cleaning, or you'll risk it becoming infected."

"I know," I say, gripping the edge of the bed.

"I will need to work quickly before the water freezes."

I peer into the bowl. The Winter King isn't wrong. Already frost is creeping around the edges of the water. "Can't you stop it?"

He says nothing as he swishes the cloth around in the water before wringing it again. I watch as my blood swirls in the bowl, mixing with the water and turning it a murky red hue.

After the initial burst of pain, my knee doesn't hurt as much as the Winter King cleans it. Once he's done, he unscrews the lid off the tin and dips his fingers into the amber balm, smearing the jelly-like substance across my wound. At first, it stings. Then it burns.

"Are you sure this will help?" I ask, wincing.

"It'll hasten the healing process by a few days." He pauses, setting down the tin. "Pass me your hands."

Frowning, I do so. He examines my palms, which are also grazed from my fall. Though they are nowhere near as bad as my knee, little more than scratches, the Winter King seems to think otherwise. His eyes sharpen.

"How did all this happen?" he demands. "Who hurt you?"

"No one," I say. "I jumped from a horse and landed badly."

"This should never have happened."

He's right. It shouldn't have. Father shouldn't be locked up in the Winter King's dungeons; Orlan and his men shouldn't be icy statues. This is all because of me.

But there's nothing I can do now to change it. I must swallow my pride and hope I can persuade the Winter King into releasing Father.

We sit in silence as he cleans the grazes on my palms and applies more balm to them. The silence continues even long after he returns the lid to the tin. Not knowing what to say, I stare at the window across from us, watching as the approach of dawn stains the indigo sky with its brilliance.

The Winter King shows no sign of leaving, though there's no reason for him to linger. Instead, he picks at the ice in the bowl, the water now almost entirely frozen.

Finally, he says, "Was it because of what I said earlier this evening?"

I tear my gaze from the window and blink at him. "What are you talking about?" I brush my skirts back over my knee, much preferring the comfort of it covering my skin.

"The reason you ran," he mutters. "Was it because of what I said about arranging a date for our wedding?"

After what's happened tonight, it's even harder to look at him and discuss our impending wedding.

"I wasn't running," I say, which is no lie. The Winter King doesn't look convinced by that, so I continue, "Believe me, I had no idea about my father's plot to rescue me." I gesture across the room to the remnants of our skirmish: the cracked and blood-stained floor. "At first, I didn't realize it was my father's men breaking into my room, and so I fought them off."

The Winter King turns and studies the disheveled floor and draws out a sigh, shaking his head. "Your father's men or not, no one should be able to break into my palace and steal my queen."

I can't help from bristling at his words, but he's turned away and can't see my face. I say nothing of it, knowing better than to protest that I am not yet his queen and am certainly not his property.

The Winter King grabs the bowl and tin and rises from his knees. "I will tell the servants to clear this up in the morning," he says, not looking at me. His hands clench around the items he holds.

He doesn't wait for me to reply before striding out of my room, shutting both doors behind him. He doesn't even bid me good night.

I stay where I am for a long while, until I'm certain that he won't return for the rest of this night. Or at least the little left of it. Then I hurry to my vanity and retrieve my dagger from the vase. With how exhausted I am, it's unlikely I'll wake before my maids enter my room, so I crawl under my bed and hide my dagger and poison in their usual hiding place, ignoring the protest in my knee as I push myself across the icy floor.

When I climb into bed and pull my blankets over me, I don't fall asleep immediately like I expect. All I can see when I close my eyes is Father shivering in the coldest and harshest of the Winter King's cells. And if it isn't Father I see, then it's the faces of Orlan and his men.

I roll onto my side and stare at the armoire, gilded by the light of dawn piercing through my windows. My gaze trails across to the door beside it.

Why did the Winter King spend so long tending to my injuries tonight? Why does he act like he cares? It's hard to reconcile that version of him with the same man who murdered Dalia and Orlan, who holds Father captive.

I let out a heavy breath. No. It's easy to make sense of all that. Tonight, the Winter King claimed that he's spent three hundred years searching for me and when we were standing out on his balcony, he mentioned about my immunity to his frost. Maybe it's true that no other Summer Bride possessed this same immunity, and this is why he believes me to be important to him. He does not care for me, but for my usefulness. I'm uncertain as to the reason he needs me, but with him being the villain I know him to be, it can only be for some dark, selfish purpose.

Chapter 18

In the morning, neither Kassia nor Elona mention the incident last night. But they'll have already heard from the guards or other servants, if not from the Winter King himself, about what happened. They clean my wounds with water like the Winter King did, and apply more of that amber balm. I tell them all I have is a few grazes but they don't listen to my protests, saying that the Winter King has instructed them to keep a close eye on my wounds until they've fully healed. It's hard not to scoff at that.

At breakfast I dine with the Winter King as usual, and I eat as little as I slept, and that is to say barely more than a morsel. He makes polite conversation with me, and I do my best to respond pleasantly, but fatigue bangs on my head like a drum, and it becomes harder to concentrate on what he's saying, let alone respond.

"Adara," the Winter King says. I realize then that he's been staring at me for some time and that I must have dozed off. "Are you all right?"

"I'm fine." I don't intend for my response to come out as short as it does. The Winter King seems unbothered by it, though he doesn't fall for my lie.

"You have eaten so little."

I gaze down at my plate from beneath heavy lids. I made an effort to pile up my plate, but I've only nibbled on my crust of bread and taken a single bite of an apple. My cheese and meat are untouched. A plume of steam wafts up and the warm smell of salted meat almost makes me vomit across the Winter King's pristine icy table.

"It was late last night," the Winter King says softly, "so I can't imagine you slept well. You should return to bed."

No matter how long I stay in bed, I will not rest. Even if by some miracle I fall asleep, it won't be a restful one. My stomach churns with worry for Father. "Will you permit me to see my father?"

"I told you last night, Adara, that you are not my prisoner. If you wish to see your father, you may. Though I would urge you to rest first."

"You don't fear that I will open his cell and free him?"

"Will you?"

I shrug. "That depends on how much he's suffering." I know I must take care with the sharpness in my words, but it's impossible with the thought of Father in a cold and lonely cell continuously stabbing at my heart.

The Winter King looks to his plate then, though he does not eat. His attention trails to his wine, to his fork. But not to me. "I'm sorry," he says to his icy utensils. It's hard not to scoff and tell him that his apology does not count unless he looks me in the eye and admits what a monster he is. "You must understand the decision to hold your father captive is not one I make lightly."

Unlike him, I don't cower as I speak. I look my opponent directly in the eye. "No. I don't suppose it is." The bitterness in my words is enough to scald my tongue. Even the Winter King flinches.

He looks up at me then, and his eyes remind me of a sorry little ice cube melting in my palm. "I did not wish for it to be like this."

"Nor did I."

He takes a long sip of his wine. "I have hundreds of guards under my employ," he says, setting down the goblet, "and I cannot easily silence their tongues. If I allow your father to walk freely, after breaking into my palace, the rest of the kingdom will believe they can do so without fear of any repercussion."

"You could cut out their tongues," I say flippantly. "Or threaten to cut them out. The threat alone would suffice after a demonstration or two."

The Winter King blinks at me. "Why would I do such a terrible thing?"

I try not to scoff and tell him he has done far more terrible things. At the least guards would still have their lives, unlike his previous victims. "It seems an easy strategy to use if you fear the gossip of a few guards."

I wait for him to agree, for him to show me the darkness I know lurks within, but it seems he's still determined to maintain this façade. He leans back in his chair and runs his fingers through his wavy, silver hair. "I would be punishing innocents."

"They wouldn't be innocent. They would be guilty of the crime of gossip. Words have great power. They can as easily build a legacy as tear it down." Of course, I don't really want the Winter King to cut out any tongues. I just want to prove he has no reason to punish Father.

"Are you asking me to maim my guards, whose sole 'crimes' are telling their wives of their hard day at work, so I can allow your father to walk free?"

"My father is innocent."

"Your father ordered his men to break into my home and steal my bride."

"He only arranged for my kidnapping because he believed I was being mistreated."

"And why would he believe that?"

I can't stop from snorting at that because it's the most ridiculous thing I have ever heard. The man whose past three hundred brides have gone missing within a year is struggling to understand why their fathers might fear for their safety?

"Perhaps it has something to do with the three hundred Summer Brides before me, all those who have gone missing," I hiss, dressing my words with my finest glare. Realizing the truth lies naked before us, I hastily add, "Your Majesty." Then, "Elaric."

I expect him to rise angrily from his seat and pound his fists against the table so hard my plate shudders, demanding to know what I mean. But he does no such thing. "I was mistaken and paid gravely for my mistakes."

I want to remind him that his victims were the ones who've paid for his mistakes and not him, but I keep my lips sealed shut. I've said more than enough already.

He sighs and slumps in his chair, his shoulders heavy. In this moment, he looks less like a terrible, immortal king and more like a mortal man. "I have never intended to hurt anyone, Adara, and I will certainly not hurt you. You have my word."

"Whether or not your intention was to hurt them," I whisper, not daring to speak my brash words above a whisper, "it does not change the fact that you did indeed hurt them. And not just them, but their families and those who loved them."

The Winter King raises his head slowly and looks at me, his eyes heavy like a blizzard. "I've hurt you once before, haven't I? You loved your sister more than anyone else in this world."

I ball my fists to restrain them. To stop myself from leaping from my chair and swinging right for the Winter King's pale face. My nails dig into my palms. "Yes," I breathe. "Yes, you have."

His eyes grow heavier still. "I'm sorry, Adara. I'm sorry for what I've taken from you."

I squeeze my eyes shut to stop him from being able to see the true depths of my hatred.

It isn't enough for him to be sorry. 'Sorry' won't bring back my sister or Orlan or anyone else. He took all those lives. He's a monster that must be held accountable for his crimes.

Chapter 19

Kassia and Elona insist I return to my room to rest. I refuse, determined to see Father first. They try to persuade me otherwise but in the end, they agree to take me to the dungeons, on the condition that I will rest straight after. Since I can barely keep myself upright, I decide it's a reasonable deal.

We cross the central courtyard to the outer wing of the palace. The entrance to the dungeons is a narrow door, with two guards standing either side of it.

"Lady Adara would like to see her father," Elona says to them.

They glance at each other, and I expect them to refuse. But they don't. They dip their heads and say, "As you wish, my lady."

I slip past the guards and through the narrow door. The passage is narrower still, and I doubt I could hold out my arms without touching the walls. The shadows are so dense that I can only see three steps ahead of me. I'm not sure how far the stairs plunge into the darkness.

Kassia and Elona follow me inside, but I turn and shake my head at them. "I wish to see my father alone."

They look to each other and then to me.

"But my lady," Elona says, "it's so dark in here. What if you miss your footing and tumble down the stairs?"

"It's also a very long way down," Kassia adds. "If you fall, you could seriously injure yourself."

These stairs are far less dangerous than scaling the palace's outer wall, but I don't tell them that. Instead I say, "I have as much chance of falling down the stairs if you are with me than if you are not."

"But we'd be there to help you," Elona replies.

"If you bring me a torch, I'll be unlikely to fall and you'll have less reason to worry."

Begrudgingly they turn and leave and then, a few seconds later, return with a torch. "Here you go, my lady," Kassia says, passing it to me. The blue light atop the icy rod flickers.

Elona eyes the torch in my hands. "We should fetch you gloves."

Before, I would play along and pretend that I felt the cold like everyone else. But now the Winter King knows the truth, what's the point in continuing the pretense? "There's no need, but thank you."

Elona frowns, unconvinced.

"I'm the Summer Queen," I say, offering the same meagre explanation as the Winter King offered me, "so I don't feel the cold."

"That's why you didn't freeze that first night," Kassia muses.

Elona offers her a warning glance, but it fades as soon as I turn to her. "We'll be here if you need us," she says.

I give her a nod, and with that, head into the darkness.

No wind blows in here as I descend the stairs. I doubt there are any cracks in the dungeons' walls, let alone windows. No wonder the Winter King doesn't mind my coming down here. The only way out is the door I've come through at the very top of the stairs, and with his guards stationed there, there is no way I could get Father out without them raising the alarm.

And I've already risked the Winter King's wrath enough as it is, between the incident last night and my brazen words this morning. He must desperately need me for him not to retaliate, and perhaps I can exploit that in order to have him release Father.

I race down the steps. The torch's blue light is bright enough to illuminate a dozen steps ahead, but I can't see at all where they end. They continue down and down. There seems to be no end, and whenever I think I've nearly reached the bottom, I'm proven terribly wrong.

My worry for Father spurs me on faster, and then I'm almost tripping over the stairs. They're uneven and coarse, having the same bumpy texture as over-trodden stone.

Finally, I reach the end.

The narrow passageway opens to a chamber, and torches filled with blue light flicker along the walls. They are distributed sparsely and are much dimmer than the one I hold, so there is little light down here in the dungeons. Everything is silent. There is no scuttling of rats nor rattling of chains. These dungeons are still.

I pass the first cell and inspect the bars. They're sturdier than the ones the Winter King crafted last night for our makeshift sleigh. The light from the torches doesn't reach far back inside the cell, so I push my torch through the bars as far as my arm can fit. The brilliant blue light banishes the shadows, allowing me to see inside.

A sculpture is huddled in the back corner, his ankles and wrists bound. He doesn't move. Like Orlan and his men, he is no longer flesh and blood, but ice all the way through.

With a trembling hand, I shove the torch even further through so I can better see his face. He's turned away from me, and it's hard to make out his features. But he's not Father.

Yet that doesn't mean Father is unaffected by the ice. He too could be huddled inside one of these cells, already frozen to the bone by the Winter King's terrible magic.

I yank my torch from the cell, and the icy bars graze my arm, their texture far from smooth. I hurry through the dungeons, shining my torch into every cell I pass and praying each time that I won't find Father frozen in them.

I find Father in the very last cell, and the tension slips from my shoulders as I realize he still draws breath, though it leaves his mouth and nostrils in powdery wisps. His wrists and ankles are bound by icy chains, and his knees are drawn to his chest.

"Father?"

He looks up as I speak, watching me through glazed eyes. "Adara . . ." His words trail off, lost to the frost. He has only spent last night and this morning inside this cell and yet he already sounds so broken.

"Have . . . have they hurt you?" I ask, my voice cracking.

Father shakes his head. The gesture is so slight I nearly miss it. "Adara," he says again, this time a whisper. "My bones feel so stiff I fear I'm turning to ice from the inside out."

Horror washes over me. I recall what Elona and Kassia said about not sleeping in the palace. How the Winter King keeps no servants overnight, just his guards who presumably go straight home to their families in the morning. Everything in these walls eventually succumbs to ice. Father won't be exempt.

"I'll get you out of here," I say, my voice solemn and low. "I promise I will. But in the meantime, you must promise you'll stay strong and fight the frost. You can't let it defeat you."

His eyes sharpen then, as if my words have stirred him from a restless nightmare. "Leave me. It isn't worth the risk. You must run while you can, as far from the Winter King as you are able. No one knows what he does to his brides, only that they're never seen again."

"I'm not going anywhere. I'm not leaving you." I lean in further, as far as the bars will allow, and lower my voice. We're far down enough that the guards and my maids won't hear me, and I've inspected these dungeons thoroughly and found not a single living soul except Father, but I fear the Winter King's power might permit him to hear through his icy walls. "Even if you weren't trapped in here, I wouldn't run. I meant what I said last night, and though you may think it foolish, someone must make him pay for all his crimes. He must be stopped, but no one else dares. Only I can get close enough and slip past his guard."

Father stares at me. His usually ruddy cheeks are colorless. I don't know how long it takes the Crystal Palace to turn people to ice, but I suspect Father doesn't have much time left. "You should run," he simply says and slumps back against the wall behind him. "But I know you're too stubborn to listen."

"I'll get you out of here, and then I'll kill the Winter King."

Father says nothing. He just gazes down at his hands and the frozen chains binding his wrists. His eyes are glazed over. With hopelessness.

"Father, come here," I say.

He looks back up and hesitates. Then he obliges and forces himself upright. It takes him near an age to do so, his movement as slow as a glacier thawing, and then he shuffles toward me, his bound ankles restricting much of his movement. When he reaches the bars, I wriggle my other arm through the gap and take his hand in mine.

"You're warm," he says with a gasp.

"Something happened after my first night here. The Winter King's magic almost froze me too, and I'm not sure how but I overcame it. Now the cold has no effect on me." I hold his hand until some of the color in his skin returns, and then I take his other. My vial of poison is yet to freeze solid, and I've been here for over a week. My blankets are the same. Perhaps objects take longer to freeze than people, but I wonder whether my touch is enough to keep the frost at bay.

And maybe I'm right, since after I've warmed Father's other hand, some of the color returns to his cheeks as well. He doesn't shiver as much, either.

"I'll come to see you as much as I can, but you must be strong and have faith. I'll get you out of here, so you can't let yourself freeze before then."

"I won't, Adara," he says. There's fire in his eyes now. The glaze of hopelessness has been banished with the warmth my hands offered. "I won't let myself freeze. But you must promise you'll be careful."

"I will. There's something else you must do for me, too."

"What do you need me to do, my child?"

"Before I move against the Winter King, I need to know that you are well and safely out of his grasp. I don't know if we will have a chance to speak privately again, so I'm telling you now. When I get you out of here and you return home, write to me immediately."

"I promise I shall."

"Include the line: '*The roses are most wonderful this time of year*.' That way, I'll know the letter is genuine and not forged by the Winter King."

"I will see it done." He squeezes my hand. "I know you are too stubborn to be swayed, but promise me you won't be reckless. That you won't get caught."

I swallow.

"Adara . . ."

"I promise," I say, not meeting his eyes. I pull my hand from his and wriggle my arms out from between the bars. I hold the torch high so its blue light illuminates the dungeons. "Be strong, Father."

I sprint back through the dungeons, not stopping along the way to peer into the cells at the frozen men, not wanting to be reminded of what Father will become if I fail. I can try to come down here each day and warm his hands, and maybe it'll slow the spread of frost, but I don't know if a morning will come where it stops working. Father's best chances are if I get him out of this frozen hell as soon as possible, and it also means that I needn't fear for Father if my plan to assassinate the Winter King goes horribly wrong.

I race up the steps, taking two at a time, and when I reach the top, I'm out of breath and my cheeks are warm. Kassia and Elona flock toward me and help me up the last few stairs and pry the torch from my grasp. I let them take it, and the guards step aside to let us through.

"My lady, are you all right?" Elona asks, peering at my rosy cheeks and my newest scratches adorning my arms.

"Take me to the Winter King," I wheeze. "Immediately."

"You must rest first. Whatever it is, I'm sure it can wait an hour or two."

"It can't. I must see him at once."

"But—"

I pull my arm from her grasp and storm across the courtyard. Elona trails behind me, while Kassia hurries to the empty bracket on the wall and slots the torch back inside. She runs after us at double speed to catch up.

Even though the Crystal Palace is a sprawling maze of icy corridors, I don't need my maids to show me the way to the Winter King's chambers anymore. Once or twice, I fear I may have taken the wrong turning, but then I recognize my surroundings and know that I'm following the correct route.

When I reach the doors to his chambers, I don't bother stopping to knock. I fling them open and march inside, and I don't need to look back to know how horrified my maids are. I can hear it in their quickening footsteps and sharp breaths.

I find the Winter King in his study, and he looks up from his desk as I shove the door aside.

"Adara?" His silver brows draw together, and he rises from his chair and paces across the room to me. "I thought you were resting. What has happened?"

"My father," I say between breaths. I wish my words were stronger, but I can barely speak after running all the way from the dungeons. I suck in a deep breath and stand taller. "My father is freezing, and if he stays there any longer, he will die."

The Winter King says nothing.

My eyes narrow. "But you already knew that, didn't you?"

"Adara . . ." He has nothing to offer except my name.

"Release him. Please."

"I cannot, as we discussed before."

"Cannot, or will not?" My jaw pulses. It's nearly impossible to stop from lashing out at him more than I have.

The Winter King sighs. "I wish it was not so."

"That's fine," I say, lifting my chin. "Let my father die to uphold your reputation. But I promise you one thing, Elaric, you will never have my heart."

Chapter 20

After leaving the Winter King's study, my maids fuss over me and usher me to bed. This time I don't resist. I hate the thought of doing nothing while Father freezes in those lonely dungeons, but exhaustion weighs on my mind and I can't think clearly. Once I've rested, I'll be more equipped to plot how to convince the Winter King to release Father. Breaking him out isn't a plausible plan. Even if I incapacitate the men guarding the dungeons, there will be more patrolling the palace. My chances of getting us both out are slim.

I'm out as soon as my head touches the pillow. I don't dream at all. There's only darkness. When I wake, I don't feel much more rested, but at least the fog of exhaustion has somewhat lessened.

My maids have drawn the curtains, but they don't hide the darkness beyond. I force myself up from my bed and walk to the window, pulling the silky curtains open so violently I'm sure I hear them rip.

Beyond my window the pale stars twinkle back at me. The waning moon is now a thin slither in its sky, but it has long reached its apex. I can't tell precisely what time it is, but there's no denying that it's the dead of night.

I curse under my breath. I must have been asleep for twelve hours, if not more. And during that time, I've done nothing to plan how to get Father out of his cell. In fact, twelve hours may have been long enough for him to freeze solid already.

My fingers dig deeply enough into the icy ledge to leave marks when I remove them. I've already tried reasoning with the Winter King, to no avail. I could try begging him day after day until he relents and visit Father every morning and warm his hands to slow the frost, but I suspect he'll have the patience of a lifetime.

No. I must try something else.

I push open the window, though it's stiff with frost and groans at the motion, and lean out, resting my elbows on the ledge. The cool night air washes over my skin, helping to further banish the fog of exhaustion and sober my mind.

My eyes trail across the palace gardens below, searching for inspiration. But there's only snow to be found. And icy hedges. I think of hiding behind them with Orlan and his men, twigs digging into my knees through the thin skirts of my chemise.

I sweep aside my skirts and stare at my knees. The wound on my left knee has faded to a rusty shade, though the scabs are still painful to the touch when I brush my fingers over them.

I know now what I must do. And if this fails to free Father, I don't know what else will work.

I pull my window shut and hurry out of my room. My attention lingers on my armoire as I leave, but I decide against wrestling into a more appropriate dress. My chemise will make a far greater impression, and shock is the weapon I intend to wield tonight.

I race down the corridors barefoot, not bothering to slow and peer behind any corners before proceeding onward. This plan will work best if all the guards take notice.

I find the first patrol of guards soon after leaving my chambers, and they shout to me to ask if everything is all right. I don't shout back a reply. Either they will follow me or report back to the Winter King that I'm sprinting through the palace. Both are what I intend. I require his attention, as well as theirs.

By the time I reach the dungeons, I have half the palace's guards chasing after me, demanding to know what is the matter.

The two guards standing watch outside the entrance to the dungeons stiffen as I race toward them. They reach for their weapons but don't unsheathe them. Instead, they glance between me and all the guards running after me.

Right before I reach them, I fall to my knees. I don't rise. I stay there, kneeling before them.

The guards chasing after me slow to a halt and surround me. At first, no one approaches. None seem sure what to do. One guard by the dungeons peels himself from the door and hesitantly steps toward me, his movements slow as if approaching a wild, injured beast.

"My lady?" His voice is rough with caution. "Are you all right?"

I don't reply. Or even blink. I continue kneeling, my gaze fixed on the doors behind him.

"Lady Adara?" he tries again.

I stay silent and still.

Other guards approach me, but I respond to none of them. One is bold enough to touch my shoulder, though it's little more than a gentle tap. I ignore it and imagine myself a frozen statue, just like the one Father will become if the Winter King doesn't release him.

After a while, the guards grow bored. Realizing that I won't react to anything they say or do, even when they're waving their arms in front of me, they begin to leave. Some remain, however, and the audience I've gathered doesn't disappear until one of the higher-ranking guards comes and shouts at them all to return their posts. His booming voice cleaves through the night air, but I don't flinch. Once all the guards have returned to their positions, he starts toward me.

"You should return to bed, my lady. Kneeling out here in the cold will do you no good."

He's wrong. I don't feel the cold. Nor do I care for the ache settling into my knees, aggravating my wounds. They're just mortal sensations. My heart must stay fixed on my goal. Freeing Father is all that matters.

"My lady . . ." the guard captain urges. He tries again and again, and when it becomes clear I won't respond no matter what he says, he turns to one of the other guards and barks at them to inform the Winter King.

The guard captain watches me for a few minutes more and then sighs and turns away, leaving me with the two guards standing sentry outside the dungeons.

By the time the Winter King arrives, dawn is spearing the heavens with its golden rays. The ache in my knees has dulled to numbness.

"Adara," he says gently, coming to a stop beside me. "The guards tell me you've been out here all night."

I don't so much as allow my gaze to flicker across to him as he speaks. I stay focused on the dungeons. I know I risk inciting his wrath with my boldness, but how can I free Father unless I am bold?

"Adara," he tries again. Still, I am silent. I even keep my breath as light as I can, so that its warmth doesn't escape in vivid swirls, and move my chest as little as possible with every inhalation.

Not once does the Winter King demand to know my reason for being here. The answer is obvious. As is the key to breaking my vigil. But the Winter King says nothing of freeing Father, so I continue to sit there. He tries to reason with me, mostly of how I should rest, and I keep my face drawn into a stoic mask. Until he announces Father's release, I won't so much as twitch. My heart burns with determination, and I will not yield.

Eventually the Winter King leaves, his footsteps heavy with reluctance.

Morning basks me with all its radiance. The breeze ruffles the delicate hem of my chemise and tugs on my curls, still messy from when I slept, though vanity isn't something I care for right now. The guards all returned to their posts a few hours ago, but I feel their stares burning into my back.

I lift my head, the slightest movement I've allowed since I began my vigil. I want every guard in the palace to see me, and I want them to report to their wives and children that the Winter King's latest bride has spent the entire evening on her knees outside the dungeons. I want the gossip to spread far and wide, blanketing the entire kingdom.

If the Winter King fears tongues talking, I'll make them talk. Father's break-in will pale compared to this. The queen sitting on her knees will damage the Winter King's reputation so much more. I don't know how long it will take for the gossip to spread, for the Winter King to start to worry, but I will force him into a corner even if I must kneel for days.

Elona and Kassia soon appear, and they are much more forceful than all the guards and the Winter King combined. Elona nudges my shoulder, while Kassia crouches before me and peers at me. I look straight past her, at the door to the dungeons.

"Has she really been here all night?" Elona asks, looking up at the two guards before the dungeons' door.

The one on the left nods. "The king came here earlier and tried to persuade her to leave."

They talk about me as though I'm not there. It's hard to stop the corners of my lips from curling in satisfaction.

"It's as if she's under a spell," Kassia says after she finishes scrutinizing me. She glances at Elona. "Do you think she is?"

Elona shakes her head. "I don't know."

"What should we do?" Kassia says.

Elona bends down and takes my hand in hers. I offer no resistance, letting her handle me like a rag-doll. "My lady, let's return to your chambers. You must be freezing out here, dressed only in your chemise."

"And hungry too," Kassia adds.

"Come," Elona urges me, "we'll get breakfast in your room. I'll send for the kitchen staff to bring some up."

When I don't reply, she presses her lips together and looks to Kassia for help.

Kassia takes my other hand. "I can't imagine it's comfortable there, my lady. Why don't we get you a warm bath?"

Both try offering me other things, like a stroll through the gardens or choosing more books from the library or even ordering Madame Bellmont to make me new dresses. My eye twitches at the last one. Though I'm sure it's from fatigue, my maids seem to take it as a positive response, and they discuss all the wonderful ideas they have to fashion into gowns. Kassia describes a lovely ebony gown with sleeves of lace and a long chiffon trail. Elona tries more tactfully with a bright yellow gown, describing it as being brighter than sunlight. They chatter on, and it becomes increasingly harder not to smile. Though they intend to persuade me to leave, their attempts only relieve my boredom and make it easier for me to continue kneeling here.

My maids request for breakfast to be brought to me and have the kitchen staff lay out a banquet before me. They leave it there for a long while, allowing the smell of warm food to waft into my nostrils. The steam swirls in a tantalizing dance. I ignore it. Elona and Kassia even go as far as eating some of the food and commenting on how wonderful it tastes. That's by far the worst torture to bear. My mouth waters, and my stomach threatens to grumble. Loudly. I grit my teeth and force it into silence. If my stomach rumbles, my maids will know what effect they're having on me and double their efforts.

Eventually, servants come to clear away all the uneaten food, and Elona and Kassia have the audacity to announce that they're going to eat it all in my room and that I should come if I wish to join them.

They leave soon after that. I have little doubt that they'll be back and are likely plotting their next attempt.

At midday, the guards swap shifts. The two who've been watching me all night and morning have grown so used to my presence that they step around me without a second glance. Their replacements are much warier. They glance at each other and then at me several times before settling into their posts.

Soon, a maid flanked by two guards approach. The maid carries a bowl of soup and a hunch of bread and a flask of water. For Father.

The guards standing sentry open the doors without a word, and the maid slips down into the dark passageway with her two guards. I stare into the shadows, imagining Father chained up and shaking in their depths. It's been a day since I saw him. How much has the frost spread? How long will my touch keep the Winter King's power at bay?

Even if I can keep kneeling without food, rest or water, that doesn't mean Father will last. If it takes days for my vigil to force the Winter King to release him, he might be frozen long before then.

I tighten my fists. I can't alter my plan now. If I haul myself up and hurry down into the dungeons, I'll ruin what I've achieved so far. I must pray Father can hold on long enough for the Winter King to be swayed.

Chapter 21

The sun begins its descent into the snowy horizon. The afternoon drags on, and long shadows stretch across the courtyard, their darkness washing over me. Soon it snows, and powdery flakes fall on my lashes. I blink them away, and at first, they're light enough for my lashes to flick aside. But then the snow falls heavier, clumping on my lashes, and I'm unable to shift it. I blink faster but the movement catches the notice of the guard on my right, and I stop until he looks away.

When Elona and Kassia return, the snow blankets my shoulders like a shawl. I didn't dare to move and shake it away, but now my maids brush it aside for me.

"My lady, look at you!" Elona exclaims. I don't turn to look at her but I hear the distress in her voice. "You'll catch your death out here!"

"It's a wonder you aren't already buried under all the snow," Kassia muses, glancing around at the snow-covered courtyard.

Both maids continue trying to persuade me into going with them. It seems they haven't thought of any better strategies, since their pleas are all the same as before. The sun vanishes into the horizon, and then the courtyard is covered in darkness.

Elona and Kassia have more food brought to me but like before, I don't so much as bat an eyelid at any of it. All I can think of is Father freezing in the dungeons beneath me, and that thought is enough to shackle my stomach. My maids take a goblet of water and lift it to my lips. I don't part them. They press the crystalline rim to my lower lip and beg for me to drink. I don't.

No moon rises tonight. The thin slither from last night has disappeared. Without its radiance, the stars seem to shine brighter.

Eventually, Elona and Kassia surrender. As they leave, they promise to fetch the Winter King so that he can talk sense into me. He arrives alone a while later, though I can't be certain precisely how long. It could be ten minutes, or half an hour. My mind has numbed to the passage of time.

He sits cross-legged beside me in the snow, and to my surprise, he says nothing for some time. Only when the guards change their shift does he say anything. And it isn't directed at me, but to the guards.

"Your Majesty," they say as they approach, dipping their heads.

"Leave us," the Winter King says, raising his hand.

"But—" the guards begin.

"There is no need for you to keep watch tonight," the Winter King replies. "Tell Varick I've relieved you both from your posts and ask him where you can make yourselves useful."

"Yes, Your Majesty," they say, bowing and leaving without another word.

Then it's just me and the Winter King and the door opposite us. What does he expect to achieve by sitting here beside me? It isn't as if it will sway me from my cause. Nothing will. Until Father is released, I will stay here on my knees.

"I am told you haven't eaten or drank all day," the Winter King says, his voice quiet. "How long do you plan to kneel here, Adara?"

My silence is answer enough.

He sighs and runs his hand through his white hair. "I could have my guards drag you back to your chambers."

My eye pulses, daring him to try.

"I must admit, I've considered it several times today, but I doubt it would inspire you to drink or eat."

I stare at the door. If he won't have me forcibly removed, then what will he do? Will he wait until I yield from fatigue or thirst or starvation?

He leans back, his elbows pressing into the blanket of snow around us, and stares up at the twinkling stars. "You have forced me into a difficult position."

Good.

"All the maids have been gossiping about this matter today, and the guards are no better." He rubs at his temple. I hope I'm causing him stress. A headache is the least of what he deserves. "I've spent the entire afternoon considering which is less kingly: releasing the man who broke into my palace or allowing my queen to kneel like a martyr before the dungeons in only her nightgown."

It's tempting to drag my eyes from the door and demand to know what decision he has reached. I don't, though. Silence is the most powerful weapon I can wield right now. This is a battle of wills, and I will prove to the Winter King I am more stubborn than he is.

"It has become clear to me which incident incites more gossip, and I have no desire for my kingdom to see me as a tyrant."

I want to tell him he should have considered that before passing laws to make it mandatory for every twenty-one-year-old girl to be presented at his Midsummer Ball and for him to have first pick of them all, like cattle. I don't, of course. Even if not for my silent vigil, I'm not foolish enough to say something so reckless out loud.

But after those thoughts fade, the weight of what he has said sinks in. My heart skips, anxiously awaiting his next words. Praying with every ounce of hope that he will say what I wish for him to say.

"How this ordeal must appear to my subjects is most troubling. They will hear that the father of their future queen attempted to steal her from the palace, which is easily addressed if he is believed to be a madman. But when they hear that same queen has spent all day and night kneeling outside the dungeon, they will wonder whether that man is truly mad or whether he was right to attempt rescuing his daughter from a vicious tyrant. Then they will begin to sympathize with his cause and wonder why their king is so unjust. All it will take is a few to complain about taxes, and then overnight, the queen's father becomes an icon to spark a rebellion. A civil war has never taken my fancy. After much consideration, it seems my choice is between freeing your father and showing how merciful I can be, or risk this spiraling out of my control. As I said, you have put me in a difficult position."

I desperately want to ask whether he has made the choice to release Father or whether he's come up with a third solution. But I don't.

"And perhaps if I thought long and hard enough, I would think of another way to solve this," he continues, as if reading my thoughts. "But this solution isn't one I loathe. Believe me, I take no pleasure in holding your father captive."

My nose twitches. I barely stop it from wrinkling.

"The reason I insisted on him remaining in the dungeons is because of the risk releasing him would pose, that it might cause others to think they too can break into my palace with no fear of retribution. But if my decree emphasizes that this man is the queen's father and that she spent an entire day and night on her knees, begging for forgiveness on her father's behalf until my heart was moved, then instead the mercy becomes a show of strength. So yes, Adara, I will free your father. I will send out the order in the morning."

Finally, I tear my attention from the door. My neck is stiff as I turn my head to face the Winter King. Only now do I realize how much snow fell upon the courtyard earlier today, and its brilliance blinds me, even with it being night. The Winter King is observing me, waiting for my response. I hesitate, fearing that his lips will twist into a smirk and tell me that everything is a lie. That he won't really free Father.

But he doesn't laugh. His brows draw together as I continue to hesitate.

When I do speak, my words are cold and hard and bitter. "And did my actions move your heart, Your Majesty?" Maybe I should jump for joy at his decision, but I will do no such thing in the Winter King's presence. What he has granted me is the bare minimum of decency: not sentencing his bride's father to death by frost. Perhaps I should tread more carefully given that Father is not yet free and that the Winter King could retract his decision at any moment, but I will not tread lightly around him. He has already seen the strength of my will, and I will no longer humiliate myself by pretending to be a scared little mouse.

The Winter King looks stunned by my question. Was he expecting me to thank him? "I . . ." His attention trails across to the dungeon's door. My body feels as if it's carved from stone, so I don't move. I just sit there, staring at his face. "I suppose so," he adds in a whisper. "Yes, you did."

I demand no more answers from him, and the Winter King sits there quietly with his thoughts.

"May I see him?" I ask.

He blinks at me, though my question should hardly be surprising. "Yes. Yes, of course you may." He rises to his feet and extends his hand toward me. I don't insult him by refusing, not when Father's freedom is mere inches away. Besides, I doubt I could stand gracefully by myself after kneeling for so long.

My legs feel paper thin beneath me, and I can't help from wobbling. The Winter King catches me before I tumble, steadying me with one arm on mine and his other around my waist. We stay like that for a long, awkward moment, the Winter King's bright eyes staring down into mine and me having no choice but to stare back at him. This close up, I can see the Winter King's eyes perfectly well. They are the color of a bright blue sky, his irises illuminated by the same glowing lights of all the torches in the Crystal Palace. Have they always been that color, have they always shone? Why do I care? My father is currently locked away in a dungeon.

His dungeon.

"Adara," he says gently, his breath brushing my brow. "I am glad you've forced me into this position."

"Why?" I don't add that he didn't think twice about taking Father prisoner last night.

"It saddens me to think you and I haven't gotten off to the best of starts," he continues, his voice still barely more than a whisper, "and I hope we can put all that has happened in the past and start anew."

I want to laugh and tell him he can hope all he wants. There's nothing he can do which will ever make me forget the past. But I can say none of that.

"Of course," I force myself to say. "I want nothing more than to start over."

The Winter King doesn't seem to see through my lie. He only smiles. "I will make it up to you. That I promise."

With that, he lets me go, releasing his arms from around me. He pushes open the door to the dungeon and holds it for me. I thank him and slip inside. The Winter King peers into the darkness, and at first, I think he will follow, but then he holds out his hand. "You will need a torch down there." His magic solidifies into an icy torch topped by an orb of blue light, like the ones illuminating the Crystal Palace. "I will wait here for you," he says as he passes me the torch.

I give him a quick nod before heading down the hundreds of stairs. It doesn't take many before the Winter King and the door at the top disappear, and I certainly don't reach the bottom quickly, but it doesn't seem to take as long as yesterday.

When the stairs open to the dungeon, I break into a sprint. My toes catch on a bump in the ice and I almost collide with a pillar ahead. The torch falls from my hand and lands on the floor with a clatter. I dive for it, fearing that it has cracked and that the light will extinguish, but upon inspection it seems to be intact. I continue through the dungeons. Though my pace isn't as reckless, my stomach churns in fear for Father.

I find him in an even worse state than yesterday. Now he does not shiver. He doesn't even twitch. I shine my torch through the cell and see that his fingers have become solid ice. The frost is spreading higher up his arms.

"Father!" I shout, squeezing my shoulder through the bars. I barely make it halfway, but it allows me to extend my torch further into the cell and get a closer look at Father. The blue light gleams on his frozen fingers. "Father!"

No matter how much I shout, he doesn't look up. My hand trembles. The torch's light flickers back and forth.

What if it's too late? What if the frost has already spread too far?

If only I could get him to sit up and come close enough for me to take his hands. Would my touch be enough to reverse the magic?

I push my shoulder further through, but then get stuck. I yank my shoulder out from between the icy bars, ignoring the pain that shoots through me. The torch's blue light gleams on the cell's lock.

If I can open the door, I won't need to squeeze through the bars to get to Father. The Winter King should still be at the top of the stairs. Maybe if I beg him enough, he'll open the cell for me. If he truly wishes to start over like he claims, then perhaps he'll agree to this to show his sincerity.

I have to try. If I can't convince the Winter King, then Father will die.

Chapter 22

I whirl around and race back through the dungeons, not caring that I trip on the uneven surface. A dark thought descends upon me, and I try to shake it away.

What if the reason the Winter King agreed to release Father was because he knew he was mere moments away from turning to ice?

I sprint up the stairs, my legs unable to carry me as fast as I'd like. No matter how hard I run, it doesn't feel quick enough. But it's fast enough that I struggle to slow myself when I reach the top and nearly collide with the Winter King.

He grips my arms to steady me. "Adara? What is it?"

"My father," I gasp. "He's almost completely turned to ice. I tried shouting, but he won't wake up. Please. You must open the cell so I can help him."

I wait for him to laugh and tell me Father can die for all he cares, but he doesn't. "So soon?" He shakes his head. "I've lingered here too long."

"Please," I try again. "He'll die if we don't hurry."

"Here," he says, holding out his hand and conjuring a key carved from ice. "Take this."

I swipe the key from his hands and don't look back as I run down to Father.

Why would the Winter King agree so readily to hand me the key? There must be a reason he wants to keep me sweet. The monster I know would never agree to something that doesn't benefit him.

By the time I reach Father's cell, the frost has spread to his elbows. I shove the key into the lock and turn it until it clicks. I throw the door aside and sprint straight for Father. He still doesn't look up. His eyes are closed.

I throw the torch onto the floor beside us and grab his hands. My stomach twists as I gaze down at his frozen fingers. They're so translucent that I can see the color of my fingers beneath his, though the image is distorted. I squeeze them, but they do not thaw.

"Father," I cry, cradling his cheek. "Please wake up." Even his face no longer feels like flesh. His cheeks are as stiff as ice. "Please don't let it be too late." I throw my arms around him and hug him tight, wishing I could squeeze the warmth back into his bones. A tear escapes, tracing my cheek. I rock back and forth with Father in my arms, begging over and over for him to wake up. I've nearly given up and accepted that it's too late when Father whispers my name. The sound is so slight I almost miss it. Then I fear it's my wishful imagination.

"Father, can you hear me?"

He croaks out my name. That's enough to know he's still alive. That there's still hope.

"You must be strong. You must fight the frost." I loosen one arm from around him and inspect his hands. His fingers are no longer translucent and the color is returning to them, little by little. The process is gradual, but I'm grateful that the spell is reversing and the ice is thawing. "I've convinced the Winter King to free you. By morning, you'll be on your way home. You can't let the frost take you now."

Father shivers, as if trying to shake away winter's embrace. "H-how?" he manages. "How did you convince him?"

"Stubbornness," I reply and hold him even tighter.

I'm not sure how long we stay like that before Father feels warm again, but it must be several hours since I feel numb all over. After longer still, I manage to get him to stand. On the first attempt, his legs give way, and he ends up tumbling to the ground. There's a terrible thud when his head smacks against the ice, and I quickly drop beside him, inspecting the back of his head. Father is dazed from the fall but quickly regains his senses and then we try to stand again. This time he's more stable, and we make it step by step out of his cell. His strides grow stronger as we leave the dungeons, though he relies on me all the way up the stairs.

The Winter King is gone and has assigned no more guards outside the dungeons, so that must mean Father really is free. It's nearly morning now, the sky a bright rosy hue.

I call over to two guards hurrying through the courtyard, and they march toward me without hesitation, frowning as they notice Father.

"My father is sick from the frost," I say, "and needs a carriage home immediately."

"Shouldn't that man be inside the dungeons?" one guard says, bristling. He looks to his companion for a second opinion.

"My lady," the other says, stepping toward me. "Allow us to take this prisoner back to his cell."

"No," I exclaim, stepping in front of Father and shielding him from the guards. "I won't let you take him back there. The frost will kill him if he stays in the dungeons any longer."

"But the king—"

"Ordered for my father to be released."

The guards glance at each other, and then shake their heads.

"I'm not lying," I say through my teeth. "If you don't believe me, ask the king yourselves."

"Adara," Father says quietly. "If this is a problem, I can return to my cell."

"No, you won't." I lift my chin and glare at the guards. "Well then, what are you standing around for? Either prepare a carriage for my father, or find the king and ask for his permission."

They choose the latter, of course. When they disappear, I help Father onto a bench. It's made from ice like everything else and unlike me, he isn't immune to the frost. I catch him flinching as he sits, and I'm sure he can feel the chill through his breeches. I could take Father back to my chambers to rest, since I don't know how long it'll take for the guards to return, but it isn't as if my chambers will be much warmer than out here in the courtyard. Wherever we go, we'll be surrounded by ice. Taking him to rest in my chambers would mean he could lie down and be wrapped up in my furs and we would be out of the wind, but it would also mean running into countless guards along the way. It seems the Winter King is yet to announce Father's freedom, and some of the other guards may decide to drag him back to the dungeons.

Father says little while we wait. Morning spreads across the sky in golden light.

Kassia and Elona soon find us, and their expressions are as confused as the guards'.

"My lady," Elona cries, picking up the hem of her skirts and rushing toward me. Kassia does the same. "Shouldn't your father be in the dungeons?"

Kassia peers at me. "You didn't break him out of his cell, did you?"

"If I did, would I currently be sitting on a bench in the middle of the courtyard for everyone to see?"

My maids relax substantially at that.

"But how did you get him out?" Kassia presses. "Elona and I both appealed to the king yesterday on your behalf, after seeing how distressed you were, and he seemed unlikely to change his mind."

I can't help but smile. Perhaps my maids are part of the reason the Winter King changed his mind. If two of his servants were sympathetic to my cause, then he'd have feared others would also be.

"Maybe you both had more impact than you realize," I say, "since the king came here earlier and said he'd release my father."

"That is most gracious of him," Elona replies.

I try not to snort. He only released Father because he feared his kingdom would see him as a tyrant, damaging his already fragile reputation. "Indeed," I say, trying to smooth the sarcasm from my voice, "how gracious of him."

"If your father is free, then why are you both still sitting out here in the cold?" Kassia asks.

"We're waiting for the guards to arrange a carriage to take him home," I say. I don't bother explaining that those guards have instead gone to find the Winter King because they don't believe that Father is free. If I tell my maids, I may also have to deal with them trying to march Father back into his cage.

"Can't you wait inside?" Elona says.

"I'm sure they won't be long." I glance at Father beside me. His eyes are closed and his head rests on my shoulder. His fingers don't seem to be turning to ice, but he looks weary and cold. "Would one of you mind fetching Father some furs?"

Kassia volunteers for the task and promises that she'll bring me some furs as well, though I have no need for them. Elona offers to get us some breakfast from the kitchens, and I certainly don't decline that—for Father or myself.

The guards return before my maids, and they apologize profusely for the misunderstanding. I interrupt their groveling by telling them to have the carriage ready immediately. Just as they leave, Kassia returns with the furs and we bundle Father up from head to toe in them. He still shivers, but not nearly as terribly, and after a few minutes of being wrapped in furs, much more color returns to his cheeks. Kassia insists on draping one around my shoulders, and in the end, I agree.

"Kassia," I say. "I was wondering if I could ask you a favor."

"What is it you require, my lady?"

"Would you mind traveling back with my father?" I ask. "I worry about him making the journey home alone, with no one to take care of him."

"Of course I don't mind," Kassia replies. "I promise I will look after him on your behalf."

Elona soon returns with several other servants and plenty of food. Steam billows into the frosty air as they approach, and I can smell the warm food even from across the courtyard. My stomach rumbles loudly enough for Kassia to hear, and she laughs.

"You have no idea how difficult it was to stop my stomach from growling yesterday," I grumble. "You and Elona really both have a wicked streak."

A smile plays on her lips. "Maybe you shouldn't have been so stubborn and just eaten, my lady."

Maybe I should have, but then the statement I made by kneeling outside the dungeon wouldn't have been as powerful and Father wouldn't be free. I don't say this though and just smile back in response.

Despite the protests from my stomach, first I try to get Father to eat. Elona and Kassia quickly take over, however, and tell me to eat as well. Though I hate eating while Father is looking so weak, my stomach doesn't refuse. I polish off half of the trays Elona brought, though Father only manages a few bites.

"I'll bring plenty of food," Kassia promises, taking my hands in hers. "I'm sure he'll be feeling well enough in a few hours to eat more, especially when we're clear of the mountain."

The guards return soon, marching alongside a carriage drawn by two horses. My maids help me get Father inside, and we cover him with furs as best we can. Father looks up as I turn to leave, and he catches my hand and gives it a squeeze.

"Adara." Father doesn't need to say any more than that. I can see exactly in his eyes what he is asking of me: to be careful of the Winter King.

I squeeze his hand back and crouch so I'm at his height. In a low voice I say, "Remember what I asked when you return home. The letter."

"And the roses."

I smile. "Yes, and the roses."

I release his hand and say my farewells. Though I know he'll be well with Kassia to watch over him, I fear this may be the last time I see him, if my attempt to kill the Winter King goes horribly wrong. But I try not to let my worry show in my face as I step out of the carriage and let Kassia inside.

They leave the palace soon after and Elona accompanies me high onto the wall, so that I can watch the carriage as it rolls down the mountain. Until eventually it disappears into the horizon.

Chapter 23

I spend most of the next day in bed, recovering from the intensity of the past few nights. On the following day, when I'm more rested and my injuries have almost healed, the Winter King asks whether I would like to spend the afternoon with him. It seems he's determined to draw a line under everything that has happened and start fresh. I can't deny that I desire the same thing. A chance to begin anew and work on regaining the Winter King's trust. Though he agreed to release Father, it was only because I forced him into a corner. And it certainly doesn't change the fact that he has taken both Dalia and Orlan from me. While my plans may have been temporarily disrupted, I have no intention of swaying from my initial cause.

The Winter King suggests a variety of activities to do together this afternoon, such as strolling through the icy gardens or visiting the library, and I instead opt for sparring against each other. It's unconventional, but the Winter King already knows I can wield a sword. He defeated me so easily the other night, and I'm determined to stand more of a chance if we are ever to face each other again. Not that I intend to end him in hand-to-hand combat. It would take several lifetimes for me to match the Winter King in skill, and if I am to defeat him, I must instead rely on the element of surprise.

Elona heads to the storehouses outside in search of suitable sparring attire. I hope my maids from home remembered to pack such clothing into my chests, even if it isn't fitting for a lady—let alone a queen. If Elona can find nothing, I'll have no choice but to duel the Winter King while dressed in a gown. Though it won't be the first time I'll have sparred in a dress, it's a disadvantage I can't afford when fighting an opponent like him.

While Elona is gone, I wait in my room and examine the flowers the Winter King has brought me today—pretty pink roses. I pluck a petal from the largest flower head and rub the silky piece between my index finger and thumb. Then I squeeze it and leave the crumpled ball beside the vase. Before I can spoil any more, the doors swing open.

I turn to see Kassia standing in the doorway.

"You're back," I say, tearing myself away from the roses. "I wasn't expecting you so soon."

"The journey wasn't that long, my lady. We arrived at your house last night and left before dawn this morning."

"How is my father?"

"Better," she says. "He started to make a quick recovery as soon as we were away from the palace. I didn't see him this morning before I left, but he looked very well last night."

"I'm relieved to hear it. Thank you for accompanying him home."

"There's no need to thank me," Kassia says with a curtsey. She pauses, glancing around the room. "Where's Elona?"

"Searching for my dueling leathers."

"Dueling leathers?" Kassia repeats.

"The king asked to spend the afternoon with me, so we'll spend it sparring."

"Oh," she replies, though she looks no less confused. "Did His Majesty wish to teach you to defend yourself after what happened?" As soon as she says the question, she clamps her hand over her mouth. "I'm sorry, my lady, I didn't mean—"

"It's fine," I say. "But no, sparring was my suggestion and not the king's. I used to train with my father's guards back at home." I press my lips together, trying to ignore the pain in my chest at the thought of Orlan.

"I didn't realize you were capable with a sword," she replies. "I'm surprised your father let you train with the guards."

I grin. "I didn't give him much choice."

She returns my smile and asks me more questions about my sword skill, and Elona returns soon after. I'm relieved to see that she brings with her my favorite training leathers from home, so I won't have to spar in a dress. She and Kassia help me into my jerkin and breeches, and once I'm dressed, they lead me down to the training yard.

The Winter King stands there alone at the center of the yard, staring up at the sky. Specks of snow drift in the wind, powdering his broad shoulders. He turns as we approach.

"Ah, Adara, you're here." When I stop before him, he offers me the sword in his hand, still sheathed in its scabbard. It's an exquisite blade, far finer than any I've ever wielded. Rubies decorate the pommel, and the scabbard is embossed with ornate detail.

I take the sword from him and unsheathe it. Without the scabbard, it's surprisingly light. I take a step back and swing the blade in an arc before me. The motion is fluid, cutting through the air like butter. My satisfaction must be clear since the Winter King smiles and says, "I thought you'd like it."

I eye the glittering jewels encrusted in the hilt. "Is this your sword?"

He nods.

"Why rubies?" I ask. "I thought sapphires would be more to your liking."

"Long ago, our kingdom's banner was crimson. My father had this blade crafted for me for my sixteenth birthday."

I frown, struggling to imagine this immortal being as a child. "Before you became the Winter King?"

"Indeed," he replies, a wistful look in his bright eyes.

I want to ask how he became the Winter King, but it's hard to know how to word the question without being too blunt. Before I can settle upon the words, the Winter King holds out his hand and conjures a sword of ice.

"I hope you will forgive me for wielding a frozen blade rather than one of steel," he says. "I assure you it will give me no unfair advantage over you. There's no magic in this blade, except that which it has been crafted with."

I examine the sword, trying to imagine how it might feel to wield. The Winter King offers it to me, and I take it. The blade is significantly lighter than my own, and I suspect I would struggle to adjust to the lack of weight without extensive practice. And of course, it isn't practical to train to fight with a frozen sword, unless you are the physical embodiment of winter and can conjure one at will.

I pass back the sword to him. "It feels exceptionally light."

"That's the reason I prefer to wield a sword of ice. I fear if I were to use a normal blade, you would win our duel. At least at first, until I became once more accustomed to wielding steel."

I arch a brow. "I didn't realize you were so competitive."

He smiles. "Perhaps, but not nearly as much as you."

"How can you tell?"

"You have this look in your eyes."

"What look?" I ask.

"Like fire."

If only he knew the truth behind the fire in my eyes.

I twirl my sword. "Are we going to stand here talking all day, or are we going to fight?"

The Winter King grins, his grip tightening around the hilt of his sword. "If my queen wishes to fight, then fight we shall."

I assume a fighting stance, knees bent to allow for ease of movement and body angled side on to reduce the target area, and the Winter King does the same. We circle each other a few times, and today I don't make the mistake of striking first. Instead, I wait him out, tracing circle after circle around him until I'm sure I must make him dizzy. Kassia and Elona soon leave, shouting that they'll see if the other maids can use their help for any errands while they aren't busy. The Winter King raises his left hand to show he's heard, but his eyes don't break away from mine.

Then he strikes, lunging at me blade first. I step aside, and his blade cuts through the air inches away from where I stand. He arcs toward me, and I don't make the mistake of parrying. I won't have the strength to hold it, and doing so will offer him the opportunity to unsteady me. Instead, I go low. His blade sings overhead. I slash at his thigh. He evades, stepping back. His sword crashes down toward me. I spring backward. The sword hits the ground with a clang. I leap upright, just in time for the Winter King's next strikes.

His attacks are relentless, as they were when we battled the other night, and I struggle to find the chance to counter. He keeps me on the defensive, and I dodge and step and lurch away from his sword. But no matter how many times he attacks, the Winter King doesn't seem to tire. Every strike holds as much strength as the last. Meanwhile, my evasions are slowing. And growing clumsier. One attack comes close to striking my shoulder. I pull back in time, and the sword brushes over my leathers. If I were wearing a tunic, the fabric would have been torn. Now there's only the slightest mark on my jerkin. On some attacks, I am forced to parry and hope I pull away in time, before the Winter King uses it to his advantage. On my last, I fail to do so. His weight bears down on me, and my sword remains locked with his. I try to pull back but stumble. My feet catch on an uneven frozen stone, and I slam into the hard surface, my sword clattering uselessly out of my grasp. My thighs bear most of the impact. I wince, but there's no time to fuss over the pain. The Winter King's sword darts toward me.

I lunge for my blade, but the tip of his sword comes to a stop at the hollow of my neck.

I look up, and he raises a brow.

"All right," I huff. "You win that round."

He laughs and holds out his hand to help me up. "You fought well."

"I can fight better." I take his hand and grip my sword, and assume a fighting stance yet again. "Ready for round two?"

The Winter King answers with the slash of his sword. Again, we fight. And again, I lose. We spend the entire afternoon sparring, and not once do I come close to beating him.

Later that evening, when we're dining in his chambers, I let out a heavy sigh and say, "How are you so good? I don't stand a chance. Even with Orlan, he was better than me, but I could see openings. Against you, there's no hope."

"Orlan?" he asks, setting down his goblet.

"My father's guard captain," I reply, fiddling with my fork. I don't add that Orlan is gone, frozen by the Winter King himself. There's no point reminding him of the incident, not when things are returning to normal.

"I see," the Winter King replies. "Does that mean you intend to give up?"

"Of course not. I'll have to try harder until I beat you."

He smiles. "You don't need to try harder, just smarter."

"What do you mean?"

"It's your tell."

I frown. "My tell?"

"It lets me know when you're about to attack."

"How?"

"Has no one ever said you tense your shoulders right before you strike?"

"They haven't." I pause, considering his words. "And I don't."

"The movement is slight, but it is enough to give yourself away."

Though I'm certain I'd be aware of what my own body is doing, I also know that he's beating me right now. And if that's his secret of how he's defeating me so easily, then there might be some truth behind what he says.

"All right." I lean back in my chair and fold my arms across my chest. "What else have you noticed that I can improve on?"

"You have a tendency to over rely on certain patterns of movements."

"Such as?"

"One of your signature moves is feinting right and kicking left. Particularly at the knee or groin."

I press my lips together, assessing his criticism. He might have a point with that one, as well. "It's usually effective on my father's guards."

"Probably because you beat them before they can learn the pattern behind your movements."

"Anything else?" I ask.

"You bend your knees a little too much."

"I can move easier that way."

"It makes you clumsier."

I frown deeper, less convinced of that one. But I'll have to trial it and see if sparring with less bend in my knees makes me any better.

I get a few more pointers out of the Winter King, such as rolling my shoulders a little more back and being less hunched over, as well as holding my sword a little looser to allow for flexibility in my wrist. And as soon as we finish eating, I return to my room and practice swinging my sword with all the Winter King's criticism in mind.

At first, it's hard to adjust, and I find myself slipping into my old ways after performing only a few strikes. Neither Kassia nor Elona are particularly pleased by my new hobby and try to persuade me to read by the fire. But I don't. If I want to beat the Winter King, I must practice. One day I might not be sparring him in the training ground but fighting him to survive, just like only a few nights ago. I never want to be in that position again, with both Father's life and mine at his mercy. Of course, now I'm fighting him only with his sword skill, and if we were truly to fight, he would also have his magic. But if being able to beat him in hand-to-hand combat increases my chances, if only slightly, then I'll practice until my feet are swollen and my fingers are bleeding.

Thankfully, they aren't by the time I finally retire to bed, though my fingers do sting from the friction. Kassia and Elona aren't happy that I go to sleep so late, though I told them to return home. As soon as they're both gone for the night, I retrieve my vial of poison and dagger from their hiding place and hold them tightly to my chest. I was so exhausted last night, and the night before I was busy kneeling before the dungeons, so I haven't held them for two nights. Already the frost is spreading across the glass, though it doesn't seem to have seeped through into the poison. Another night or so and I fear it would have frozen the Nightshade completely, and I'm not sure my touch would return it to its original state. The Crystal Palace has plenty of icy furniture, and my fingers have thawed none of it.

I sleep with my dagger and the vial cradled to my chest, and by morning, the frost is gone. I awake at dawn, leaving plenty of time to return my weapons to their hiding place.

Like yesterday, I spend the afternoon dueling with the Winter King, but he's busy in the morning and we only have a few hours to ourselves. I duel him as I practiced in my room last night, with my shoulders rolled back, my knees less bent and my grip looser around my sword, but fighting like this feels uncomfortable and I come no closer to beating him. Neither do my attempts help the following day, and the day after that we don't have a chance to duel since the Winter King is busy. I spend time in the training yard by myself, practicing some more so I can become more accustomed to this new way of fighting.

By the end of the week, Kassia brings me an envelope with Father's wax seal stamped onto it. So eager to read the contents, my fingers nearly tear apart the paper in my haste. I scan over Father's scruffy writing, the ink blotched in places, and read two lines at a time.

My Dearest Daughter,

I am writing to let you know that I am faring much better since returning home and am already feeling much more like myself.

I hope you are also well in the Crystal Palace, and I am regretful that you are not home this Summer to enjoy our gardens. The roses are most wonderful this time of year.

Kind regards,

Your Loving Father

I read the letter twice. My fingers claw at the paper, crumpling the edges.

'*The roses are most wonderful this time of year.*'

Father will have sent this letter no later than this morning, and writing this line means that he is already on his way to leaving home and keeping a low profile. Of course, Father can't be missing for weeks, especially if the Winter King holds meetings and Father is absent. It'll be fine at first, since everyone will know that Father left the Crystal Palace far from his usual self and will suspect him to be bedridden. But if they question our staff or demand to meet with Father, the truth will escape. I may have a month before questions start getting asked. I need to strike sooner rather than later.

I must slay the Winter King before anyone can discover that Father is on the run.

Chapter 24

Two days later, I finally find an opportunity to poison the Winter King. This afternoon, he suggests we take a break from sparring and spend it inside the palace's gardens. There isn't much color, but the snow fluttering down and the stillness of our surroundings makes it rather peaceful.

We sit in a pavilion, built from ice, and the Winter King asks my maids to retrieve an old chessboard in the storehouse. Apparently, it was one from his childhood, which he used to play with his father and sometimes his older brother. This is the first time he has ever mentioned any siblings, but I don't squeeze out any information other than his brother being called Caltain. I don't press for anything else, since the knowledge of his brother won't help me in my quest to vengeance.

The set Elona and Kassia return with doesn't look as old as I expect, not centuries old. The corners of the wooden board are slightly scuffed and some of the black paint marking the squares is patchy and peeling in places, but it looks remarkably good for its age. They set it down on the small table between the Winter King and me.

"Can I get you anything else, Your Majesty?" Kassia asks, bowing her head.

The Winter King turns to me.

"Some wine?" I suggest.

"Wine it is then," the Winter King says.

With that, Elona and Kassia leave in search of wine.

The Winter King opens the box containing the chess pieces and sets them one by one across the board. "Have you played before?"

"Just a little, with my father. And only ever on days where it was raining. Even then, I couldn't ever sit long enough to learn. Dalia was much better than me, and she and Father often used to play."

The Winter King smiles at that. "Well, hopefully you will manage to sit still long enough today to learn."

"I suppose we'll find out," I reply, returning his smile.

He holds up each piece in turn, explaining their role and the rules of the game. Somewhere in the back of my mind I recall learning them, and as we begin to play, that knowledge comes to the forefront of my mind. I lose, of course. Just like with dueling, there seems to be no way I can beat him. When I was younger, I would always lose to Dalia or Father and would end up getting into such a strop, I shoved the board across the table and sent all the pieces flinging across the room. The first time I did that, the chess set was Father's finest, and I ended up chipping one of the jade pieces. He was furious and then I was only ever allowed to play with wooden sets, though I never bothered with any. Today I certainly don't send the Winter King's board flying across the gardens, not when I know it's as old as he and may crumble during its flight. I'd be lying if I said I didn't contemplate it at least once, though. On our first five games, I lose within five minutes. After that, each round becomes slower as the Winter King points out each mistake I make. I ensure I don't repeat them, and a few hours later, we begin to have actual games. I still don't pose much of a threat to his reigning status of champion, though.

In the late afternoon, our game is interrupted when a servant arrives and informs the Winter King that some lord or other has requested to meet with him.

"I doubt it will take too long," the Winter King says after apologizing for the interruption. "Not more than an hour."

"I'll wait here for you," I say, leaning back in my chair.

"Surely you can't be comfortable sitting out here?"

"We've already been sitting outside for several hours," I point out. "Besides, we can finish our game when you return. I'm certain I'm winning this time." I'm not under any illusion that I'm close to winning, but I desperately want to stay out here and finish our game. The Winter King's gaze sweeps over the chessboard and then he looks up at me. He isn't able to hide the dubious look in his eyes, but he doesn't point out the fact I'm by no means winning.

"All right," he says, and then steps down from the pavilion. "I won't keep you waiting for long."

I watch as he follows the path back to the palace. After he disappears, I wait a long while and stare out at the barren gardens, watching the snow descend upon the icy shrubs and thorns.

The gardens are so still and silent, with few servants around. I scan across every inch of my surroundings and when I'm sure

I'm alone and can hear no footsteps approaching, I pull the glass vial from under the neckline of my dress and yank the chain over my head. Under the table, I pop off the wooden cork with my thumb and lean across to the Winter King's goblet.

There's just enough wine left in his goblet that the poison will mix thoroughly with it, though I will need to give it a shake to ensure it all swirls around. Though Nightshade has an incriminating dark hue, it will blend perfectly with the red wine we're drinking and, if anything, will only make it darker by a slight shade. Nothing that the Winter King will notice. And the wine is sweet enough that even if it tastes a bit sweeter, the Winter King certainly won't suspect Nightshade has been slipped into his drink.

I hold the vial above his goblet. Blood pounds in my ears.

Once I tip this poison into his drink, there will be no going back.

Am I making the right choice? What if the Winter King doesn't deserve to die?

No. This is the right choice. It has to be. He is the one who stole Dalia from me, and now Orlan, as well. Not only am I doing this for myself, but for everyone else in the kingdom who has suffered from the Winter King's selfishness. All those who mourn silently.

Just as I'm about to tip the vial and let the poison drip into the wine, snow crunches to the left.

I snap back the vial and hide it under the table, blanketing it with my skirts. Maids appear from the hedges. I steady my breathing as they approach, doing my best to look as relaxed as possible.

"My lady," one of them says, curtseying. "The king sent us to check if you need anything while he's busy meeting with Lord Farrows."

Can they hear the frantic pounding of my heart? I swallow and will my blood to slow its relentless thrum.

"Cake," I blurt. "I'm quite hungry and would be grateful if cake or something else sweet is brought to me."

They dip their heads and say together, "At once, my lady." Then they scurry off, leaving me alone in the gardens once more.

I heave in a shaky breath and peer under the table at the vial. It's tilted and the stopper is off. If I'd tilted it over any further, it would have splashed across my dress and stained it. Then I'd have to explain that—though I could probably get away with blaming the wine—but more importantly, I would be without any Nightshade to poison the Winter King.

Again, I lean over the table, and this time I don't hesitate before letting all the poison drip into the Winter King's wine. The incriminating splash of each drop makes me flinch, but no one else appears from around the corner. The Nightshade seeps into the wine, and I lift the goblet by the stem and give the wine a swirl until the poison mixes seamlessly with the wine.

I slink back to my side of the table—and just in time. A servant hurries past, though he's too focused on going about his business and doesn't turn to look at me even once.

Soon, the maids return with several dishes filled with cakes and other sweet treats. There's much more than I could usually eat, and my appetite is lacking right now. The poisoned wine sits just mere inches away, and I can all but smell it in the frosty air. My stomach churns. What if the maids decide to clear away the Winter King's goblet and pour out the wine? What if he doesn't return at all this evening? If either happens, then I will have wasted my poison and won't get another chance.

I force myself to eat while the maids are watching. As soon as they leave, I set down the cake I was biting into and wrinkle my nose. It tastes like ash. I doubt I can get away with spitting out the mouthful of cake, so I force myself to swallow it and then I touch no more of the dishes. I stare out at the fluttering snow once more, praying the Winter King will soon return.

He does, though it feels like it takes forever. His cloak billows out around him as he walks through the gardens, and the snow falling on it makes it look like stars glittering across the midnight sky.

I can barely look at him as he slides back into the chair opposite me. I feel nauseous, and the smell of all the sweet treats around me doesn't help to steady my stomach. Any moment now, the Winter King will peer into his goblet, or sniff it, and realize what I've done. He doesn't, though. Instead his gaze rakes across the board, and then he looks up at me and raises a brow.

"I hope you haven't tampered with the board."

I have to force a laugh, hoping it doesn't sound as hollow as it feels. "It's your fault if you don't remember where they were."

"Hm." He leans forth, resting his chin on his fist, and examines the board more closely. "I'm sure my bishop was here." He taps the adjacent black square.

"If that's what you want to believe, then move the bishop. But if you do, you'll be cheating because I haven't touched a single piece."

"Do you swear it?" he asks with mock solemness.

I press my hand to my chest. I can feel the frenzied beat and suck in a sharp breath. I do my best to relax my shoulders. After all, the Winter King's eyes were astute enough to see that I tense before striking when we were dueling. I worry he will also be sharp enough to see through me.

"I swear it on all my honor," I say, dipping my head.

He watches me for a long while and then I'm forced to look up and meet his bright eyes. I do my best not to flinch. I hold myself perfectly still. "All right," he finally says. "Perhaps I believe you." His eyes sparkle with amusement.

I turn my gaze back to the board, desperate for a distraction. "Whose turn was it last?"

"That I can't remember, so it seems you should go first."

"You don't need to take pity on me for my awful chess skills. I'm sure it was your turn next, now that I think about it."

"I insist. Ladies first."

I scan across all my remaining pieces on the board and decide to move a rook. It turns out to be the wrong decision since the Winter King takes it on his next move.

"Sloppy," he says, his lips twitching. "It seems you've already forgotten how to play. What was it you said about winning before I left?"

He's right that I'm sloppy now. All I can think of is the poison in his goblet. The thought consumes all others and makes sensible thinking hard. Instead, I lift my chin in what I hope looks like mock indignation. "Has no one taught you it's rude to gloat?"

"Not once in my three hundred years," he replies, his smile growing. "It seems you'll have to be the first to teach me."

"I'm certain it would take you another three hundred years to learn humility," I huff.

"It's never too late."

"If you say so." I move a pawn forward by a square. "Your turn, Your Majesty."

He responds by claiming that pawn with a knight. But I'm not too annoyed. If I hadn't sacrificed that pawn, he would have taken my bishop.

Despite my efforts, I still lose. We play another game after that, but by then the sun has already set and night is falling upon us, shadowing the snowy gardens.

"It's late and you haven't eaten," the Winter King remarks, looking out at the night sky beyond the pavilion. "You must be hungry."

"Not particularly." I point to the cakes still lying uneaten in their dishes. "Or else I would have eaten them."

"I suppose," the Winter King says. "Though you should still attempt to eat, or else you'll feel terrible later." He stands. My attention drifts to his goblet. Though he returned an hour ago, he hasn't drunk a single drop of wine. If only I can get him to stay here a little longer.

"All right," I reply. "But why don't we eat out here tonight for a change?"

"Out here?"

"Unless you would prefer to eat inside?"

"I have no preference," he says. "I was thinking out of concern for you."

"I don't feel the cold at all, and it's rather peaceful with the snow."

The Winter King nods. "If you wish to eat out here, then we shall. I'll inform the maids that we will dine out here tonight instead of in my chambers." With that, he leaves in search of maids.

When he's gone, I lean over the table and peer into his goblet. The poison is still untraceable inside it, and the wine is as full as when I poured it in. Can he sense, even without drinking it, that I've poured Nightshade into his goblet? Is that why he hasn't touched his wine? Unless he's forgotten it's there.

Under the table, I clench my fists. When the Winter King returns, I must ensure he drinks every drop. Nightshade is expensive and difficult to acquire, so I only had enough for a fatal dose. He must drink it all, or else the poison will just make him sick. A few drops will be no good.

The Winter King soon returns with an entourage of maids. They clear away our chess board and the dishes of cakes. Thankfully, they see that our goblets are still full and leave them where they sit. They disappear with the dishes and promise they won't keep us waiting long for dinner.

When they're gone, I turn to the Winter King and say, "I was wondering something."

He raises a brow at me. "What?"

"You always mention that I must be hungry or thirsty, and never that you are yourself."

"And you're wondering whether I too feel hunger or thirst?"

I nod.

"I don't require either, and can go months without eating or drinking anything. Neither food nor wine has tasted the same since I became immortal. Everything tastes bland now."

"Since you became immortal? That was three hundred years ago?"

"It was."

"And how did you become immortal?"

The Winter King pauses, pressing his lips together. The whir of the wind feels our brief silence. "I cannot say," he finally replies.

If he isn't willing to answer, then it'll do me no good to keep pressing him about it. I let a moment pass and then another. The Winter King says nothing either. I'm too preoccupied plotting how to get him to finish his wine to make conversation. By the time the maids show up with our food, an idea has come to me.

"Thank you for teaching me how to play chess today," I say once the maids finish setting our table and leave. "My father would be surprised that I managed to play a full game of it. In fact, he would likely fall out of his chair with surprise."

The Winter King laughs. "You are most welcome. I thought it would be something different to do, other than sparring. We can play chess tomorrow if you would like, or we can duel again."

I smile. "Let's spar again tomorrow. I think I have more of a chance of beating you with a sword than with my chess skills." What we decide to do makes no difference to me. If all goes according to plan, he won't live to see tomorrow.

"Your chess skills have vastly improved from this morning," the Winter King offers.

"Only because I was so terrible to begin with." I take my goblet and hold it up to him. "Let's toast to my newfound chess skills."

The Winter King answers as I hoped. He reaches for his goblet and raises it in the air. We clink our goblets together, and then I drink. So does the Winter King.

Except he doesn't drink it all.

I make sure I drink every drop of my wine and set my goblet down on the table with a dramatic thud. Then I point to the wine still inside his goblet. "You're meant to drink it all!" I exclaim, hoping I sound jovial enough. "Now you've ruined our toast, and my chess skills will be cursed with bad luck. You're just worried I'll start beating you, aren't you?"

"I'm not worried," the Winter King says. He picks up his goblet again and drinks every drop of wine. I watch him carefully. When he sets his goblet back down on the table, I make a show of peering inside.

"Good," I say. The enormity of what I've done crashes into me like a tidal wave. My heart swarms with fear, relief, and triumph all at once.

I settle back into my chair and try not to let my raging emotions show. At least eating provides the perfect excuse to not have to make conversation. It's hard to eat, but I force down every mouthful.

"Adara," the Winter King says when we've nearly finished.

I look up from my plate. "Yes?"

"I was thinking about arranging for musicians to play in the hall tomorrow night."

"For what occasion?"

"Not for any particular occasion," the Winter King replies. "It occurred to me the other day that you must find the Crystal Palace far too quiet."

"Are you planning to hold a Ball?" I ask, frowning. Other than the Midsummer Ball, the Winter King isn't known to host Balls.

"No, I was intending for it to only be the two of us."

"Oh," I say. The idea of a private Ball sounds too romantic, more so than an evening sitting out in the gardens together in the snow.

"What do you think?" he asks when I say nothing else.

I'm not sure how I feel about the prospect of dancing with him. Though sparring requires us to stand close together, dancing requires a certain level of intimacy.

But it doesn't matter. He'll be dead by the evening.

"Yes," I say quietly, since there's nothing else I can say. "I would like that very much, thank you."

He smiles at that, and my stomach knots.

By the time we finish eating, the Winter King doesn't look any paler than usual and there's no sign of poisoning. That isn't too surprising, since it takes a few hours for Nightshade to work, but I expected to see some sort of change in his appearance to indicate my crime.

We stay out for another hour after dinner, but even by the time we return to the palace for the night, the Winter King still isn't showing any outward signs of poisoning.

Morning soon comes, and when my maids come to wake me, I expect them to burst in and tell me that the Winter King has mysteriously died in the night. Except they don't. They instead take me to his chambers, where I find the Winter King sitting at the end of his table.

Perfectly well.

The Winter King says something as I sit down, but I don't hear it. Blood drums in my ears.

Elona shakes my shoulder. I'm delayed in looking up at her. "My lady, are you all right?" I have to read her lips to make sense of her words.

"Air," I gasp. "I need air."

At once, the Winter King orders my maids to escort me outside. His words sound hollow beneath the frantic pounding of my pulse. I barely register as my maids lead me through the palace and into the gardens, and once we're outside, I stare at the gnarled, icy branches around us.

How is he still alive? I watched him drink every drop of wine from his goblet. The dose of Nightshade in my vial was more than enough to kill a man. There's no way he should have survived.

I hate that I've failed, and I hate even more that a small, treacherous part of me feels some relief in that failure.

I crush it and burn it until it dies.

Kassia and Elona fuss over me, desperately trying to get me to drink water, to help my breathing steady. It takes a long while for me to recompose myself, to accept the fact that a man who should be dead is somehow alive.

When they're convinced that I'm fine, they take me back up to the Winter King's chambers, where I force myself to eat and act as normal as I can.

Not once does the Winter King mention poison, not even by the time we finish breakfast. As I stalk back to my chambers, my shoulders are heavy with the burden of truth.

The Winter King is too powerful for poison to work on him.

Now I must hope a dagger through the heart will be enough to kill him.

Chapter 25

The following evening, Kassia helps me dress into one of the most luxurious gowns Madame Bellmont fashioned for me. She tames my vibrant curls into a neat updo, powders my freckles, dabs rouge onto my lips and cheeks, and then whisks me off to the great hall. It feels a lifetime ago since the Winter King called my name there. It's been barely two weeks, but so much has happened since then. Father's attempted rescue, Orlan and his men frozen solid, and my failed attempt at poisoning the Winter King.

I thought long and hard last night in bed about how I could seize another opportunity tonight to kill the Winter King while we're dancing. There's only a slight chance I'll retrieve my dagger from beneath my gown when he isn't looking and stab him with it. A sword would be more effective, but I won't be able to hide one well enough and still dance. Besides, the Winter King doesn't need a blade to be armed. He has his magic at his fingertips. Always.

The best chance I have at successfully stabbing a blade through his chest is when he's asleep. But the Winter King said the other day that he doesn't need to eat or drink if he doesn't want to. It's possible that he doesn't need to sleep, either. All I can hope is that he opts to sleep, just as he opts to eat and drink, though he doesn't require it to survive.

The Winter King is already in the hall when Kassia and I arrive. On the balcony high above, there's a group of musicians gathered on the platform, just like there was at the Midsummer Ball. There are more than I expected, as many as there would be for a real Ball, though the Winter King and I are the only ones attending.

Tonight, he wears a deep blue silken tunic with silver thread embroidered into it so that it looks just like the night sky, and his icy crown sits atop his head as usual. His white hair gleams with a hint of blue from the braziers and torches scattered across the room.

I curtsey as I reach him, and the Winter King bows and extends his hand toward me. I accept, and his slender fingers close around mine.

"You look splendid tonight," he says, his gaze trailing down the length of my gown. I don't miss the fact it momentarily lingers on my plunging neckline.

"Thank you, Your Majesty."

Hand in hand we descend the stairs, and step out onto the empty sprawling floor of the ballroom. When we are at the center, the Winter King raises his palm and the musicians play. The sweet strings of violins fill the empty hall, vibrating off the domed icy ceiling.

"Would you care to dance?" the Winter King asks with a smile.

"It would be my pleasure."

His left arm slips around my waist, pulling me close. Far too close. He smells of pine and frost—of Winter. At first, I try to avoid inhaling his scent, to give myself the illusion of distance, but as we sweep back and forth across the empty hall, it becomes increasingly difficult to do so. Little by little he pulls me in closer, until my body is pressed against the hard planes of his chest and we dance as one.

"That night at the Midsummer Ball," the Winter King whispers, his breath tickling my ear, "all I wanted was to leave my throne and come down here and dance with you. Instead, I had to watch countless young lords bear that honor, and imagine myself in their place."

"Why didn't you?" I ask, focusing on my words rather than his closeness, as difficult as that is. "You're the King of Avella. You may do as you please."

He shakes his head. "It's best I stay far away from crowds."

"That's why you kept our ball for just the two of us?"

"Indeed."

"Why?"

"The frost," he simply says.

I frown at that. Some servants come fairly close to him, and he has frozen none of them. Or at least not so far that I've seen. It must be mostly the fear of accidentally freezing guests which keeps the Winter King far away.

The musicians play harder and faster, and our steps quicken to fit their rhythm. The Winter King sweeps me across the center of the icy hall, his hand only leaving my waist to twirl me around. When the music slows, the Winter King leans in once more to whisper in my ear.

"Adara." He speaks each syllable of my name like a caress. "I realized the other day that we've still yet to arrange a day for our wedding."

My steps falter. I drag the Winter King to a halt with me, and the two of us stop in the middle of the hall. The musicians continue serenading us with their strings. "Our wedding?"

His silver brows knit together. "You are to be my queen, and for that, we must marry."

"Of course," I say, hoping my words sound even. "Have you given thought when our wedding should be held?"

"I wished to consult you about it first," he replies. "Although we spoke about it several weeks ago, we reached no conclusion, and I fear that perhaps circumstances have changed since then?"

While I have no wish to marry the Winter King or rule at his side, a wedding sooner than later would be to my benefit. I don't know how long I will have before Father's absence from court will be noticed, and I'll have the opportunity to assassinate the Winter King on our wedding night when he's sleeping. Even if the thought of *marital duties* fills me with nausea.

All things considered, our wedding should be no later than by the end of the month.

I force a smile. "Whenever is most convenient for you, Your Majesty. Though with the incident with my father, it would be more beneficial for your reputation if we marry sooner than later. That way, the kingdom will know that I am well, and that my father had no reason to take me from the palace."

The Winter King pauses, considering my words. "You aren't wrong," he says. "That thought has also concerned me. If that is what you wish, then we will marry as soon as we are able. I will speak to some of my advisors and discuss which date would be the soonest feasible date."

I give him a nod, and we continue to dance. It must be nearly midnight by the time the Winter King dismisses the musicians and escorts me back to my chambers.

"Thank you for tonight," I say when we reach the door to my room. "I really do appreciate all that you have arranged for me tonight."

The Winter King dips his head. "It's nothing, but you're most welcome." There's a long pause, as I wait for him to bid me good night and leave, but he doesn't. Instead, his attention sweeps from the door to my room and back to me. "Your maids will have already returned home for the night." He gestures to the length of my dress. "Will you manage alone?"

I arch a brow at him. "It seems I'll have to manage alone, won't I?" I meet his gaze. "Unless you were offering your assistance, but that would be highly inappropriate considering we are yet to wed."

"I . . ." He clears his throat. "That wasn't what I meant."

"So you weren't offering to help? But what if I'm here all night, wrestling with my dress? Would you not feel duty bound to help a damsel in distress?"

He takes a step forward. Instinctively, I take one back, and my back meets the door. The handle digs into my hip. I can't read the Winter King's expression. Have I infuriated him?

But then amusement cracks across his face. "I find it hard to imagine you a damsel in distress. If your dress was causing you annoyance, you would no doubt tear it apart. And I imagine that is how you handle all your problems."

I've only been here two weeks, and yet he already knows me well enough to know that. Does he realize I intend to handle my problem of him murdering my sister in that same way? That I've already tried to poison him and am now plotting to slay him on our wedding night?

"Although," the Winter King continues, taking another step forth, "it would be a shame to ruin such a lovely dress."

He reaches out, slowly and tentatively, and I focus on the feeling of the solid door behind me, forcing myself not to jerk away. His fingers skim across the golden silk, following the neckline from my shoulder and to my collarbone. My gaze lowers. I don't breathe as I watch his fingers brush inward toward the hollow of my neck. I hope they won't plunge any lower. That they won't trail down to my chest. My skin is on fire.

When I look back up, he's staring at me. I wonder whether he can see the battle raging within me through my eyes. "Adara," he says slowly, savoring every syllable of my name. His fingers sweep up and brush my cheek. "Will you allow me to kiss you?"

I can only nod.

He must notice my reluctance, since he hesitates. Those moments stretch on. I watch in slow motion as he leans forth, and as he draws near, it feels as if I'm watching through a window rather than through my own eyes. But then he kisses me, and there's no mistaking that it's my lips he is kissing.

Me that he is kissing.

I focus on the sharp ache of the door handle digging into my hip. I push against it harder, wanting the pain to drown out the burn of the Winter King's lips on mine.

He pulls back slightly and gazes down at me with his bright eyes, as if he can't tell whether I wish to kiss him or not. I do my best to hide my heart, but then he begins to pull away. I feel my chance slipping through my fingers. In desperation, I force myself forward, tearing my hip away from the door handle, and catch his lips with my own.

The Winter King is surprised at first, and just stands there, letting me kiss him. Then his hand reaches behind my head, his fingers weaving through my curls, and he pulls me closer to him, deepening our kiss. He seems to mistake my desperation for desire as he claims my mouth with his. He presses into me and my back is flush to the door once more, and there is no escape.

His kisses are relentless, as if driven by hunger, as if tonight was not the first time he has longed to kiss me. Without the handle pressing into my hip, I have nothing to distract myself from the way his lips feel against mine. Every place his lips touch tingles, and then he lifts his mouth from mine and leaves a trail of kisses down to my neck. The tingling travels further down my shoulders, my arms, my chest. It reaches my stomach and sparks spread.

His lips find the spot between my neck and shoulder, and when his teeth graze that sensitive place, lightning courses through my veins. The sensation is so powerful that a moan escapes from my throat. I curse my body for betraying me and remind myself that this man is responsible for so much pain, but every touch of his lips extinguishes each thought before it can fully take root in my mind.

I can't think of anything but the tidal wave of pleasure crashing into me, especially when his lips trace lower, across my collarbone and down to my chest. His kisses stop just short of my breasts. I imagine him delving lower, his fingers pulling down the shoulder of my dress and exposing my chest. I crush the image as quickly as it blooms in my mind. But the shadow of the thought lingers, and I can do little to rid myself of it.

Right now, I am nothing but a slave to my selfish mortal body.

His lips trail upward, and his teeth graze my earlobe. My back arches off the door, pressing into him, though this man is my most hated enemy. Warmth pools in my lower stomach. I hate it. All of it.

And yet I want more.

"Adara," he breathes, his voice thick with need. "We must stop."

My stomach plunges like a dead weight. I wrap my hands around his neck, pulling him closer. "Stop?" I ask, struggling to keep my voice steady. "Why?"

He swallows. "I can't bear any more of this."

"Of what?"

"You," he growls. "If we keep doing this, I'll end up ripping your gown off right here."

I don't want him. I don't really want this to happen. But I've come so far in earning his trust, in making him believe I am falling for him as he seems to be falling for me. To back out now would mean shattering all I've accomplished. I must commit both my body and heart to this path. If I can lure him into my bed, I'll be able to strike him tonight. I won't have to wait until our wedding night.

"Then why don't you?" I tell myself the reason I'm daring him is so I can stab him in his sleep. Not because my treacherous body is yearning for his touch.

"I will only have you when you are my queen, and not before." He cups my cheek and presses his lips against mine in a chaste but firm kiss. "On our wedding night, I will savor each and every moment with you." His fingers brush across my temple, sweeping a stray lock of hair from my face. My skin tingles at his touch. "Good night, Adara. Sleep well."

I bid him good night too, though I don't know how I'll sleep with the conflicting forces of hate and desire raging through my entire being.

Chapter 26

That night, sleep feels an eternity away. I toss and turn, and no matter how hard I try, I can't shake away the echo of his lips on mine. The scorch of my skin as his fingers trail over me.

I tell myself the reason the memory is branded so deeply into my mind is not because I enjoyed it, but because it was my first kiss. Real kiss, if you're counting the frozen one the Winter King gave me during my first night here.

That lie doesn't hold for long. I know what I felt. The sheer pleasure, overwhelming desire, coursing through my body. Even if he is my most hated enemy. The man who murdered my sister. Orlan. And so many countless others.

The bile which rises from my stomach is so intense that I think I really will vomit. Only by swallowing down forcefully do I hold it at bay.

The disgust I feel isn't directed at the Winter King, but at myself. For desiring the monster who inflicted such suffering and pain on those I love dearly.

But somewhere, in the back of my mind, a small voice whispers that a true monster would not kiss me so tenderly, would not gaze at me with such softness in his eyes. And that maybe Dalia's death is somehow a misunderstanding.

No.

I clutch my blankets.

How can it be a misunderstanding? I was there when he called Dalia's name. I was there when he froze Orlan, not sparing him even a moment's hesitation.

He is a monster. He has to be. And either he has somehow fallen for me, or intends to use me for some dark purpose.

And it might be for the best that my body is so readily accepting of his touch. It enables me to play my part so perfectly the Winter King will never see me coming. There is no way I can defeat him in hand-to-hand combat. My only chance of killing him is to stab him through the heart on our wedding night, when his guard is well and truly lowered.

Enjoying the feel of his lips on mine is not a betrayal. It's an opportunity.

Only when I repeat that thought over and over do the chains of guilt loosen around me, allowing sleep to drift over me.

When I wake, it's to the sound of my door opening and Kassia and Elona entering my room. Kassia pushes aside my icy curtains, allowing the glorious morning rays to spill in. Elona brings me a steaming hot mug of juice and casts me a bright smile as she hands it to me.

"Did you sleep well, my lady?" she asks.

The question catches me off guard, and my shoulders stiffen. All I can think of is the conflicted storm of emotions raging through me last night.

I quickly draw my lips into a smile, and since it likely looks fake, I blow across my mug. Tendrils of steam waft out. "Well, thank you." To further mask the lie, I sip on the juice, though it scalds my tongue.

My maids help me dress, and when they're brushing my hair, a knock sounds on my doors. Most likely a servant bringing word that the Winter King is ready for me to dine with him, though I don't know how I will face him after what happened last night.

Kassia sets down her brush, leaving Elona and me, and rushes to the doors. When she opens them, surprise ripples across her face.

"Your Majesty," she says, dropping to a deep curtsey.

"Is my queen suitably dressed?" comes the deep, gravelly voice which haunted my dreams last night.

At the Winter King's words, I bolt up, almost sending the hairbrush which Elona holds flying across the room. Muttering her a quick apology, I join Kassia and the Winter King at the door.

His glacial eyes meet mine, burning into me despite their coldness. I can't look away. I stand there frozen in place. All I can think of is the two of us against those same doors behind him, me trapped between their hard planes and his even harder chest. Whatever this is that I'm feeling might prove an invaluable weapon for achieving my ends, but I fear I too will succumb to its steel. Unless I seize control of this explosive energy and keep it on a short leash.

The images of Dalia's and Orlan's faces do wonders for restraining the emotion swelling within me, smothering the building heat until the flames are nothing but dying embers.

My attention flickers down from his cold eyes and to the bouquet of roses in his hands. Red, like the color of my curls.

My heart skips at the sight. I remind myself he has brought them to win me over. For whatever he is scheming.

The edges of the roses are already being claimed by the frost, much quicker than the other flowers around my room. I suppose the fact they're currently clutched in his icy hands has much to do with that.

He bows deeply at the waist, which shocks my maids even more than the roses in his hands. Elona has left the vanity to come and watch us both. Though the Winter King has been sending me flowers for countless weeks, they must have thought he was only doing so out of a sense of duty. As for me, I know this villain is willing to do whatever is needed to achieve his own ambitions.

"I wanted to bring you the roses myself this morning," he says, "after our dance last night." His gaze drifts from me and back to the roses, a heaviness settling in his bright eyes. "Except it seems I'm best sending a servant to deliver them. I did not think they would succumb this quickly to the frost."

It's nearly impossible to prevent the narrowing of my eyes. Here's yet more evidence of the Winter King's inability to control his frost.

Why can't he control it?

He glances back up at me, his lips pulling upward into a small smile. "I hope you like them, nonetheless."

I force myself to return his smile. "I like them very much."

I maintain my smile as he passes them to me, and I gaze down at the pitiful flowers, doing my best to look grateful, and then hand them to Kassia. "Can you put these in a vase for me, please?"

Kassia takes them from me. "I'll put them in the empty one beside your bed."

When she leaves, the Winter King returns to me, his eyes drifting across my face and down my dress. "You look magnificent."

"You said the same thing last night," I say, doing my best to dull the sharpness on my tongue.

His smile grows. "Only because you look magnificent every day, no matter what you wear."

I stamp down the heat that flares at his words. Fortunately, Elona saves me from having to figure out how to respond to him.

"I just need to finish her hair," she says, ushering me back toward the vanity. "And then she'll be all yours."

The Winter King waits by my door, even when Kassia offers for him to come in and sit down. He stands there, with his hands clasped behind his back, not venturing even a step forward.

Once Elona finishes tending to my hair, I join the Winter King, and he offers his arm. Gingerly, I take it.

We traipse through the tangle of frozen corridors, taking the long way back to his chambers, though it would be quicker to take the door on the other side of my room.

A tense silence consumes us for most of the way to his chambers. As if, like me, all he can think about is our kiss last night.

Finally, when we reach his chambers, he speaks. "This morning, I spoke to my advisors regarding what we discussed last night."

I blink.

"The date of our wedding."

"Oh. Of course."

He frowns. "It is still what you want?"

Of course it's still what I want. A perfect opportunity to plunge my dagger through his chest. "It is," I say with a smile. "Did you decide on a suitable date?"

"Yes." He pauses. "Not this Friday, but next."

My stomach dips. "That's nearly two weeks away."

I don't know whether I'll be able to afford two weeks before killing him. Will Father's disappearance be noticed before then?

"We will need to send invitations across the kingdom," the Winter King replies. "And those invited will need to travel to the palace. Next Friday is the soonest that we will be able to hold it. Unless you would prefer to hold the wedding the following week or the one after?"

I swallow. "Next Friday will be perfect."

One morning the following week, when we're strolling through the courtyard, the Winter King says, "What do you think of the flowers?" He nods at the servants carting in wagons full of red roses and golden pansies. During the past few days, countless flowers and decorations have been brought to the palace to prepare for our wedding on Friday.

I turn back to the Winter King. "It's as if you've stripped the entire kingdom of its flowers."

He drops to a bow, takes my hand, and kisses the back. Though he is a being of frost, my skin scorches where his lips touch. "You deserve nothing less, my queen."

I shuffle in place, debating whether to tear my hand out of his. I opt to return my attention to the servants and their carts of flowers instead. "Why red and gold? Shouldn't flowers be white at weddings?"

He straightens, though he doesn't release my hand, and he follows my gaze back to the flowers. "For you, of course," he says, turning back to me. He sweeps a lock of hair from out of my face. His touch is light, but my brow stings. "I have ordered for the hall to be decorated with the colors of Summer. Besides, I don't see why weddings should be white. This palace sees enough white all year."

"White is supposed to symbolize purity and innocence."

He scoffs at that. "I hardly think you could ever possibly be called pure and innocent."

I clasp my chest in mock offense. "Are you questioning my virtue, Your Majesty?"

His expression grows serious. "That wasn't what I meant. I was only joking." He holds my hand tighter and leans forth and lowers his voice. "Whether your virtue is intact or not would not change my opinion of you."

"It would not bother you if I had lain with another man first? You would still take me as your queen?"

"I'd kill him and then take you as my queen."

I glance at him, my eyes narrowing. I would expect no less from this villain.

He lets out a laugh. "I jest. Your past doesn't change who you are."

"Good," I say, and we continue through the courtyard, hand in hand.

A few steps later, he peers at me.

"What?" I ask, raising a brow.

"Have you?"

"Have I what?"

"Lain with another man," he hisses.

"I thought you said it doesn't matter either way?"

"It doesn't."

"Then what difference does knowing make?"

He frowns at that, and it doesn't relent all the way back inside the palace. He doesn't ask me again, however, and I can't help my satisfaction at knowing I've ruffled his feathers over the matter. Actually, the truth is that I have not had a lover before— how could I when I spent the last three years planning to infiltrate the palace and kill him? But he doesn't need to know that. I would much rather torture him by making him wonder.

At dinner that evening he asks, "Should I prepare the palace for any more rescue attempts? Or other disruptions to our wedding?"

"What do you mean?" I ask, though I suspect what he's referring to. "My father knows now that I'm not in need of rescuing. He hasn't fully recovered, either. I'm not sure he'll be able to make it to our wedding on Friday." I decide it best to plant the seed of my father's absence earlier rather than later.

"I didn't mean your father," he says. "I meant whether I should expect any past lovers to crash our wedding."

I offer him a mischievous smile. "You'll have to wait and see."

The Winter King's eyes twinkle. But his amusement is short-lived. "Your father," he says with a frown. "If he is too ill to make the wedding, then we can delay it."

"We can't delay it now," I reply, my pulse quickening. As it is, I'm risking Father's disappearance being noticed, hoping that it will go undetected for two more days. "You've already announced to the kingdom that our wedding shall be held on Friday, and that's just a few days away now. Some, on the far reaches of the kingdom, may have already left for the Crystal Palace."

"They aren't as important as your father," the Winter King insists. It's hard to bite my tongue and stop myself from pointing out that just a few weeks ago, my father almost died from his frost while being locked in his dungeons, so how can he claim that my father holds such importance to him? When I don't reply, the Winter King adds, "If your father isn't present, who will give you away?"

"Why must someone give me away?"

"It is a marriage tradition," he says, as if I've never attended a wedding in my life.

"I'll give myself away," I say, with a firm look.

The Winter King looks as if he wants to say something, but then bites his tongue and smiles. "It would be unconventional, but since I'm marrying an unconventional bride, I can think of no one better to give you away than yourself."

Chapter 27

Today is the day I will marry the Winter King. The day I finally stab my blade through his heart and end his frozen reign.

I awake long before dawn. When I push aside my blankets and peek through my curtains, the sky is still stained ink black.

If I succeed in killing the Winter King tonight, what will happen to this palace? Without him, will all of it melt away and it'll be as if the Winter King was never here?

When the Winter King falls, what will happen to our kingdom? Who will take his throne? Though I'll officially be the queen, the dukes and lords comprising the kingdom's council will never allow a woman to rule. And that's assuming I survive killing the Winter King and avoid being caught. I have no escape plan, but that's because I've never thought further ahead than vengeance. If I'm caught afterward, so long as he's dead, what will it matter? Father has already long fled. If he's sensible, he will be far away from this kingdom.

What I need is a way of killing him tonight, a way of smuggling a weapon into his room. The easiest way to do that will be to carry my dagger under my wedding dress, in the same way as I sneaked it into the Crystal Palace. But in a few hours, my maids will flock into my room to bathe and dress and decorate me until I'm painted into the queen they desire me to be. I will need to secure the dagger after I've changed into my wedding dress, when my maids aren't present.

My dagger is under my pillow, since last night I wanted to sleep with it in my hands to ensure it wouldn't suddenly freeze and render all my plans useless. Unless I hide it elsewhere, Elona and Kassia will find it under my pillow when they come to make my bed. Usually I'd return it to its hiding place under my bed, but there's no way I'll be able to slip through the narrow gap between my bed and the floor in my extravagant wedding dress, and there's even less chance of emerging without a single crease to incriminate me. I'll need to leave it somewhere more easily accessible. But wherever I choose will need to be hidden enough that Elona and Kassia don't spot it while helping me get ready for the wedding.

I return to my bed and snatch the dagger from under my pillow and scan the room. The vanity will be of no use. Though it has countless drawers, all are left empty. Elona and Kassia bring everything I need every morning from the storehouses outside so that they don't turn to ice inside the palace. The same goes for the rest of the useless furniture in my room. The armoire is nearly always left empty, and only a few books sit on the icy shelves on the other wall. Not nearly enough for me to hide my blade behind.

My gaze snags on the armoire. Though it's empty and I won't be able to hide my dagger inside it, maybe I will still be able to use it.

The gap between the armoire and the floor is much smaller than the one under my bed, just wide enough for the dagger to slide under. It isn't hidden as well as under my bed, where it was buried in ice, and when I shove it under the armoire, my cheek pressed flat against the floor, I can see its outline glinting amid the darkness. When the sun rises and light pours into my room, the dagger will be even more noticeable. Yet I can't push it much further under without risking being unable to retrieve it when I need it. I'll just have to hope that no one looks closely enough until I strap it to my thigh. At least there's less risk of being found under there than behind the books, and I can see nowhere else I can hide it.

Hoping it'll suffice, I climb back into bed and wrap my blankets around me. Though I've hardly slept and dawn is still far away, sleep doesn't claim me. I stay wide awake, thoughts of what is soon to come weighing heavily on my mind.

I pick at a loose thread in my blanket, imagining myself killing the Winter King. Will I have the strength to drive my dagger through his chest? When his eyes snap open and fill with the pain of betrayal, will I stay true to my purpose? Can I keep my blade pressed deeply into his chest until he draws his last breath?

I swallow, recalling the feel of Orlan's blood on my hands. As much as I long to kill the Winter King, I have never claimed a life and I worry that my heart will falter at the last moment. Or that my treacherous body will betray me, distracted by the thought of his lips burning across my skin.

And is killing the Winter King the right thing to do? While he might be a cruel tyrant, what if the next king—whoever he may be—will be far worse? What if the lords and dukes don't easily decide on a successor and our kingdom is plunged into civil war, claiming countless innocent lives and ruining many more?

All that chaos, that blood, will be on my hands and mine alone. My actions will cause far greater suffering than the Winter King murdering a bride every Summer for the past three hundred years.

Is killing the Winter King the moral thing to do? Does he even deserve to die? Or is there more to Dalia's disappearance that I need to know?

I tighten my jaw, shattering all those doubts. These thoughts are the ones that will deliver me to my failure. To succeed, I must bury them until even their shadows are vanquished.

With only fire and fury in my heart, I stare at the ceiling once more and count until the end begins. Until my plans are set into motion.

I am a weapon, and weapons do not think. They do not feel. They only strike.

So deep in my trance, my mind barely registers the sound of my maids entering the room.

"Are you awake, my lady?" Kassia calls.

Anxious for it all to begin, I bolt up. "Wide awake."

They waste no time in readying me for the ceremony. I eat without the Winter King this morning in the confines of my room, for which I'm grateful. Stomaching food is hard enough, let alone when sitting across from the man I'm plotting to marry and bed and kill.

After I'm finished, Elona and Kassia have a bathtub brought to my room and scrub my hair and skin until I'm smelling like a bouquet. Then they set to work with painting my face with so many cosmetics that when I gaze in the mirror, I no longer recognize myself. It's as if I'm wearing a mask. But it's better this way. A mask will help me to hide my heart, to allow me to become the person I must be today. When the lords and ladies of this kingdom look upon me, they will only see the face of a grateful queen.

Not the knife clutched behind her back.

Though my maids brush through my unruly locks and pat out the excess, my hair remains damp and won't dry for some time. At least the wedding ceremony isn't being held until the afternoon. Then the wait is painful, and every time Elona and Kassia glance at the armoire, I fear they'll see the shadow lurking beneath. The glint of silver. Each time I hold my breath, but they don't seem to notice. I hope it stays that way.

I read for a while, or try to. My mind struggles to focus on the pages, the words blending into a maelstrom of parchment and ink. I rise from the soft cushions of my frozen armchair and head to the window, gazing out at the gardens.

Though this morning, when I first awoke, the palace's gardens were nothing but a bleak landscape of ice and frost, it seems the servants were busy while my maids were preening me. Now flowers and banners are draped across nearly every wall, and the gardens are bursting with color.

The color of Summer.

Magnificent golds, bold reds, fierce oranges. As if a fire is raging across the snowy gardens.

And when I kill the Winter King, that fire will be me.

When my hair is nearly dry, Elona and Kassia twist and twirl it into an elaborate updo, leaving a few strands at the front to frame my face. They decorate my hair with golden pins and rubies, though they are careful not to place too many on the very top of my head.

"You won't want them to dig in," Elona says with a smile when I ask her about it, "when you are crowned as the Summer Queen and the crown is placed upon your head."

My stomach dips at the thought of the crown's weight. How will I bear it when I have no intention of being queen longer than tonight?

Finally, when there's nothing else left to be done, they wrap me in the crimson and golden silk of my wedding gown. Madame Bellmont designed it for me, and I've only tried it on once before. Tuesday, when she had me try it on to see if any adjustments were required. She'd made it perfectly for me, and the only change she needed to make was to tighten the fabric around my arms. I suspect that's less to do with Madame Bellmont's skill and more to do with the fact she went off my previous measurements. At home, I spent nearly every day training with the guards, honing myself into the sharpest blade I could, and though I've sparred occasionally with the Winter King, it isn't enough to maintain the strength in my arms. It shouldn't prove a problem in my plan, however. Not when it all hinges on my ability to seduce him enough to drop his guard and drive my dagger through his chest while he sleeps.

I gaze at myself in the mirror. The paint and silk are excessive, but no less than the Winter King will have ordered. He's made it clear on several occasions before that appearances matter to him, and right now, I look like the embodiment of Summer. A force great enough to rival Winter.

I pray that will prove true.

BRIDE OF THE WINTER KING

When Kassia leaves to fetch my veil, I realize the opportunity which stands before me. The wedding ceremony is to begin shortly, and unless I act now, I will have to enter battle unarmed. I will have no choice but to strangle the Winter King with my bare hands—a method which would likely fail due to both his magic and physical strength.

I turn to Elona and suck in a breath. There are few excuses I can think of which will allow me long enough to wade beneath the heavy layers of my trailing skirts and strap the blade to my thigh. If I ask for a drink, she will likely ask for another maid to retrieve it in her place. If I ask to use the chamber pot, she will have to assist me with how cumbersome my dress is.

So I say the only thing I can think of. A reason which isn't too far from the truth.

"I . . ." I close my eyes and swallow. "Is it all right if I have a moment alone?"

I open my eyes slowly, fearing how Elona will react. That her gaze will sharpen with suspicion. Instead, she presses her lips together in pity and takes my hands, squeezing them in hers.

"No wedding is easy, for it means promising your heart to another," she says gently. "But marrying a king means becoming a queen, and that is yet another burden on top of becoming a wife."

I lower my head, not sure how to respond. The uneasiness I feel isn't over promising my heart or becoming a queen. It is for sacrificing my body, my life, to kill my husband.

Lowering her voice, Elona continues, "If it makes it any easier, I'm certain the king cares deeply for you, and I know he'll treat you well. These last few days I have noticed him smiling much more than usual, my lady."

None of this makes it any easier. It just makes my chest constrict.

I lift my head in a nod. After all, I don't want the maids to think I'm having too many doubts and report it to the Winter King, who then may decide to delay the wedding.

"I'll be fine," I mumble. "I just need a few moments to compose myself."

"I understand, my lady. All we need to do is to secure your veil, and that won't take long. There's an hour until the wedding starts, and I'll come and fetch you shortly before it begins."

I crush the pang of guilt which lances through me. "Thank you."

With that, Elona turns and leaves, granting me more time than I hoped for.

Chapter 28

By the time my maids return, I've long secured my dagger and smoothed out any creases in my skirts. Elona quickly adjusts a few of the strands which have fallen out of my updo, and once satisfied with my appearance, Kassia places a crimson veil over my head. My world is stained with red. Like blood.

As my maids escort me through the Crystal Palace, I have to hold their arms to keep from tripping over any steps. With how greatly this veil obscures my vision, maybe I should have asked the Winter King if my maids could walk me down the aisle instead of walking by myself.

The wedding is held in a different hall to the one which held the ball. Though this hall is smaller, it contains much more usable space thanks to its rectangular shape. Countless chairs have been crammed into the hall, though those at the back are left standing. The crowd is parted down the middle, forming an aisle which leads to the dais on the far side of the hall.

The Winter King stands there, dressed in his finest embroidered silk. Navy, as usual. Does he own any other color?

His shoulders are held tensely, as if he fears something might go wrong. I hope his instincts aren't causing him to suspect my intentions.

It seems every noble man and woman has come to attend my wedding today, painting the icy walls and floors with a rainbow of color.

All heads turn to me as we reach the doorway. I swallow, immediately grateful for the veil obscuring my face. Otherwise they would see the fear and doubt clouding my eyes.

Maids flock toward me, more than I realized the Winter King employs. They smooth out the trail of silk behind me, scrutinize my dress for even the slightest wrinkle, and when their inspection is complete, Elona signals to the musicians at the back of the hall, and they begin to play.

With a shaky breath, I start down the aisle, every footstep ringing in my ears. Though the musicians' strings sing loudly through the hall, it isn't loud enough to drown out the sound of my marching to battle.

As I pass through the hall, I keep my gaze fixed to the Winter King at the far end, his bright eyes tracking me every step of the way. Not once do I turn my head to view the nobles staring at me. I wonder what they must be thinking. This is the first time a Summer Bride has been seen after being chosen at the Midsummer Ball, the first time a queen has ever been crowned. And yet tonight I will disappoint them all. Not only will they lose a queen on the same day as gaining her, but they will also lose their king.

I do my best not to think of the civil war my actions may plunge this kingdom into. I focus on the music, my footsteps, to drown out the echo of the clang of steel and drums of war. The destruction which has yet to come. All I can tell myself is that no matter what the consequences for this kingdom are, whether the matter of replacing the Winter King is peaceful or not, every outcome is better than allowing a murderer and a tyrant to continue reigning over us.

Finally, I reach the dais and ascend the steps, coming to a stop beside the Winter King. Though he doesn't turn to look at me, his gaze staying on the hall, I notice that his lips are curled upward into a gentle smile.

The priest steps forth, giving a speech of God and duty and love. His words fade beneath the relentless rush of my blood, my attention pinned to the large arched doors on the other side of the hall. Unable to look down at the crowd, or at the king I intend to betray.

"Do you, Elaric, King of Avella, vow to love and honor and cherish this woman from this day forth, to be a faithful husband to her as long as you both shall live?"

The king's smile does not falter as he says, "I do."

Then the priest turns to me. "Do you, Adara, Daughter of Duke Darrell Lansford, vow to love and honor and cherish this man from this day forth, to be a faithful wife to him as long as you both shall live?"

The words love and honor and cherish grate in my ears. What the priest asks of me is the opposite of what I intend to do, and yet there is nothing else I can say, except for: "I do."

The priest gives a nod solemn enough to be fitting for a funeral. "Then from this day forth, I pronounce you as one, as man and wife, as King and Queen of Avella."

The priest takes both our hands and raises them high, and when the crowd cheers, he joins our hands, and we become one.

As the Winter King's fingers tighten around my hand, I hope he cannot tell how clammy my palms have become. How quickly my heart thrums, as if I am facing my end.

The priest retrieves the crown from the altar behind us, the crown which is to be mine. It's a stark contrast to the frozen one fixed upon the Winter King's brow, which I have never once seen him without.

When the crowd falls silent once more, the Winter King releases my hand and takes the crown from the priest. My shoulders stiffen as the Winter King addresses the crowd.

"For three hundred years, I have searched for my rightful queen," he says, his voice ringing out through the hall's icy walls. "My Summer Queen. For three hundred years, I have searched for a bride who is bold and passionate, whose heart possesses enough fire to rival Winter. To be my equal and opposite in all things."

His fingers wrap around my wrist, his touch burning my skin, and he turns me to face him. I have no choice but to stare up at his glacial eyes, the crimson veil doing little to dull their luminescence. I pray the thin fabric hides the tightening of my jaw as my gaze meets his.

"And now," the Winter King continues, his eyes on me as he addresses the crowd, "I have finally found you. Adara, it is my honor to be your husband, and I vow I will treasure you every day for the rest of our lives."

I swallow. My saliva burns my throat.

"Not only will you be my wife, but you will be the queen this kingdom deserves. With your intelligence and kindness, I know you will help me lead this kingdom justly and wisely, to serve all our people."

Kindness? What kindness does the Winter King see in me? Never once has there been kindness in my heart, at least not directed at him.

He releases my wrist and reaches for the veil. I brace myself as the fabric slides away, exposing my face to the hundreds gathered in this hall. The air feels hot against my cheeks.

The Winter King hands the veil to the priest, and with both hands, he places the crown atop my head.

The crown is as heavy as I feared, and it's all I can do to keep my head held high, to prevent myself from being crushed beneath its weight.

The Winter King turns back to the crowd and takes my hand in his, raising my arm once more. "All hail the Summer Queen!"

The rest of the afternoon is a blur of music and dancing and feasting. Following our wedding ceremony, the Winter King and I lead the audience to the Crystal Palace's great hall, the one in which the Midsummer Ball was held. The lowest floor of the hall has tables situated around its perimeter, which the lords and ladies of Avella sit upon. During the banquet, the Winter King and I remain on the highest tier, away from the crowd, and we eat up there. Afterward, the nobles dance but not once do the two of us dance with them, though the Winter King proved he was perfectly competent when it was just the two of us in this hall.

The music is too loud for us to have any extensive conversation, but on several occasions, he takes my hand in his and offers a gentle squeeze. I return the gesture because not doing so will demand more questions.

Throughout the afternoon of celebrations, I'm painfully aware of the dagger digging into my leg. The heavy crown on my head. I can't but help draw a parallel to the first night I came here, when I feared that the dagger and poison vial I concealed would be exposed. When I was determined for the Winter King to choose me.

And here I am now, sitting beside his frozen throne on one of my own, though mine is smaller and is constructed from gold. It can't stay here without turning into ice like everything else in the Crystal Palace, and hours later, when the music draws to an end, I can already see the frost creeping across the gilded arms of my throne.

My throne might succumb to the frost, but I will not.

The lords and ladies empty from the hall, and then only servants are left below, tidying up the floor beneath us. The Winter King watches them for a while before rising from his throne and holding out his hand to me, bowing deeply at the waist. "My queen."

I take his hand, and he helps me from my throne and guides me through the door to the right.

As we traipse through the Crystal Palace, the band securing my dagger to my leg rubs against my skin, burning it bit by bit. I keep my head held high and my shoulders rolled back as I march to war.

To my wedding night.

When we arrive at his chambers, the Winter King holds open the door and I suck in a breath as I slip inside. He takes two goblets from the table in his dining room, along with the bottle of red wine beside it. The servants must have placed it there several hours ago, since the bottom of the glass bottle is already decorated in whorls of frost.

The Winter King continues through to his bedroom. It's nearly impossible to stop the tensing of my shoulders, the hardening of my jaw. If all goes according to plan, this will be the last room we ever enter together.

And only one of us will emerge from it.

The Winter King pours the wine into both goblets and passes me one. He pauses as I take it from him, his bright eyes scanning across my face. "Are you all right, Adara?"

My fingers grip the goblet's icy stem. I need to relax. Just for a few hours more will I need to continue this pretense.

Yet no words come to me. I manage a small nod, staring into the red wine which looks eerily like blood.

The Winter King's gaze softens. "Nothing has to happen tonight."

My head snaps up. "What?"

Everything must happen tonight.

He clears his throat. "Between the two of us." He raises his hand, and a crack sounds as the door which leads to mine opens slightly. Another crack echoes from within, presumably as the other door at the end of the passage opens. "You may return to your chambers whenever you wish." His voice lowers, barely a whisper. "There is no need for us to consummate our marriage tonight."

I scan across the Winter King's face, looking for a clue that this is some trick. Why else wouldn't a tyrant like him demand that which is owed to him?

There's a small part of me which considers agreeing to his suggestion. But if I don't act tonight, I'll have to act tomorrow night or the night after. I might manage to convince him to leave the passage between our chambers unsealed and sneak in and kill him, but it won't be as effective. After all, how will I know when he's asleep? By staying here tonight, I will be better able to identify the perfect moment to strike.

I swallow and say, "And if I choose to stay?"

The Winter King pauses, as if he had been expecting that I would choose the other option, and his lips pull upward into a gentle smile. "Then you are more than welcome to stay, and I will worship you as a queen deserves to be worshipped."

My treacherous heart flips at his words. At first, I curse myself for the reaction, but then I banish all resistance. For this next part, I must surrender to my body's will, or else he will suspect that something is amiss.

To mask my hesitation, I raise my goblet and say, "To our marriage."

To justice.

The Winter King clinks his goblet against mine. "To our marriage."

And then we drink.

I doubt the wine is that strong, but tonight it burns me as it washes over my tongue. It scalds my throat. Yet I drink more, enough to free my inhibitions, but not too much that my blade will miss my mark in his chest.

We take our goblets out onto the balcony overlooking the frozen gardens. With every sip of wine, I imagine the color seeping back into the withered flowers when the Winter King meets his end.

Leaning on the balustrade, the Winter King says, "I meant what I said in the hall."

I turn to him and raise an eyebrow.

"About how precious you are to me."

I set down my goblet on the icy rail. "Elaric . . ." His name is the only way I can think to reply.

"I will do everything in my power to be the husband you deserve," he continues. "If there is ever anything you feel I can do better for you, if there is ever anything you are lacking in—"

Unable to listen to his words, I cut him off with a kiss. I fear if I hear him to the end of whatever he wants to say, then he will inject doubt into my heart. Doubt I can't afford.

Thankfully, my kiss is distracting enough. The Winter King doesn't try to continue his speech, and the words fade into the night, entirely forgotten. He places his goblet beside mine, and his fingers tangle through my hair, pulling me closer.

I kiss him as hard as I can, my lips fueled by the determination burning within me.

I need this.

I need him.

And not only because this will open the doorway to justice. The feel of his lips on mine makes my body yearn for more, and when his tongue brushes over my lips and then delves deeper, the sensation causes that yearning to reach a crescendo.

His lips leave mine, and he brushes aside my hair, trailing hundreds of kisses down my exposed neck. My back meets the balustrade, the edges digging into my skin, and I arch against it as his lips dance over my collarbone. Every touch sends more warmth surging through me, until an aching inferno of need is roiling through my stomach.

His hand skims up the inside of my leg, pushing aside the heavy layers of crimson silk, and I savor the feeling for a moment too long. The leg he's slowly working his way up is the one to which my dagger is secured.

With his fingers mere inches away from the leather band, I have no choice but to jerk away. The silk falls back into place, concealing the weapon.

The Winter King's gaze sweeps over me, his brows drawing together.

My breaths are heavy gasps, from both the exhilaration of his kiss and the fear of being caught. Of all my plans being crushed by a moment's weakness.

"Adara," he says, his voice strained with the conflicting forces of hesitation and desire. "If you've changed your mind, we can stop. We don't have to do this."

But I can't stop.

Nor do I want to.

I must remove this dagger and hide it before it's too late.

"I want to," I say, my words slow and careful. "I do want this. But . . ."

He closes the distance between us and takes my hand and presses it to his chest. "If you are not ready, we can wait."

I am ready, and it will be tonight. I allow hesitation to wash over my face, and seize the few precious seconds it gives me to think clearly about how I will remove the dagger and hide it without the Winter King seeing.

"I was only teasing you the other day," I begin.

His cold eyes sharpen. "About what?"

"About all those previous lovers," I reply, glancing down at the floor. "The truth is, I've never once been with a man. All of this is new to me. But I want to do this tonight. Tomorrow will no longer be our wedding night."

And that is the truth. Though it isn't the reason for my hesitation.

His gaze softens. "We don't need to do this, Adara."

I look back up at him, meeting his eyes. "I *want* to."

The Winter King is quiet, his fingers clasping mine tighter. Finally, he says, "Then we will do this on your terms."

Chapter 29

Holding his hand, I guide him away from the balcony, leaving our goblets forgotten, and lead him toward the bed.

"The lights," I say softly, my gaze on the sconces around his room, filled with flickering blue light.

The Winter King lifts his hand and all the lights fizzle out at once. Now the only source of illumination is the pallid moonlight filtering in through the balcony.

This is the first step. Darkness. But I can't be certain it'll offer me all the cover I require.

The Winter King places his icy crown on a small counter, and I leave him sitting on the edge of the bed. I swallow, allowing all my nerves to show on my face. I hope he mistakes them for shyness rather than the fear of being caught.

"Turn around," I whisper.

It seems I've already earned the Winter King's trust, since he turns around without hesitation. I stare at his back, thinking of how I could seize my dagger and kill him now. Yet he would hear me approach and be able to stop me before the blade even drew near him.

The very best opportunity will be when he's asleep.

Not daring to waste another second, I walk to the icy armchair and pull down the sleeves of my wedding dress. The silk spills down my chest and pools at my feet, leaving me in my corset and the chemise beneath.

The corset is harder to remove than my dress, and pulling at the laces only seems to tighten it. At first, I fear I'll have to ask the Winter King to help, but then the laces give way, and I'm able to discard the corset onto the armchair. I drape the wedding dress over it, too.

Now comes the most important part.

I glance back at the Winter King, but his head is still turned, his attention glued to the doors on the other side of the room. I don't breathe as I reach beneath the thin skirts of my chemise and unbuckle the leather strap from my leg. Once it's removed, my skin is left slightly pink, but I hope it's dark enough that the Winter King won't notice its incriminating mark.

Doing my best to stop the steel from clinking, I slip the dagger underneath the heavy silk of my wedding dress, burying it as deeply as I can. Since no servants can stay in the Crystal Palace overnight without risking being frozen, I pray that will remain the case tonight, and they won't move my dress until the morning. Not until long after the Winter King is dead.

I slide my feet out of my heels, leaving them beneath the armchair, and then remove my chemise and lay it at the top of the pile. Then I'm left there naked, the moonlight gleaming across my bare skin.

With a deep breath, I turn and pace back to the bed, where the Winter King still sits turned away from me. My bare feet brush across the icy floor, and though he must hear me approaching, he doesn't stir. Even when I sit on the bed beside him, his back is rigid.

"You . . ." I begin, my voice cracking with the anticipation of what is to come. "You can turn around now."

The Winter King turns slowly, and his surprise at my nakedness is clear by the way his silver brows rise. Never have I seen the Winter King so caught off guard.

His gaze drifts downward, but before it can reach my breasts, his eyes snap up, fixing on my face. "Adara," he says, his voice coarse like the scraping of steel against ice. His jaw tightens. It must be taking all of his willpower to keep his eyes on my face and to stop them from drinking in every inch of my naked body.

I take his hand and lift it to my breast. A breath shudders through his lips as his fingers meet my warm skin.

"Are you sure?" he asks, hesitation clouding his eyes.

"I'm sure," I say, the words hot on my tongue. "I want this. I want you."

The Winter King holds my gaze and then the last strands of his restraint fray and crumble.

His fingers brush across my breast, caressing me. He pulls me closer, and his breath is warm against my ear as he says, "You're beautiful. Even more beautiful than I ever imagined. Many times have I dreamed of this night, and the Adara in my dreams pales compared to the one before me now."

His words send another lance of doubt ricocheting through me, and I feel my resolve crumbling.

I tell myself they're just pretty words he's spent three hundred years reciting—that when they were first spoken, they weren't intended for me.

That thought helps crush the doubt preying on my heart.

To silence any more of his pretty words, I claim his mouth with mine. The Winter King groans, his fingers grazing over my peaked nipples.

Heat burns in my core, my thighs slickening with need. I lean into the feelings building within me, allowing instinct to guide every movement.

I banish all my thoughts. Right now, all that matters is being fully immersed in this moment with him. I can worry about everything else afterward.

The Winter King leans me back until my head meets the soft blankets. My breath hitches as he lowers his mouth to my nipple. His tongue rolls over it, desire burning hotter within me.

His lips trail lower, tracing a burning line down my abdomen. His hands drift up my thighs, and the skin where the leather band sat is especially sensitive to his touch.

His bright eyes seem to shine brighter, his lips curling into a smirk, as he lowers his mouth and kisses the apex of my thighs.

My legs buck against him, but his grasp is firm, holding me down as he wrenches a symphony of moans from my lips. In this moment, there's only pleasure—doubt and fear and hatred all extinguished with the heat of his lips, his tongue, against me. There is no mournful past, no violent future. Just the sweet bliss of the present.

His fingers slip inside me, and I clutch the soft blankets beneath. At first the sensation is foreign, painful even, but then all those feelings are drowned out by the tidal wave of pleasure seeking to drown me.

His tongue consumes me as his fingers strokes deep inside me, and bit by bit the pressure within builds until it's too much to bear. His fingers find an especially sensitive spot within me, and then I'm unable to withstand the tension any longer. Heat bursts through me, flames devouring every inch of my heart, and I'm left trembling and gasping, struggling to regain my breath.

The Winter King reaches over and brushes away the hair which has fallen over my eyes and presses his lips to my forehead in a kiss so tender it feels like he's driving a knife through my chest.

Tenderness is not something I want nor can afford, so I grab his broad shoulders and pull him down to me, claiming his mouth in a forceful kiss, tasting myself upon his lips. I need to get this over with before he can penetrate any further through the fractured walls around my heart.

"Why are you still dressed?" I demand between kisses, pulling at the buttons on his tunic. "It isn't fair that I'm naked, yet you're still fully clothed."

A low chuckle rumbles through him and he helps me as I undo the buttons and pull aside his tunic. It's no pretense when I reach up and run my fingers over the hardness of his chest, the edges well defined enough that it's as if he's a statue carved from alabaster.

My hands delve lower, until they reach his breeches, and as I push aside the button securing them, his shoulders tense. The fabric slides down, revealing him in his entirety. That he wants this as much as me. Or at least as much as my body does.

I reach out for him, to wrap my fingers around him, but the Winter King catches my hand before I can, pinning them both to the bed.

"Adara," he breathes, "are you sure this is what you want?"

"I'm sure," I whisper. "I want you. All of you."

His chest heaves with a deep exhalation, and then he climbs over me, his hands caressing every inch of my skin. But the gesture is too light, too *loving*.

I wrap my legs around his waist, pulling him against me. I kiss him fiercer, with desperation, urging him to finish what we have started.

Though the Winter King shudders as I draw him closer, he does not quicken his pace. His kisses trail over my arms, my breasts, my legs, my stomach—worshipping me as he promised he would.

"Please," I say, every part of me aching.

But the Winter King only smiles. There is no mercy in his bright eyes. "I have waited three hundred years for you, my queen, and I will not be rushed."

All I can do is lie there and brace myself as each and every gentle kiss needles my heart, some digging in deeper than others.

It feels like an eternity passes before he finally grants me mercy, his hips driving down as he plunges into me.

At first there's a sudden, sharp pain as my body struggles to accommodate him, and I can't help wincing.

The Winter King freezes, his shoulders going rigid. "Adara?"

"I'm fine," I say, my voice coming out in gasps.

The Winter King hesitates, so I clench my jaw and push my hips against his, forcing him deeper. He takes that as a signal to move, though he does so slowly in several long, steady thrusts. The pain soon gives way to a river of pleasure, and then my hands trace over his back, feeling the firm lines of his muscles.

Every stroke grows harder and deeper, and each time he buries himself to the hilt. Though I relish the way he feels inside me, I hate how he's the one in control. I want him to be the one yielding to me, not the other way around.

I push him upward and over, and surprise causes him to easily fall to my will. I offer no hesitation before climbing on top of him, straddling him with my thighs as I press against his hardness.

The Winter King does not push me back over and demand control once more. He simply reaches up, his fingers brushing my cheek. Before he can torture me with any more tenderness, I slowly slide myself down his length.

"Adara," he groans, his voice cracking around the syllables of my name. Triumph sparks through me at the sound. The knowledge that he is at my mercy.

It's impossible to stop the smirk which dances on my lips and then I move upward, before forcing my hips down. Once more, he groans.

Over and over, I slide myself up and down, but then his resolve breaks and he grips my waist, guiding each thrust. His other hand grazes my breast, skimming over my hard nipple and then back down.

I will make him yield to me. That thought drives me onward, my rhythm frenzied with determination and desire until I push the Winter King to his release and he cries out my name between ragged breaths. The sight of him beneath me, slave to the pleasure I have wrought upon him, is enough to undo me. My head falls back as I too am pushed over the edge and claimed by those tantalizing waves.

When his breathing steadies, the Winter King scoops me into his arms and stares at me. The devotion in his bright eyes is so intense that I'm the first to break our stare, and I tuck my head against his shoulder so that he can't see my face.

Why is this part more difficult than when we were one?

The Winter King holds me, his breaths slow and heavy, and then he presses his lips to my forehead. "My queen."

Chapter 30

For a long while, I lie there in the Winter King's arms, rigid and still. I don't twitch. I barely dare to breathe.

My heart is battered and bruised as an onslaught of emotions rage war on each other, dominated by guilt and desire.

I can still feel those all-consuming waves of pleasure washing over me, and though I had no choice but to surrender to desire, I question whether I enjoyed it too much.

But more than that, it's the feeling of the Winter King's lips brushing over my forehead, his fingers cupping my cheek, which tightens my chest. No matter how tenderly he may have made love to me, it doesn't change the fact that he stole both Dalia and Orlan from me.

Even if he can induce such pleasure upon my body, I will never forgive him for what he has done.

Just like that, their faces cause my blood to run cold. The violent clash of emotions in my heart comes to a sudden halt, wrath emerging victorious.

He may kiss me tenderly, stare at me with such devotion, but it does not change the fact he is a monster. A wicked villain who has ruined countless lives.

Tonight, he will finally pay for his crimes.

I shift back and stare at him. I do my best to ignore the calm contentment on his face. I expect his eyes to snap open and for that bright blue to stare back at me, but he doesn't stir. He seems to be asleep, but the problem is that I don't know whether this immortal king even sleeps.

"Elaric," I say softly. I use his name infrequently enough that it should cause surprise to flicker across his face if he's awake.

I hold my breath and study his face. But even after several seconds, his expression doesn't change.

"Elaric, are you awake?" I whisper, keeping my voice low enough to not disturb him if he really is asleep.

Again, there's no response.

The Winter King must be asleep.

And I finally have the opportunity I need.

My stomach flips. I've waited so long to strike, to end his frozen reign, yet never once did I imagine I'd arrive at this moment with nausea swarming over me.

I tell myself it's just a side effect of giving my body to him, and in the morning, these fleeting feelings will be long gone. I can't allow myself to be distracted from what must be done.

Little by little, I slide myself back until I have escaped his arm. Before each movement, I pause, fearing the Winter King will awake and all hope will be lost. But he doesn't. Even by the time I reach the edge of the bed, he remains asleep.

With a deep breath, I slip from the bed and my feet meet the icy floor. I tip-toe across to the armchair, constantly glancing back, fearing he will bolt up and demand to know what I'm doing, sneaking around his room.

When I reach the armchair, I push aside the silk, careful not to disturb it too deeply. My fingers close around the hilt of my blade. Slowly, I draw it from its sheathe. Only the slightest scratch of steel escapes. Holding my breath, I turn back to the Winter King.

He hasn't moved.

I tuck the blade behind my back, the hilt burning so hot against my fingers that it's a struggle not to drop it. My pulse drums so wildly in my ears that it's a wonder the Winter King doesn't awaken to the maddened rush of my blood.

My shins meet the frozen bed frame. Swallowing, I bring one knee onto the bed and then the other, careful not to disturb the blanket. One advantage of sleeping on a bed carved from ice is that the solid mattress doesn't shift beneath my weight.

As soon as I can, I slip the dagger beneath my pillow and out of sight. Then I wait. Painful minutes stretch by. Still, the Winter King doesn't wake.

This is it.

Now or never.

I must act.

Yet my hand refuses to move. It's as if my body has betrayed my heart for him, after just one blissful night of pleasure.

I crush all doubts.

He must die.

Before my selfish mortal body can douse the fury burning within me, I pull my dagger from beneath my pillow. In one fluid motion, I drive it straight through his chest.

The force is great enough that he is flung aside, and I climb on top of him, pressing down as hard as I can, even as irrational tears spill from my eyes and distort my vision.

But my sight is clear enough that I can see the Winter King's eyes snapping open. Pain and anguish and betrayal rage across his face. Blood spills out, hot and sticky against my hands.

I had no other choice.

I had no other choice.

I tell myself this over and over, but it doesn't stop the sob which wracks through me. I always imagined I would feel relief at the Winter King's death, not a pain so intense that it feels as if I'm driving the blade through my chest as well.

"Adara," he chokes out, his voice broken and lonely and hurt.

My hand trembles.

I press deeper.

But then I'm no longer sinking through soft flesh, and the tip of my blade clinks against something solid. Though the surface scratches, it does not yield. I force my dagger down harder, driven by fear, but I cannot break his frozen heart.

"Adara."

This time his voice is less broken. Angrier.

Though I've driven a dagger through his chest, it doesn't sound like he's dying.

With a growl, he shoves me aside with far greater strength than a man bleeding as greatly as him should. Though I cling to the hilt with all my might, the steel slips through my fingers.

The Winter King grabs both my hands and pins them to the bed. I struggle and wrestle against his grasp, but I'm no match for his strength. He pulls the dagger from his chest. Blood spills out, pooling across both my skin and his.

I have failed.

Even a blade of steel is no match for the Winter King.

Every inch of my flesh burns with the devastating crush of defeat.

He throws the bloody dagger off the bed. I flinch as it clangs against the floor.

Neither of us says anything. Both our breaths are haggard rasps.

The Winter King is the first to break the deathly silence.

"You . . ." His voice breaks. He closes his eyes, drawing in a deep breath. "You tried to kill me."

The thundering of my heart drowns out his words.

What use is there to continue pretending? I've tried to kill him, and failed. He already knows of my murderous intent. Now it has been exposed, it can never again be concealed.

Fury blazes in the Winter King's eyes. "All this time . . . You wanted to kill me."

A hysterical laugh chokes through me, though when it leaves my lips, it sounds more like a strangled sob. "Do you think anyone would *want* to marry you?"

His grasp around my hand tightens hard enough that it hurts. "Then none of this was real."

"Who would ever fall for a tyrant?" I sneer. "A monster?"

A growl escapes him. I wait for him to conjure a blade of ice, to slit my throat.

He does neither.

"Do it," I dare. "Kill me. Murder me like you've murdered all your other brides."

It's better to die a martyr than a villain. If he kills me now, he will only prove me right, that he is a cold-blooded murderer. That attempting to assassinate him in his sleep was the right choice.

He raises his hand. I brace myself. Prepare to meet death head on.

But death does not claim me.

Instead, frost snakes around my wrists, binding them together.

In the next moment, he grabs my waist and hauls me over his shoulder. Already the wound I carved through his chest is healing, the hole to his frozen heart filled with blue light.

I put up as much resistance as I can, thumping his back, but it's no use. It only annoys him more.

He passes the armchair and grabs my chemise from the top of the pile and then continues toward the door which leads to my chambers.

My shouts echo as we pass through the dark passageway, but the Winter King ignores all of my taunts. No matter how hard I try, I can't goad him into setting me down and letting me fight him.

We reach the end of the tunnel and he shoves open my door. Not once does he pause as he crosses the room to my bed. He drops my chemise at the center, and then he deposits me unceremoniously beside it.

The Winter King doesn't look back as he turns away.

I scramble upright, though it's hard with my bound wrists, and chase after him. His pace doesn't quicken, continuing his stoic march all the way to the door, even when I'm but a few yards behind him.

Just as I lunge for him, the Winter King raises his hand. A wall of solid ice rises from the floor, stopping me from reaching him.

I bang on the ice as hard as I can. It doesn't fracture.

"Elaric!" I yell, slamming into the ice.

At the sound of his name, the Winter King glances back over his shoulder. Even through the thick wall of ice, his eyes burn into mine. Though he stays silent, there's no mistaking his wrath.

"Elaric!" I shout again. "Stop being a coward! Face me!"

The Winter King says nothing as he turns away, and the door slams behind him. The manacles around my wrist dissipate into blue light.

And then I'm alone in the darkness.

I sink to my knees, defeat dragging me down like an anchor.

I have failed to kill the Winter King.

Adara and Elaric's story will continue in...

HEART
OF THE
SUMMER
QUEEN

To learn more about HEART OF THE SUMMER QUEEN *(Winterspell, #2)* and find out how to get a copy, you can visit here:

www.hollyrosebooks.com/heart-of-the-summer-queen

Want to read a bonus scene of Elaric's point of view of their wedding night? You can head to the link below to find out how.

www.hollyrosebooks.com/botwk-bonus

ABOUT THE AUTHOR

Holly Rose has been obsessed with high fantasy since the age of 5, when she first watched The Fellowship of the Ring (her parents raised her right). After realizing she couldn't become an elf, she decided to start writing about them instead. She also grew up on World of Warcraft and copious amounts of anime.

She was born and bred in Wales, United Kingdom, where she currently spends her days terrorizing teenagers with mathematical equations (and sometimes teaching them useful things). When she gets home from school, her real work with writing about magic and mayhem can begin.

You can find her online at:
http://hollyrosebooks.com/
https://www.instagram.com/hollyrosebooks
https://www.facebook.com/hollyrosebooks